BAIt

NICK
BROWNLEE

Minotaur Books   New York

For Janey – who always kept the faith.

This is a work of fiction. All of the characters, organizations, and events portrayed in this novel are either products of the author's imagination or are used fictitiously.

A THOMAS DUNNE BOOK FOR MINOTAUR BOOKS.
An imprint of St. Martin's Publishing Group.

www.thomasdunnebooks.com
www.minotaurbooks.com

Library of Congress Cataloging-in-Publication Data

Brownlee, Nick.
    Bait / Nick Brownlee. — 1st U.S. ed.
        p. cm.
    "A Thomas Dunne book." —T.p. verso.
    ISBN-13: 978-0-312-55021-9
    ISBN-10: 0-312-55021-9
    1. British—Kenya—Fiction. 2. Ex-police officers—
Fiction. 3. Detectives—Kenya—Fiction. 4. Murder—
Investigation—Kenya—Fiction. 5. Fishing—Fiction.
6. Mombasa (Kenya)—Fiction. I. Title.
PR6102.R73B35 2009
823'.92—dc22
                                                2009004488

First published in Great Britain by Piatkus Books,
an Hachette Livre UK Company

First U.S. Edition: July 2009

10 9 8 7 6 5 4 3 2 1

Acknowledgements

This book was inspired by the remarkable country of Kenya, and by the warmth, wisdom and optimism of its people.

In particular I would like to thank Damian Davies of Watamu beach for his insights into White Mischief, 21st-century style, and Edward Bejah of Mombasa for sharing his knowledge, enthusiasm and irrepressible good humour.

I would also like to thank Jane Gregory and Emma Dunford for taking a punt and making it all happen – and for allowing me to fulfil every unknown writer's dream of one day having lunch with his agent and editor.

Day One

Chapter One

As a boy, George Malewe had gutted thousands of fish for the white men who came to catch game off the coast of Mombasa. But, as he plunged the blade of his favourite teak-handled filleting knife into the soft underbelly and eased it upwards through the stomach wall with a smooth, practised sawing movement, it struck him that he had never before gutted a white man.

A man, George concluded, was not so different from a large karambesi or marlin. The guts spilled out on to the cockpit deck with the same moist splash. And the pool of blood that hissed between his bare toes had the same warm tacky consistency as that of a big game fish.

Admittedly, there was more of it. It would take him a lot longer to swab down the deck and hose the entrails out through the scuppers in the stern of the boat when he was done.

And, George reflected, he had never before gutted a game fish that had been bound to the fighting chair with fishing line.

Nor one that screamed as he eviscerated it.

'George – move your arse, will you?'

He jumped suddenly at the harsh voice from above. 'Yes, Boss.'

The scrawny African moved to one side, so that instead of hunkering between the bound man's knees he now leaned against the outside of his immobilised left thigh.

'Smile!'

George turned and looked up into the lens of a camera pointing down at him from the flying bridge. He knew all about cameras, and this one was top of the range. Very expensive. He beamed, revealing a decimated set of yellow teeth beneath the peak of his New York Yankees baseball cap.

The Boss Man holding the expensive camera pulled away from the eyepiece with a snarl of annoyance.

'Not you, you stupid *kaffir*. *Him*. You get on with your work.'

George's face fell and he turned silently back to the gaping abdomen of the man who sat bound by his wrists, forearms, ankles, upper thighs and knees to the steel struts of the fighting chair.

'Come on, Dennis!' the Boss Man said cheerfully. 'Say cheese!' Again he snorted with annoyance. 'George – lift up his head, will you?'

George went behind the fighting chair and wrenched the bound man's head off his chest by a hank of silvery hair.

'Up a bit, up a bit . . .'

From his position on the tarpaulin-covered flying bridge, overlooking the cockpit and the stern of the boat, the Boss Man wobbled on his feet slightly as he adjusted the focus on his camera.

'He don't look too clever, does he, George?'

George glanced down at the grey upturned face.

4

The mouth hung slackly and the open eyes had rolled upwards.

'He look dead to me, Boss.'

'Mmm.'

The Boss Man put down the camera and clambered gingerly down a set of iron ladders connecting the superstructure to the cockpit. He was thickset and the way he staggered drunkenly as the boat pitched and rolled on the swell indicated that he was no sailor.

But then George had known that anyway. The skippers who worked these fishing grounds for a livelihood knew every inch of the reef, knew precisely where the snag-toothed coral lay near enough to the surface to rip the bowels out of a thirty-foot twin-engined game-fisher like *Martha B* as easy as tearing paper.

The Boss Man didn't have a clue.

George did; but then you didn't crew fishing boats from the age of eleven without learning how to navigate into open sea, how to read the currents and how to anticipate the waves that could pick you up and smash you into matchsticks.

That was why he was here.

That and the five hundred dollars the Boss Man had promised him for navigating *Martha B* through the reef, gutting the white man in the chair and asking no questions.

George felt a flutter of excitement as he thought about the money. Five hundred dollars was a fortune in a country where the average monthly wage was less than ten. With five hundred dollars, he could *be* someone. There would be no more scraping a living on the streets of Mombasa, no more stealing from white tourists just to put food on the table for Agnes and little Benjamin. With five hundred dollars, he could set himself up in business, be one of the smartly dressed *tausi* like Mr Kili who drove around in expensive cars and could order things done simply by snapping his fingers.

'Yep. He's dead all right,' the Boss Man said, a hint of disappointment in his voice. 'Cut the line, George.'

Five hundred dollars.

Gutting the white man had not been as hard as George had imagined. Once the Boss Man had smashed him over the head with the metal claw of the grappling hook, the rest had been relatively straightforward. In fact, he had quite enjoyed it. It certainly beat stealing wallets, cameras and cell phones. Of course, George had been puzzled as to who this white man was, and what he had done to deserve such a fate. But the Boss Man seemed to know him, so that was OK.

Ask no questions.

As the last of the fishing line was cut from the dead man's wrists, George looked at his face and shuddered.

'Right. Get him to the back of the boat.'

The Boss Man was back on the flying bridge now, issuing his orders against the increasingly excited cawking of the seagulls circling overhead.

George manhandled the body out of the fighting chair to the stern rail.

'OK. Get rid of him.'

The body splashed into the ocean. It floated face-up for a moment, but only until the empty abdominal cavity filled with water and sent it swiftly beneath the surface.

'Right,' the Boss Man said. 'Now get that shit cleared up.'

As he got to work with the hosepipe and the stiff brush, George reflected that the body would not last long in these waters. The blood and entrails siphoning from the scuppers would soon attract a hammerhead or a bull shark, and tuna or sailfish would consume what was left.

As he worked he hummed a tune, 'Wana Baraka', which was a traditional folk song he used to sing with his mother in the shanty church of Likoni when he was a boy. It was about how those who pray will always be blessed, because Jesus himself said so. Nowadays George sang it to his own son, Benjamin, and just the thought of his little boy brought a broad smile of joy to his face. There were not many things in George's wretched life that he was proud of, but Benjamin was one. Today was his third birthday, and five hundred dollars would buy him a present he would never forget.

But, suddenly, George's beatific expression turned to one of puzzlement. Putting his hand to the peak of his cap, he stared out across the grey water towards the western horizon. A boat was approaching, low in the water, and, judging by the cascades of spray it threw up as it smashed against the swell, it was travelling fast.

George looked up to the flying bridge, but the Boss Man was hunched over, fiddling with something under the steering console.

'Boss!'

'What is it, George?'

'Boat coming.'

The Boss Man appeared at the rail, squinting through his sunglasses at the rapidly approaching vessel. He smiled. 'Right on the money,' he said, and turned back to the wheel again. 'Get on with your work.'

As he swabbed the deck, George watched the other boat out of the corner of his eye until it drew near enough for him to identify it as a high-powered speedboat, the kind he sometimes saw moored near the rich tourist resorts at Kikambala, Bamburi and Watamu. There was a white man at the wheel, hunched down behind the Perspex windshield. George did not recognise him. As the boat drew alongside *Martha B*, the man tossed a mooring rope across. George took the rope and secured it to one of the deck cleats.

'Right, Georgie-boy,' said the Boss Man, 'I'm afraid this is where I'm going to have to bid you *kwaheri*.'

George watched him negotiate the whitewashed iron ladder on the side of the boat. The expensive camera was now secured in a padded shoulder bag slung across his broad back. The Boss Man tottered unsteadily on the leading rail before sitting down and easing himself into the bobbing speedboat. He turned and smiled at the bemused crewman.

'Hope you don't mind – but I'm sure you know how to drive, don't you, George? It'll be a little treat for you. And you know that bloody reef like the back of your hand.'

George nodded dumbly.

'Nearly forgot.' The Boss Man rummaged in the pocket of his shorts and flung George a ten-dollar bill. 'You'll get the rest back on dry land.' He grinned. 'Then you can buy me a beer, eh? Maybe some girls. Lots of pretty *manyanga* for Georgie-boy, eh?'

Then the Boss Man said something to the man in the speedboat, and the craft's mighty engines coughed into life. George watched as it moved away from *Martha B* in a lazy arc, and saw its stern bite into the churning water as the turbos kicked in and fired it towards the distant mainland.

George shrugged. *Five hundred dollars and no questions asked.* He stared at the ten-dollar bill in his hand, then put it under his cap and shinned up the ladder to the flying bridge. He'd been on the flying bridge of one of these game boats before, of course. But always at the shoulder of the skipper. Bait boys weren't allowed near the wheel or the controls, not unless they were trusted.

When he'd been a bait boy, George reflected bitterly, he'd never been trusted.

He had watched though. He knew how to steer, how to ease forward the throttles and make the engines throb – and, although he wasn't sure how the compass worked, he knew every last inlet of the coast. George settled himself in the cushioned pilot's chair and sighed contentedly.

Five hundred dollars. Yes, he would soon be like Mr Kili in Mombasa. Maybe one day he would have his own boat. Yes, that would be good. Little Benjamin would like that.

He reached forward and jabbed the starter button.

A mile away now, the Boss Man winced in his seat in the rear of the scudding speedboat as *Martha B* disintegrated in a ball of flame. Splinters of wood and debris rose on the back of an oily black mushroom cloud, drifted lazily in the air, then fell back to the ocean in a cascade of tiny splashes. Eventually the smoke dissipated into a single thin swathe high above the surface, then vanished altogether. Of the boat, there was no sign.

'*Kwaheri*, George,' the Boss Man muttered as the powerful boat swung round and headed south. '*Kwaheri.*'

9

Chapter Two

Ever since the elections of late 2007 and the damn-near civil war that followed, Ernies had been scarce in this part of Kenya. Too many killings. *Too much heavy shit going down.* But scarce did not mean extinct – and thankfully there were always a few gunslingers determined to prove that tribesmen with machetes and cops with batons and semi-automatics couldn't spoil *their* fun.

'Aw – sonofa*bitch*! I've done it *again*!'

Up on the flying bridge of *Yellowfin*, Jake Moore sighed and killed the thirty-footer's twin engines and tried to remember that in these troubled times the Ernies and their money were just about all that kept his boat – and his livelihood – afloat.

'Mr Jake! Mr Jake!'

'OK, Sammy,' he said, wearily swinging his legs from the dashboard and easing himself out of his chair. 'I heard.'

His accent marked him out as an Englishman, and the faint north-east twang betrayed his Northumbrian roots. He certainly had the rugged look of a Cheviot hill farmer – and there were those who said he had the cussedness too. It was a comparison that always

10

amused him, because Jake had never been to the Cheviots in his life. He belonged to the sea. And no matter how many times he tried to escape its grip, he always found himself coming back.

Down in the cockpit, Sammy the bait boy had clambered barefoot on to the stern rail and was peering out at the ocean. Behind him, strapped into the fighting chair, the overweight Ernie in the shop-new bush hat scratched the back of his neck, leaving livid white marks on the red raw skin. He spun round and smiled stupidly as Jake came down the ladder.

'It slipped out of my hands,' he said sheepishly. 'Sorry, man.'

There was a guffaw from the shade of the cabin awning beneath the bridge, where two more Ernies sat in deck chairs and tinked their beer bottles together.

'That piece of kit has got to be worth twelve hundred bucks *at least*,' one of them announced. 'You're a goddamn liability, Ted.'

'I'm real sorry, Jake,' the Ernie in the chair repeated.

'Not to worry,' Jake said evenly, thinking only of the hundred bucks an hour these bozos were each paying for the privilege of dropping his fishing rods in the ocean. 'You see it, Sam?'

'I see it, Mr Jake,' the boy said, his eyes never leaving the water as he stripped off his sun-bleached T-shirt.

'OK.'

He nodded to Sammy. Without hesitation, the boy launched himself from the back of the boat and arrowed into the fizzling remains of its wake. The Ernies under the awning levered themselves from

11

their deck chairs and lumbered unsteadily to the stern rail, beers clutched to their bare chests.

'This I *got* to see,' one of them said, resting a broad buttock on the gunwale. The four men watched as Sammy moved smoothly and rapidly through the water, tacking left and then right like a porpoise to take account of the swell.

The Ernie in the fighting chair shook his head in admiration. 'I'll be damned. You train him to do that?'

'I guess it's just a talent he was born with, Ted,' Jake said.

The Ernie, gawping out at the ocean, did not register the sarcasm in his voice.

Fifty yards out, Sammy suddenly disappeared under the water. When he resurfaced a few moments later, a twelve-foot fishing rod was clasped in his hand and a huge smile split his face.

'Sonofa*bitch*!' exclaimed Ted. He said something else, but the whooping and high-fives of his buddies drowned out his words.

Jake permitted himself a self-satisfied smile as Sammy returned to the boat. He reached down and retrieved the rod, then hauled the bait boy over the rail and into the cockpit.

'You oughtta get that kid on TV!' one of the Ernies exclaimed. 'I know a guy who's pretty high up in CBS. You're talking big money contracts, man—'

'Sammy's not for sale, pal,' Jake said, clambering back up to the flying bridge.

Although he had to admit the money would come in mighty handy.

The sun was setting by the time Jake cracked open his

first Tusker of the day. The Ernies, lobster red and worse the wear for drink, had been deposited at their hotel marina, and Sammy, having cleared up after them, had dived overboard at Jalawi Inlet to swim back to the shack on the edge of the jungle he shared with his mother and younger brother. Now, as he steered *Yellowfin* through the narrowing channel of Flamingo Creek towards the boatyard a mile upriver, Jake took a long luxurious pull on the ice-cold beer. The first mouthful tasted of the sea salt caked on his lips, and he wished – as he always wished at this time of the day – that he still smoked. Packets of nicotine gum were no substitute for the harsh impact of Marlboro smoke on the back of the throat. Once the pharmaceuticals companies could replicate that sensation, tobacco's days would be truly numbered.

After anchoring the boat, he jumped into a motor launch moored in the shallows. He ramped up the outboard and directed the craft towards a row of bare lightbulbs strung along the length of the jetty. The jetty led to the workshop, a large breezeblock and corrugated-iron structure on the south bank of the river. From one corner of the building came the low thrum of a generator. In another corner, barely insu-lated by three large panes of clear plastic, was the office of Britannia Fishing Trips Ltd. Inside, looking for something in a pile of dog-eared papers stacked on a battered metal filing cabinet behind the desk, was Jake's business partner.

'Evening, Harry,' Jake said.

Harry Philliskirk grunted and wafted a hand in greeting, but did not turn.

'What have you lost?'

'I can't remember,' Harry said. 'But I will when I find it.'

13

'Good luck,' Jake said.

As far as he could see, it was a miracle that Harry could ever find anything in his self-imposed chaos of paperwork. But Harry – as Harry kept reminding him – had a *system*. 'Don't ask me to explain it, old man,' he would say, 'but it works.'

He was forty-two years old, but age meant nothing to the tall Londoner with the crisp Home Counties accent. As far as Harry was concerned, he simply *existed* – and, if you wanted to demarcate that existence into years, that was your concern. In any case, Harry was one of those people who defied any sort of pigeonholing. He stood six feet four inches in his sandals – Harry rarely wore shoes – and the shapeless clothes that hung from it exaggerated his spare frame. His usual choice of attire was a grubby vest and ancient army camouflage pants, a combination which was not helped by the grimy lime-green I RAN THE 1ST LONDON MARATHON baseball cap that he had worn with pride for over a quarter of a century. Unruly sprigs of greying greasy hair sprouted from under the cap, framing a narrow, almost morose face dominated by a large bony nose.

'There you are, you see!' Harry exclaimed triumphantly. 'Always trust in the system!'

He waved a piece of paper between his forefinger and thumb like Chamberlain returning from Munich.

'What is it?'

'An invoice for seventeen thousand dollars' worth of diesel fuel.'

Jake felt a knot tighten in his stomach. 'What about it?'

'I told the Arab that we had paid it. He said we hadn't. This would appear to prove that he was right and I was wrong.'

14

'Oh shit.'

'Hmm,' Harry said. He sat down on the corner of the desk and stared out of the office's single exterior window at the twinkling lights of the smart new marina complex that had been built on the other side of the creek. 'Still – not to worry.'

'We don't even have seventeen *hundred* dollars, Harry,' Jake reminded him.

'No.' Harry grinned, wagging his finger. 'But we've got the Arab's fuel.'

'Yes. And the Arab has got associates with guns.'

'Don't you worry about the Arab, old boy,' Harry said. 'Business will pick up. I can feel it in my water.'

Jake drained his beer and tossed the bottle through the office door and into an old oil drum in the workshop. 'Jesus Christ, Harry.'

He went to the window. Through the thickening gloom, it was still possible to make out the crisp modern angles of the brick and smoked-glass boat-houses, clubs and diving schools which had sprung up seemingly overnight on the opposite bank. Their own premises were like an outhouse by comparison. Jake could imagine the blazered clubmen and their wives staring across from the veranda of the Flamingo Creek Yacht Club and wondering when the developers' bulldozers were scheduled to obliterate the squalor that gave such a sour taste to their gin and tonics.

'How were the Ernies?' Harry asked breezily. 'They were from Detroit, weren't they?'

It was Harry who had coined the term 'Ernies' to describe the pale-skinned tourists who came to Kenya in search of big fish. Jake didn't pretend to know about literature, but Harry assured him that

15

every one of them, whether from the USA or the Ukraine, imagined themselves to be Ernest Hemingway, and that every puny baitfish they heaved aboard would have become a two-hundred-pound marlin by the time they returned home. Jake wasn't about to argue. Harry was an educated man. As long as the Ernies paid, Jake didn't care what he called them.

He reached into a pocket of his shorts and dropped a wad of bills on the desk. 'They paid up in full and in cash.'

Harry rubbed his hands and placed the cash in a tin box. 'God bless America.'

He put the box in a floor safe, then stood and rubbed the base of his crackling spine. Jake watched him closely. Ever since he'd got back, there'd been something about his partner that didn't seem quite right. The good humour and the bravado were in place, but then those were Harry's default settings. Jake had known Harry long enough to tell when he was hiding something.

'What is it, Harry?'

'Eh?'

'Out with it.'

There was a moment when Harry debated keeping up the pretence, but then it passed and his long face fell into an expression of weary resignation. 'Oh, Christ, Jake. I was hoping you might have already heard.'

'*Harry* . . .' Any number of apocalyptic scenarios suddenly flashed across Jake's mind. Had there been a bombing? Was the country about to erupt into bloodshed once again? Had the government in Nairobi imposed martial law and ordered all foreign nationals to get the hell out?

16

Harry slumped down behind his desk and removed his cap. 'It's Dennis Bentley.'

Jake almost laughed with relief. 'Dennis? What about him?'

Harry nodded in the direction of a ship-to-shore wireless positioned by the door. 'It's been on the radio all day.'

Jake scowled. 'Well, since *Yellowfin*'s radio is still in bits, you can assume I'm in the dark. What's happened to Dennis, Harry?'

'Well, that rather does seem to be the point, old man.' Harry shrugged. 'Nobody appears to know.'

Chapter Three

From the elevated third tee of Monte Julia golf course, Norrie Barclay could see for more than thirty miles beyond the scalped, arid foothills of the Serr de Ronda mountains to the hazy blue smudge of the Mediterranean sea. On a clear day, it was possible to see even further to the jutting black tooth of Gibraltar nearly fifty miles to the south.

Norrie couldn't care less. The only view that concerned him was down into the steep-sided ravine that separated the tee from the handkerchief-sized green 219 yards away. This unforgiving bastard had already swallowed three top-of-the-range Titleists and wrecked his scorecard. Anyone else would have cut their losses and walked away – but not Norrie Barclay. There was the small matter of pride to consider. After careful deliberation, he selected a six iron from his golf bag, removed another gleaming Titleist from the ball sleeve and approached the tee-box.

'Come on, Norrie! This time!'

Norrie turned and smiled grimly at his playing partner lounging in the shade of the golf buggy.

'I'm going to whip its arse, mate,' he said confidently.

His playing partner swigged from a bottle of San Miguel he had plucked from an ice-box attached to the back of the buggy. He was slim built, and Norrie guessed maybe in his early thirties. He wore pressed slacks and a maroon golf shirt. Norrie Barclay knew him as Whitestone, but what he didn't know was that Whitestone had many names.

'Here's to fourth time lucky,' Whitestone said, and raised the bottle in a toast.

Arrogant prick, Norrie thought as he dug the point of his tee into the bone-hard earth. Just because his guest had fluked a drive to within five feet of the pin he thought he was Tiger fucking Woods. But just as quickly Norrie reprimanded himself. There was no need to be like that. All in all Whitestone was a decent bloke. Strange fellow, admittedly. A bit *intense* at times – and even now Norrie still couldn't place that accent of his. Was it European? Was there a touch of Kraut in there? It was hard to tell. Anyway, it didn't matter where he was from. What mattered was they'd done some good business since he'd flown in this morning. They could do with a few more like him on the Costa. And, it had to be said, Whitestone's merchandise was top class. Everyone thought so – which was why Norrie was making a healthy little earner for himself by reselling Whitestone's goods to his associates in the Balkans. All right, it wasn't strictly kosher business protocol, but you got nowhere in this world unless you were prepared to bend a few rules.

'Nice and easy, Norrie,' Whitestone said.

Norrie took a deep breath, exhaled slowly. *Backswing, hold, downswing . . . Thwapp!* The contact was fat and healthy and echoed satisfyingly from the steep sides of the ravine.

'You're the man!'

With mounting excitement, Norrie shaded his eyes from the sun and attempted to get a bead on his ball. There! A speck of iridescent white against the blue sky, soaring high and handsome and on a perfect trajectory. Christ – maybe he *was* the man! The ball pitched ten yards on to the green, bounced once and then—

'Hold up! Hold up!' Norrie wailed. *'Nooo!'*

The ball bit into the turf and spun backwards, gathering speed as it approached the lip of the ravine. For a moment it seemed as if it might catch on the unruly tuft of marron grass that fringed the green, but instead the ball bobbled once and dropped over the edge, bouncing crazily on the rocky outcrops as it plunged into the abyss.

'Bad luck, Norrie,' said Whitestone, as he stepped from the buggy and made his way to the tee-box.

Norrie leaned on his golf club like a bent old man. 'I do not fucking believe what I have just seen. I *never* get backspin. *Never!'*

'Of course, it could be worse,' Whitestone said.

'I don't see how.' Norrie shrugged, staring balefully down into the crevasse.

In a single fluid movement that would have graced anybody's golf game, Whitestone swung a Big Bertha War Bird with nine-degree loft into the side of Norrie's head. Norrie staggered across the tee-box, blood pumping from a two-inch gash, then fell on his backside on the artificial grass.

'What did I tell you about business etiquette, Norrie?' Whitestone said calmly, the club resting on his shoulder like a parasol. 'About doing deals behind my back with *my* merchandise?'

'Wha—' Norrie said, his eyes spinning in their sockets.

20

'Now maybe you people here think it's acceptable to do that. Maybe you think it's all part of the rough and tumble. But it's not how I do business, Norrie. So as of now our arrangement is terminated. Do you hear me?'

Norrie attempted to swipe the blood from his eyes but succeeded only in overbalancing and slumping over on to his side.

'*Terminated.*'

Whitestone broadened his stance and drove the club head into Norrie's face. Three more swings, and what was left of the Englishman's skull had turned to pulp.

Whitestone scooped up the inert body with a single easy movement and dumped it behind the wheel of the golf buggy. After wiping the blood from the clubface with a towel, he replaced it in the bag tied to the rear of the buggy and then jammed the gear lever into the forward position. By standing on the running board, Whitestone was able to direct the vehicle to the lip of the ravine. As its fat front wheels went over the edge, and the buggy and its single passenger plunged two hundred feet on to the unforgiving rocks below, he noted with irritation that there was a single spot of fresh blood on his brand-new $300 golf shoes.

Chapter Four

Suki Lo's skull-face cracked open as Jake and Harry walked into the bar and her Nike-tick eyes all but disappeared in the harsh creases of skin.

'Hey, boys – how you doin'?' she called out in a shrill voice that some of her regulars said could cut through fog better than the siren at Galana Point.

'A bottle of Mr Daniel's finest, Suki, my pet,' Harry said. 'And two large glasses.'

Suki smiled again. Her teeth were mottled and crooked; as long as they'd known her, she'd insisted that one day she was going back to Malaysia to get them replaced because dental work across there was dirt cheap compared to Kenya, and a million times safer. She claimed to know a dentist in Penang who would, for just one hundred US dollars, pull those rotten pegs right out of her head and replace them with gleaming white porcelain tombstones. Jake didn't know how gleaming white porcelain tombstones would look in her mouth. Suki Lo had the kind of lived-in face that suited the teeth she'd got.

She placed a bottle of bourbon on the bar and skimmed across two half-pint glasses.

'God bless you, my darling,' Harry said, tipping

22

two large measures into the glasses.

Suki Lo's bar was three hundred yards along the dirt track from the boatyard and blended in perfectly with the rest of the ramshackle buildings on the south side of the creek. It was a rudimentary drinking den with nicotine-brown walls and bare wooden floors eroded by cigarette butts and spilled liquor. Along the length of the bar, shallow grooves and nicks had been carved by the elbows and gutting knives of Suki's regulars, mostly game-boat skippers and mechanics, a few of whom now sat in dark corners hunched protectively over their bottles of hooch. Normally they talked about money and women. Tonight they were talking about one thing and one thing only.

'Terrible 'bout Dennis,' Suki said in a low voice. 'Fuckin' uh-believable.'

'We heard,' Harry said, nodding. 'Shocking business.'

'Fuckin' uh-believable.' She shook her head and, muttering to herself, wandered into the kitchen.

Yes, Jake thought, sucking back a mouthful of bourbon. *Fuckin' uh-believable* just about summed it up.

Dennis Bentley was a white Kenyan who ran a game boat called *Martha B* out of a yard up near the mouth of the creek. He had a reputation as a loner and a cantankerous bastard, but then who didn't round here? Like most of the longtime independent operators in this part of Kenya, Dennis was more concerned with keeping his shoestring outfit solvent than affecting pleasantries. Jake remembered him as a tall, rugged-looking man in his mid-fifties who occasionally dropped into Suki's for a shot of rum.

According to Harry, Dennis had set out shortly

23

before dawn that morning to pick up some Ernies from one of the all-inclusive hotels at Watamu beach, thirty miles to the north of Flamingo Creek. It was a routine job – the punters wanted to see some humpbacked whales – but *Martha B* had never arrived. After an hour waiting for him to show, the Ernies predictably kicked up hell; and it was this, rather than any concern for Dennis's welfare, that had persuaded the hotel owner to contact the coastguard. By then, however, a sugar freighter bound for Mombasa had already sighted oil and debris on the water around twelve miles east of Watamu. Fishing boats in the area had picked up the chatter on their radios and immediately switched course – but after six hours trawling the open sea they had found nothing.

And all the while Yellowfin *had been blithely chugging along with a boatload of Ernies and a radio that didn't work.*

'You OK, Jake?' Harry asked.

He nodded, but in reality he felt sick to his stomach – because as far as he was concerned there was an extra repugnant twist to Dennis Bentley's apparent demise. The Kenyan skipper's bait boy was a thirteen-year-old kid called Tigi Eruwa who lived with his mother and his elder brother Sammy at Jalawi Inlet.

The same Sammy who that afternoon had been amusing the Ernies with his swimming prowess, unaware that his kid brother was missing, presumed dead.

'Fuckin' hell,' Suki said, lighting a menthol cigarette and blowing the smoke in the direction of a long-defunct ceiling fan. 'How the hell does a boat just *blow up*?'

Harry shrugged. 'Who knows?'

'We don't know for sure that's what happened,' Jake said, but his words were greeted by a harsh cackle of cynical laughter from the other end of the bar.

A man in a khaki shirt and a greasy Peugeot cycling cap sat nursing an open rum bottle.

'*Martha B* was a fine boat – but she was fifty years old,' the man said in clipped South African tones.

'Good evening, Tug,' Harry said without conviction. 'Are you well?'

'As well as can be expected, Harry,' the man said, splashing three fingers of liquor into his glass and raising it in salute. 'To absent friends, eh? Absent fucking friends.'

Tug Viljoen could have been anywhere between forty and sixty, but his deeply etched, leathered face made it difficult to tell. Behind his back Suki's regulars reckoned he looked like one of the mouldy old crocodiles he kept in his reptile park up near the Mombasa highway, but he always reminded Jake of the Tasmanian Devil cartoon character of his youth – a squat, powerful torso supported by unfeasibly spindly legs, and with a similarly wild look in his eyes.

'Yeah, *Martha B* was a bloody fine boat in her day,' Viljoen growled. 'But, when Dennis bought her, she was rotting away in a dry dock. I kept telling him he should get a new boat, but he treated her like a vintage car.' He drained the glass and immediately refilled it. 'Trouble is, vintage cars aren't as robust as new ones. *Martha B* was designed for rich piss-artists to go cruising up and down the coast, not for belting the shit out of for fifteen, twenty hours a day chasing marlin. The parts get old, they get worn.

Pipes can start to leak. All it takes is a spark, or some drunken fuck to drop his cigarette end between the boards and . . . *kaboom!*'

'Aren't you a ray of fucking sunshine?' Jake said.

Viljoen swiped his mouth with the back of his hand, revealing an ugly stitchwork of scar tissue on the underside of his arm.

'Just being realistic, son,' he said. 'Used to happen regular round here. Long before you pair of English *conquistadors* arrived. Speaking of which, how old is that bucket of yours?'

'Fifteen years.'

'Hah! Then you want to think about getting a new one before it's too late.'

'We'd need to think about robbing a bank first,' Harry admitted.

Viljoen stared at him for a moment, then laughed gruffly and turned back to the already half-empty rum bottle.

'Anyway,' Harry continued, 'as Jake said, we still don't know what's happened to Dennis. And, knowing that old bastard, there's still every chance he might be found drifting on a plank of wood.'

'You really think that?' Viljoen said sceptically.

'Always look on the bright side, Tug.'

'Bright side?' Viljoen said. 'I don't recall seeing one of them round here recently.'

26

Day Two

Chapter Five

The reward for professional diligence, Detective Inspector Daniel Jouma of the Coast Province CID reflected, was a sore head from bashing it against brick walls. And, right now, he had a splitting headache that was not being helped by Detective Sergeant Nyami's tea.

'How did you make this?' Jouma demanded, pointing at the insipid white liquid in the cup on his desk.

Nyami glanced up from the sports pages of *The Daily Nation* and furrowed his brow. 'With a teabag.'

'*Details*, Nyami,' Jouma demanded.

'I put hot water in the cup, then added a teabag and milk. How else do you make tea?'

'And for how long was the teabag in the cup?'

Nyami sighed theatrically and flung the newspaper on his desk. '*I* don't know!'

'One minute? Two minutes?' Jouma stared at Nyami. The sergeant's eyes fell. 'Ah! *Less* than one minute! Thirty seconds? Forty-five?'

'I do not remember,' Nyami mumbled.

Jouma stood and carried the cup across to a tiny sink fixed to a wall in the corner of the office.

'Sergeant Nyami, I firmly believe that tea only becomes tea when the bag is allowed to infuse in hot water for a minimum of two minutes. Otherwise, it is not tea – it is slightly stained hot water. This—' he held the teacup between his finger and thumb '—is slightly stained hot water.'

Jouma dismissively poured the contents of the cup down the plughole, then turned on the tap. There was an ominous clunking sound, before the tap juddered twice and spat filthy brown water into the sink. The inspector felt a sudden overwhelming pressure above his eyes. Some days it was advisable to remain in bed rather than experience a day like the one he was having. It was not even three o'clock in the afternoon, but already it seemed the day had lasted a hundred years.

That morning Jouma had spent three interminable and frustrating hours waiting for a case to be called at the law court in downtown Mombasa, only for it to be adjourned in less than twenty seconds. Upon his return to Police Headquarters on Mama Ngina Drive shortly before midday, he had found Agnes Malewe and her son sitting on a wooden bench in the corridor outside the office he shared with Nyami.

'Who is that woman in the corridor?' he had asked the sergeant, who was slumped at his desk, reading a magazine and eating a jam sandwich.

Nyami did not look up. 'She is still there?' he grunted. 'I told her to go home an hour ago.'

'Who *is* she?'

'Her name is Agnes Malewe.'

'Why is she sitting in the corridor?'

Nyami shrugged. 'Those idiots at Likoni Station sent her here. Now she refuses to leave.'

30

Jouma went across to Nyami's desk and snatched the half-eaten sandwich from the sergeant's fingers. *'What does she want?'*

'She says her husband did not come home yesterday.'

'Who is her husband?'

Nyami looked at his boss as if he was a simpleton. *'George* Malewe.'

Jouma groaned inwardly. George Malewe was a lowlife from Mombasa Old Town. His speciality was stealing wallets, cameras and phones from gullible tourists, before returning them to their grateful owners in return for tips far in excess of what he could get by selling them. Not that George saw any of the money, of course. Almost all of his earnings went directly to Michael Kili, the gang boss who controlled the port and the Old Town. George Malewe was a big-time loser. Until that moment, Jouma had not known he had a wife.

'Then he is drunk somewhere,' he said. 'The docks most probably. You know what George Malewe is like.'

Nyami whipped back his sandwich. *'That's* what I told her. But she refuses to accept it. She says he should have been back yesterday.'

'Why?'

'It was their son's birthday.'

Jouma rubbed his face with his hand. 'Tell her to come in,' he sighed.

Agnes Malewe was perhaps nineteen years old. She sat primly and defiantly in a chair on the other side of Jouma's desk, her three-year-old son sitting cross-legged at her feet.

'My husband has been slain, Inspector,' she stated matter-of-factly. 'Of that I am sure.'

31

Jouma leaned forwards across his desk and smiled. 'Mrs Malewe. Just because your husband failed to turn up for your son's birthday does not mean he is dead.'

'*Slain*, Inspector Jouma,' Agnes said forcefully. 'It is the only possible explanation for his behaviour.'

'Perhaps he is visiting friends. Perhaps he will have returned by the time you get home.'

Agnes shook her head. 'My husband *never* misses Benjamin's birthday.'

Jouma leaned back in his chair. 'Well, Mrs Malewe, I'm afraid there is not a great deal I can do, other than ask Sergeant Nyami to help you fill in a missing persons report.'

'I see,' Agnes said curtly, standing up from her chair. 'Then I bid you good day, Inspector.' She tapped Benjamin on the head, and together the pair of them left the office.

At twelve forty-five, Jouma had been flicking through the overnight crime sheet – thirteen robberies, two abductions, two suspected arsons, a streaker on Moi Avenue and a chicken thief in Likoni – when the telephone rang. It was an internal call from his superior, Superintendent Teshete.

'Daniel,' Teshete said, in a perfectly reasonable voice that Jouma knew from long experience meant trouble, 'I have a Mrs Malewe with me here in my office. I understand you sent her to see me?'

Jouma's heart sank even as he marvelled at the girl's persistence. 'Not exactly, sir.'

'I see. Well, Daniel, Mrs Malewe is quite insistent that one of our detectives looks into the disappearance of her husband.'

Jouma could imagine the insincere smile that

Teshete would be flashing Agnes Malewe at that very moment.

'Her husband is *George* Malewe, sir.'

A pause. 'I am aware of that, Daniel. But I am sure that you will be able to make some *initial* enquiries into the matter now. Just to put Mrs Malewe's mind at rest. *To reassure her that she doesn't have to pay a visit to Provincial Criminal Investigation Officer Iraki.*'

Police Criminal Investigation Officer Iraki was Teshete's immediate boss. Jouma put down the receiver and picked up his jacket.

So it was that, at one-fifteen, when he had a million and one better things to do with his time, Jouma had found himself threading his 1984 Fiat Panda through the traffic-choked thoroughfares of Mombasa Old Town, tooting the horn at the thronging vehicles and pedestrians, and ignoring the disgruntled protestations of Sergeant Nyami, who sat with his arms folded in the passenger seat beside him.

'You know that this is a waste of time,' Nyami said for the third time since they'd left the police station.

Jouma nodded. 'Perhaps – but it is our duty to make enquiries.'

'Pah!' Nyami snorted. 'You take too much notice of Teshete. And too much notice of that hysterical woman. She would have gone home eventually. If George Malewe is dead, then he will be doing us all a favour.'

'Sergeant Nyami,' Jouma said, wagging an admonishing finger, 'I accept that George Malewe is not a model Kenyan citizen. Nevertheless, he has a wife and a son who have a right to know what has become of him.'

33

As he spoke, Jouma hoped he sounded more convincing than he actually felt. In truth, he felt like the very worst sort of hypocrite.

Fifteen minutes later, they were in the upstairs office of an Old Town strip joint called the Baobab Club, for an unscheduled audience with a twenty-three-year-old gangster named Michael Kili.

With his pointed face and dead eyes, Kili reminded Jouma of a shark. Were he ever to smile, the detective imagined he would see scraps of flesh hanging between the gangster's teeth.

But Kili was not smiling. He was sitting in a battered armchair behind a leather-topped desk, fingers steepled under his chin, face impassive behind expensive wraparound shades. There was a sofa and some wooden chairs against the wall, but they were not offered. Instead, Jouma and Nyami were made to stand before the desk like two naughty schoolboys in the headmaster's study. A shaven-headed bodyguard filled the doorframe, twitching with aggression.

How you must be enjoying this, Michael, Jouma thought. *How it must please you to have me standing before you, awaiting your benediction. How many years has it been since our paths first crossed? Ten? Twelve? You were such a clever boy. You could have achieved so much. But here we are. You in your chair and me standing before you. You must think you have the world in your hands. You must think that becoming God was so easy.*

'We are making enquiries into a missing person,' Jouma announced with as much authority as he could muster. 'His name is George Malewe.'

'Mr Kili does not know of anyone by that name.'

34

The speaker was a thin bespectacled man wearing a plain white cotton *khanzu* robe and a *kofia* on his head. He stood attentively at Kili's left shoulder, like a carved giraffe bookend from one of the trinket stalls on Digo Road.

'I understand Mr Malewe was one of your employees,' Jouma continued, his words directed at the gangster behind the desk. Jouma saw himself in Kili's mirror lenses: a small impossibly deformed figure.

'Mr Kili does not employ anyone of that name.'

Jouma flashed the bespectacled man a withering glance. 'You seem to be very well informed about what Mr Kili does and does not know. Who, might I ask, are you?'

'My name is Jacob Omu. I am Mr Kili's representative,' the man said calmly.

Kili's *representative*? Jouma thought. It was indeed a strange and troubled world when murderous thugs employed agents to do their talking for them.

'Then perhaps you would be good enough to tell Mr Kili that this is a routine enquiry and Mombasa CID would be very grateful for any information he might have regarding the whereabouts of Mr Malewe,' Jouma said.

'Mr Kili has no information that would assist you.'

'Then would you be good enough to tell Mr Kili that a CID investigation into the illegal practices carried out in this area is long overdue, and that any such investigation would inevitably bring Mr Kili's activities under the most painstaking scrutiny.'

Omu smiled. 'Are you threatening Mr Kili?'

Jouma smiled back. 'Does Mr Kili have any reason to feel threatened?'

Omu shook his head. 'Certainly not, Inspector.'

35

Jouma stared at Kili. No, he thought. He most probably didn't. There were more than enough Mombasa police officers and civic officials receiving regular backhanders from Michael Kili for him not to be worried about any investigation into his affairs. *It had ever been thus in this city. Only the faces changed.*

The detective reached into the breast pocket of his jacket and removed a card, which he placed on the desk. He addressed Kili. 'This is my telephone number. I would be grateful if either you – *or your representative* – would give me a call if you hear anything about Mr Malewe.'

Kili slowly reached across and picked up the card. He handed it to Omu without looking at it. Omu handed it back to Jouma.

'Mr Kili does not know of anyone by that name,' he repeated.

Jouma looked at the face of the Mombasa gangster, and as he did so Kili slowly removed his sunglasses. The small cold eyes seemed to glitter.

I had rather be a doorkeeper in the house of my God, Jouma thought, *than to dwell in the tents of wickedness.* His headache was starting to throb and something told him it was only going to get worse before it got better.

Chapter Six

At that moment, in another part of Mombasa, the man known as the Arab stuck the end of a sharpened twig between two of his upper-right molars and twisted it until a fingernail-sized morsel of chewed lamb flew from his mouth and landed in the dirt at Harry Philliskirk's feet.

'What is this?' he said, holding up a thin sheaf of dollar bills.

'Think of it as an instalment,' Harry said. 'A gesture of goodwill until full payment can be resolved.'

'This is neither of those things, Mr Philliskirk,' the Arab said matter-of-factly. 'This is an insult.' He opened his fat fingers and the bills fluttered to the ground.

'Abdul,' Harry said placatingly, scooping up the money, 'surely our credit with you is good enough to see us through this temporary cash-flow problem?'

The Arab removed the stick from his teeth and spat derisively on the ground. '*Credit!* It is always credit with people like you! What is credit but a convenient way of not paying your debts?'

Standing beside Harry, Jake shrugged. 'Abdul, you

know what business has been like since—'

The Arab sat forward in his deckchair and cocked his head expectantly. '*Since*, Mr Moore? Since what?' He waved his stick dismissively. 'Don't expect my heart to bleed for you because a few thousand madmen in the Rift Valley decided to kill each other over a crooked election. I am interested only in *business*. I don't give a fuck about anyone else's problems. Yours or theirs.'

In the open compound of the fuel depot, the heat was oppressive. The Arab knew this, which was why he was sitting in the shade of a canvas awning strung between two diesel sumps while the two Englishmen were standing out in the sun. As if to emphasise their discomfort, the Arab reached down for a cold can of Coke and brought it to his wet lips with relish.

'When I first came to this country, one of the first things I saw was a dead body on the Mombasa highway,' he said. 'It was flat as unleavened bread, the trucks and the cars just driving over it as if it was a dog. Later, I discovered that the body had been there for nearly two days because the police in Mombasa and Malindi couldn't decide under whose jurisdiction it lay. It was at that point I realised that my business here would be a success.'

The Arab shifted in his seat and scratched his backside with the stick. 'This country is not like yours or mine, gentlemen,' he continued. 'It lies somewhere in the middle, and what happens here is not controlled by either the east or the west. Here you must make your own destiny – or be crushed flat beneath the wheels of progress. Do you understand what I am saying?'

'Does that mean you'll give us more time?' Harry asked.

'You have five days,' the Arab said. 'At twelve per cent interest per day.'

'Fuck the Arab, that's what I say!' Harry said, weaving through the potholed suburbs of Mombasa in his twenty-year-old Land Rover. 'He thinks he's the Sultan of Oman. We'll just have to teach him the real meaning of a market economy, that's all.'

'And how do you propose to do that?' Jake said.

'The Arab isn't the only diesel supplier in Mombasa.'

'He's the only one who'll give us credit,' Jake pointed out. 'Even if it is at twelve per cent.'

'I'll think of something,' Harry said.

'Then you'd better make it fast – or else start learning how to make sails.'

Or how to catch fish ...

That morning, head throbbing from what had turned into an impromptu and lengthy wake for Dennis Bentley in Suki Lo's the previous night, Jake had stared out from *Yellowfin*'s flying bridge and wondered if even that fundamental requirement of running a game-fishing business had deserted him. Since just after dawn, they had been chugging in figure-eights in the area east of Kilifi where the tuna schools normally congregated, but without a single bite. Now they were heading home. The Ernies from Düsseldorf who had paid three hundred bucks for this abortive half-day excursion sat in ugly brooding silence in the cabin below. Of course, the Indian Ocean was a big place and big fish were capricious. But Jake knew that was no excuse. There were old salts who drank at Suki Lo's who claimed to be able to sense shoals by the strength of the current or the colour of the sea, but these days most skippers preferred hi-tech sonar systems to voodoo. At the very least they had functioning radios so that they could communicate with each other to find out where the fish were.

Yellowfin had neither. Such was the parlous state of Britannia Fishing Trips Ltd's finances, they didn't even have credit for a mobile-phone contract. Jake stared at the dead radio and cursed it. Two weeks for replacement parts from Nairobi. *Two fucking weeks!* It was all very well for Harry to deal with the vicissitudes of life with a wisecrack and a dismissive swipe of his hand, but without a radio *Yellowfin* shouldn't even have been on the water. If anything went wrong, all Jake had was a box of flares. And, if the disgruntled Germans knew *that*, it would certainly take their minds off the lack of fishing.

Harry's argument, of course, was that what the Ernies didn't know wouldn't hurt them, and that in any case they simply could not afford to take *Yellowfin* out of circulation. But that was the kind of logic that got people killed. And it turned Jake's blood to ice that, despite everything he knew about the actions of desperate men, he should find himself complicit in just such an act of desperation.

He adjusted the bearing slightly then watched as Sammy once again reeled in each individual line from the booms and diligently rebaited them with slivers of pinky-white flesh. It was a fruitless task because they were now approaching the reef, but it gave the impression that at least one member of *Yellowfin*'s crew knew what they were doing.

Sammy. Christ, Jake thought, the kid was incredible. His brother was missing presumed dead less than twenty-four hours, but when Jake had gone in person to the boy's house at Jalawi that morning Sammy had insisted on working as if nothing had happened.

'Tigi will come back,' was all he would say on the matter as he sharpened his filleting knives on a leather strop nailed to the door.

Inside, his mother filled a canvas musette with dates and slivers of dried meat for his lunch, busying herself the way only parents can when the alternative is too terrible to contemplate.

They were on the outskirts of the city now, stalled in traffic a quarter of a mile from the Nyali Bridge, which connected Mombasa island to the north mainland. Ahead was a cacophonic lottery of carts, cars, trucks, *matatu* taxis, motorcycles, pedestrians and animals, all competing for the same inch of empty road at the same time. Harry's left hand maintained a steady rhythm on the horn, as if that would make a blind bit of difference. After five years in Kenya, Jake knew all about Mombasa traffic jams. All it took was some rickety old pick-up to shed its load of goats and the city could be gridlocked for hours.

Five years. Was it really that long since he'd arrived at Moi Airport with nothing more than a suitcase and the Kenyan guidebook he'd bought at Heathrow? Even now he marvelled at how wonderfully naive he had been that day, striding out into the sapping Mombasa heat like some latter-day colonial adventurer straight off the steamer.

His old man would have laughed his head off if he could have seen it.

'Look at him!' Albie Moore would have said, leaning forward on his bar stool in the taproom of the Low Lights Tavern in North Shields. 'He used to

41

think he was Dixon of Dock Green. Now he's Gordon of Khartoum!'

And that low bronchitic laugh would have rumbled out again until it was doused with a mouthful of Pusser's Rum, his fifth since stepping off the trawler at four that morning.

But of course Albie Moore never saw the day his son arrived in Kenya. The old man was long dead, killed by too much drink and too many hand-rolled cigarettes, but mostly by the crushing realisation that his life, which had been so unimaginably hard, should have ended up meaning nothing at all.

Jake stared through the grimy window at the clutter of rundown shacks and jerrybuilt stalls constructed from corrugated iron, chicken wire, salvaged wood and knitted palm leaves that hugged the verges on either side of the road, selling everything from hand-stitched *kanga* shawls to 100 per cent hooch. The ingenuity never failed to amaze him. Nor did the grinding poverty that made it necessary. He wondered what his old man would have made of it all. Albie, he knew, would have understood it more than he ever understood his son.

'There is, of course, another solution to all this,' Harry said suddenly.

'What?'

He waved two hundred dollars under Jake's nose. 'I know a bar not half a mile from here.'

'I thought that money was for the Arab.'

'You heard what he said: he considers it an insult.'

Jake rubbed his face wearily. Through his fingers he saw the traffic jam stretching to infinity, and the thought of getting drunk again was suddenly hugely appealing. Then something – a sudden blur of movement – caught his attention.

'Maggie's Den is the name,' Harry was saying. 'Overlooks the dhow harbour. A bit rough, perhaps, but not without character.'

'Stop the car,' Jake said suddenly.

'What?'

'Stop the car. Now.'

Harry swerved abruptly across the road and all hell erupted behind him as the traffic slowed from a crawl to a dead halt – but the passenger door was already swinging open and the seat was empty. Jake was visible only for a moment, slaloming through the nose-to-tail vehicles in order to get to the far side of the road. Then he was gone.

Chapter Seven

The girl was perhaps sixteen years old. She was slumped against the hand-painted raffia frame of a fruit kiosk, legs splayed across the pavement, blood seeping from a wound to the side of her head. She was wailing, her eyes rolling wildly in their sockets, her hands fluttering on either side of her face. A crowd of curious onlookers were gathered around, staring down at her but seemingly unwilling to help in case she was possessed by a demon. Jake surmised she was in shock, which did not surprise him. Less than thirty seconds earlier, he had watched from the Land Rover as a tall man, his face hidden by a hooded sweat top, had run up behind her, snatched the baby she had been carrying in a cotton sling around her neck and pushed her roughly to the ground.

He knelt and quickly assessed the injury. It was superficial, despite the blood.

'You,' he snapped at the stall owner, a spindly man with tobacco-stained teeth and alcohol-induced shakes. 'Get this woman a bandage.'

The man looked at him blankly.

Jake pointed at the wound. '*Gango!*'

The man nodded frantically, repeating the Swahili word over and over as if to ensure he did not forget it. But Jake did not wait to see if he understood.

The abductor had sprinted from the main highway and on to a narrower adjacent road that looped down towards the vast concrete supports of Nyali Bridge. Jake followed until the road abruptly stopped. Ahead of him was a breaker's yard, situated on scrubland beneath the span of the bridge itself. It was filled with teetering piles of rusting vehicles, most of them mangled out of all recognition by the collisions that had ended their useful lives. Over the angry blare of stalled traffic on the carriageway high above him, Jake could hear the urgent keening of a child as he approached. It was coming from a tar-paper cabin on the far side of the compound. He moved forwards, grabbing the nearest weapon to hand, a foot-long piece of virtually carbonised exhaust pipe. He hoped to hell he wouldn't have to use it because it felt like it would crumble in his fingers at the slightest impact.

Jake waited outside the cabin, listening. The crying was relentless, like a buzz saw. There was a window. He peered in and saw the baby, still wrapped in its cotton sling. It had been dumped in an in-tray on a metal desk in one corner of the room. The abductor sat with his back against the opposite wall near the door. Jake could see now that he was no older than the girl he had left bleeding on the street. *Just a kid.* His head was between his knees, his hands clamped to his ears. His foot was jiggling nervously. Suddenly, he sprang to his feet and opened the door. Jake flattened himself against the flimsy wall of the cabin until the door slammed shut again.

Waiting for someone?

He placed the pipe on the ground, wiped the shit off his hands and knocked on the door.

The door flew open.

'Good afternoon,' Jake said pleasantly, then rammed his fist into the abductor's solar plexus.

The kid's eyes bulged, and with a retch of pain and surprise he crumpled first on to his knees and then on to his side in the foetal position. Jake stepped over him and went to the desk. He picked up the baby, saw that it was unharmed and replaced it in the in-tray.

'I think you've got some explaining to do, son,' he said.

The kid had dragged himself into a corner of the cabin like a wounded animal on the highway. His dark skin had turned grey, and his face was full of fear.

'You are the police?'

'No. I'm not the police. What's your name?'

Total confusion now.

'I won't ask you again.'

'Adan. Adan Mohammed.'

'You want to tell me what's going on, Adan?'

'*Who are you?*'

'Why did you take the baby?'

The kid's stupefied expression hardened. 'I am his *father!*'

Oh shit, Jake thought.

'And the girl you just knocked for six is the mother?'

'She told me I could not see him again,' the kid protested. 'She said I am a bad father.'

'Seems to me that she's got a point.'

Adan shook his head. 'Shahira's father never liked

46

me. He has poisoned her against me.'

Jake sighed. By now the traffic on the approach to Nyali Bridge might have unglued itself. He and Harry could have been home free. To hell with Maggie's Den, in a little over an hour they would have been ensconced in Suki Lo's.

'So what's the plan, Adan? Tell me you've got a plan. Who are you waiting for?'

'My friend Lucas has a truck. He will drive us to Nairobi. Then I will write to Shahira instructing her to join us. Once she is free of her father, I am convinced we will be happy. I will find a job. I will provide for my family.'

'You're meeting Lucas here?'

Adan nodded.

'Forget it. He's not coming.'

'Lucas will come.'

'No, he won't, Adan. Because any minute now this place will be crawling with police. It tends to happen when you kidnap a child in broad daylight on the busiest fucking road in Mombasa.'

At that moment, a look of utter despair crossed Adan Mohammed's thin face.

'But Oki is my son,' he whispered.

Jake looked at him, and any anger he felt towards the boy evaporated. 'How old are you, Adan?'

'Seventeen.'

'OK. Get up.'

Adan gingerly levered himself to his feet. Jake passed over the baby. The boy held his son with an unmistakable tenderness. *No – he wasn't a bad father*, Jake thought. *He was just a stupid, headstrong teenager*. He deserved a clip round the ear. Him and his flaky girlfriend.

Whether Mombasa police would share Jake's

opinion was a different matter, however.

'Where are we going?'

'We're going to hand ourselves in, Adan.'

Chapter Eight

After his abortive meeting with Michael Kili, Jouma had returned to Mama Ngina Drive, his headache building. He was fifty-one years old, and on days like these he felt every one of those years. How much easier life would be if he shared Sergeant Nyami's attitude to policework, he reflected. What had he hoped to achieve by investigating the disappearance of a lowlife undesirable like George Malewe anyway? Some sort of professional satisfaction? The eternal gratitude of a young wife and a small boy who had just celebrated his third birthday? No, Nyami was right: if Malewe was indeed dead, then it was probably nothing more than he deserved. There was an old saying that, if you swam with sharks, sooner or later you were going to get eaten by them.

Yet, almost as soon as the thought entered his head, Jouma felt ashamed. Was this what he had been reduced to? Thirty-three years a serving police officer, only to end up turning his back on everything he had sworn to protect? He thought about the riots in the Nairobi slums and in the Rift Valley, about the violence and bloodshed that had stained his country in recent months. How he, like everyone else who was a proud Kenyan, had stared with disbelief at the television images that were being beamed around the world. He'd watched young men, many barely older than boys, descend into unspeakable savagery with breathtaking ease, in the blink of an eye almost; and it made him realise that the barrier that held back such raging bestial instincts in a man must be so paper-thin as to be almost invisible. As churches burned and mothers wept for their dead children, Jouma had concluded that, if all that was good was not to be consumed by all that was evil, this flimsy barrier had to be protected at all costs.

How quickly you forget, Daniel.

'Put the kettle on, Nyami,' he said wearily. 'I will show you how a cup of tea should be made.'

It was five minutes past three. In two hours he could go home and forget about this day. Then the telephone rang, and even before he answered it Jouma knew that another test awaited him.

The Englishman from Flamingo Creek was sitting quietly in the interview room, his left wrist manacled to a metal loop on the table in front of him. Jouma knew the creek. It was situated between Mombasa and Kilifi, and was well known as a habitat for that most peculiar of species – the fishing boat skipper.

He had never heard of Jake Moore, however.

For a moment the two men sized each other up across the room.

'Mr Moore?'

'Inspector Jouma?'

Jouma gestured irritably, and a uniformed officer standing by the door moved sharply across the room to unlock the cuffs from Jake's wrist.

'I apologise,' he said, sitting down on a plastic

50

chair that was bolted to the floor on the other side of the table. 'Standard procedure, I'm afraid.'

'I understand.'

'Then you will understand that, if there is one thing that we frown upon most severely, Mr Moore, it is vigilantism. We simply cannot have members of the public taking the law into their own hands. Mombasa is a dangerous place. The consequences do not bear thinking about.'

'Of course,' Jake said. 'How is the boy? Adan?'

'He is downstairs in the cells, considering the error of his ways. I intend to let him consider them for the rest of the day.'

'And then?'

'It depends whether the girl wishes to press charges. I will be strongly urging her not to.'

'A compassionate copper?' Jake smiled. 'Now there's a rarity.'

'Compassion has nothing to do with it,' Jouma said. 'Paperwork does. And so do lawyers. By the time this case reaches any sort of fruition, the baby you rescued will be in long trousers. But then I suspect you know that anyway, Mr Moore.'

'I don't understand.'

'It takes a policeman to know the many pitfalls of the judicial system, does it not?'

Jake looked at him across the table and nodded admiringly. 'You've done your homework, Inspector.'

'It is standard procedure to run background checks on foreign nationals held in custody. All it took was a telephone call to your Consulate here in Mombasa.'

'Then I hope they told you that I haven't been a policeman for quite some time.'

Now it was Jouma's turn to smile. 'Indeed they did, Mr Moore. Six years, to be exact. But it would

51

appear that living in Kenya hasn't dulled your instincts.'

'Old habits die hard, Inspector,' Jake said.

Jouma stood, and the interview room echoed to the sound of cracking knees.

'This has been a long and tortuous day for me, Mr Moore,' he said, looking at a clock on the wall. The time was now four o'clock. 'I don't think we need to take this matter further.'

'Thank you, Inspector.'

'Don't thank me. Just remember that we too have laws here, and we employ officers to enforce them.'

Jake extended his hand and Jouma took it. The inspector was a small man, but his grip was surprisingly firm.

'Goodbye, Mr Moore. Constable Walu will show you out.'

Day Three

Chapter Nine

In Baghdad, a motorcade had been ambushed as it made its way from the airport to an anti-terrorist summit at the headquarters of the latest ruling council, and the Iraqi security minister and six UN officials were dead. Two thousand miles away in Amsterdam, the man who had supplied the four Russian-made SA-7 missile launchers used by insurgents in the ambush emerged from the bedroom of a two-thousand-euro-a-night hotel suite and lit a Turkish cigarette.

The room had been conscientiously furnished with every imaginable accoutrement of eighteenth-century French period ware: intricate walnut fauteuils, bergère armchairs, cabriole-legged commodes and bureaux, Quimper earthenware and gilt wood mirrors – but, in one corner of the room, an ultra-modern plasma TV screen showed CNN footage of bodies being extricated from the twisted and burning wreckage and placed into waiting ambulances.

'Happy, Mr Dzasokhov?' Whitestone said from a tan leather sofa on the other side of the room.

The man with the cigarette puffed contentedly. 'Extremely.'

Whitestone reached for the remote control and switched off the TV. 'Would you like a drink?'

Dzasokhov grunted and walked across to a picture window that overlooked Prinsengracht and the queue for the Anne Frank Museum. The windows were silvered from the outside, so it did not matter that his silk dressing gown hung open and his reddened genitals were exposed beneath an expanse of pale-white gut.

Whitestone filled a thumb-sized glass with chilled Stolichnaya. Dzasokhov drained it in a single throw and returned the glass for a refill.

'They are all like that?' Dzasokhov said, nodding towards the bedroom and wiping his mouth with the back of his hand.

'I like to keep my standards high.'

'I am impressed, Mr Whitestone. And I have many friends I know will be impressed too. I think we will be doing more business together.'

'Maybe,' Whitestone said. 'Maybe not.'

Dzasokhov took another drink and looked at him curiously. 'I don't understand.'

'I'm not over-keen on long-term contracts, Mr Dzasokhov. That's how you get your name in the *Yellow Pages*.'

Dzasokhov laughed and moved away from the window, idly tightening the sash of his dressing gown with one hand.

'You are right to be cautious, Mr Whitestone,' he said. He crossed the room to a mahogany writing desk and flipped open a slim leather briefcase. 'But at the same time it would be a pity to be so modest – especially when the service you provide is so unique.'

He handed Whitestone a plain white envelope. 'A

little extra thank-you for services rendered.'

Whitestone opened the envelope. Inside was a single sheet of paper with a series of numbers printed on it. He refolded the sheet and placed it back in the envelope. 'This is very generous. But I cannot accept it.'

Dzasokhov puffed out his chest. 'I believe in rewarding those who do good work for me. If it is not enough—'

'I expect only the second half of my fee, as agreed. Like I said, Mr Dzasokhov, it's not to my advantage to be beholden to anyone.'

For a moment, Dzasokhov appeared to be on the brink of losing his temper. But then he smiled and shrugged his shoulders. 'It is an indication of how the world has changed when a Russian is being lectured about the benefits of commercial restraint by a capitalist.' He laughed at his own joke and sat down on the sofa with his legs apart. 'You know, I never did find out her name,' he said, nodding once again at the closed bedroom door.

'Is that important to you?' Whitestone asked.

Dzasokhov thought for a moment. 'No – I suppose it isn't,' he said. Then he laughed. 'I suppose I can call her anything I want.'

Chapter Ten

That night a summer storm swept in from the east. In the shanty communities dotted along the Kenyan coastline, the locals had smelled the copperish tang on the dry air long before the first fat droplets of rain reached them. It was the signal for mothers to quickly round up their children while the old men packed away their backgammon boards and glanced up warily at the sky. Oxen, goats and other livestock were herded into wooden corrals or simply tied to the nearest tree.

As the first lightning ripped across the sky and the deafening thunder made the children scream, families headed for the strongest-built of the houses and huddled together for safety. They listened to the rain clattering against corrugated-iron roofs, and to the wind that threatened to lift those roofs into the sky with every venomous gust. To pass the time, they told stories. As usual, the stories that scared them the most were of the souls of the drowned dead, raised from their slumbers by the storms, that came ashore on nights like these looking for human souls to take back with them to the deep.

Day Four

Chapter Eleven

Margaret Tambo had lived through more storms than she cared to remember, and at the last count had seen fourteen of her houses blown away. But, at the age of seventy-two, she ascribed her longevity to the fact that every night she prayed to God that she might survive to see another day. For the last two years she had included her boar Mwitu in her prayers, because without Mwitu, and the few shillings she made by selling his potent semen, Margaret knew that not even the Good Lord could save her from destitution and death.

Margaret lived alone near Bara Hoyo beach, ten miles up the coast from Mombasa, in a shack built from breezeblocks left over from a half-built hotel and from the rusting metal hull of a fishing trawler that had run aground the previous summer.

The day after the storm, she woke at dawn with a feeling of utter dread. Despite her prayers the previous night, she knew that something very bad had happened.

Something very bad indeed.

As a rule she kept Mwitu tied to a rope that was fixed to a palm tree close to her shack. The rope was long enough for him to roam and forage, but lately the boar had been visibly irritated by his constraints. Margaret, while concerned about Mwitu's stress levels and the effect it might have on his semen, dared not let him free. When she first smelled the storm approaching on the air the previous evening, she had fastened the rope tighter.

After seventy-two years, Margaret's eyesight was little more than a smear, but as she stepped out of her house she did not need eyes to sense that the boar was gone. Normally, she could smell his pungent scent and hear his snorts. Today she heard only the sound of the breeze in the palm leaves and the crunch of the surf on the beach near by. Sure enough, as she approached his tree, she reached out and to her dismay felt that the rope hung slack, its fibres gnawed away.

Oh, Saviour, please spare the life of my Mwitu.

She called his name, her voice hoarse with worry. Nothing.

Margaret began to follow the outer rim of trees, increasingly concerned that the boar had escaped along the beach in the direction of the expensive tourist hotels at Kikambala. If he had, she knew all too well that he would most likely be shot dead by the guards who patrolled the private beaches. Slowly and arthritically, she made her way through the trees, her cries growing ever more desperate.

Suddenly, her heart leaped. There, no more than fifty yards away, was the unmistakable pot-bellied shape of the boar! *Oh, thank you, Saviour, for thy mercy and wisdom!* He was standing near the tree line, his snout buried in a pile of debris thrown high on to the beach by the force of the previous night's storm, making grotesque snorting noises of satisfaction.

'Mwitu!' Margaret scolded. 'What are you doing escaping like that and frightening your momma?'

The boar lazily lifted his head, and Margaret saw what she at first thought was a tuna carcass dangling from his mouth. But as she approached it became clear even with her blighted eyesight that the object was in fact a human leg, connected by a few scraps of skin and tendon to what remained of a human torso and a man's head.

Chapter Twelve

The boatyards and marinas of Flamingo Creek were too far upriver to have been greatly affected by the previous night's storm that had battered the coast, but that morning saw Jake, Harry and a handful of Suki Lo's regulars manhandling fallen palm trees that were blocking the track along the south bank of the creek. The work was more self-serving than community minded: the trees had blocked all road access to and from Suki's bar, and Suki was threatening to stay closed until they were moved. But, for the two Englishmen, keeping busy provided a welcome distraction from their empty bookings ledger.

'Are you still pissed off with me, Harry?' Jake asked.

Harry looked up from the rope he was tying to the trunk of a tree. 'I wasn't pissed off. But when you go gallivanting off like the Lone Ranger I get worried.'

'You shouldn't be. I'm a big boy.'

'You were a big boy in London, too. Look what happened then.'

'Adan Mohammed is not the Canning Town Firm,' Jake said.

'Yes. And isn't hindsight a marvellous thing?'

That, Jake reflected, was debatable. He thought about a framed photograph tacked to the wall of the office back at the boatyard. Harry and Jake, standing together in *Yellowfin*'s cockpit, arms folded and big grins on their faces. A local kid had taken it on a cheap Instamatic. The kid had later stolen the camera, but back then they could afford to laugh about it, because it didn't matter. Business was good. *Life* was good.

The photo had been taken the day they took delivery of *Yellowfin* from a secondhand-boat dealer in Ramisi. She was ten years old, with one rather careless owner judging by the scuffs and scrapes along her hull and the scabrous condition of her cabin; and her engine was so cooked she'd needed a tow to get her the last few miles along the coast and up the river. But she was beautiful in her own battered way, and both Harry and Jake immediately fell in love with her. For Harry, she represented the day Britannia Fishing Trips Ltd stopped being a pipe dream and finally became a reality. For Jake, it was nothing less than the start of a new life – one that had begun six months earlier with a small ad in the classified section of the *Sunday Times* one gloomy and rain-sodden English day.

> *Wanted: free-spirited soul to invest time, love and £20,000 of own money into marine venture in Africa. Experience preferred. Baggage, emotional or otherwise, optional.*

With his pension and his compensation in his back pocket, Jake had the money all right. And the shrink at Scotland Yard would have probably argued that he had the emotional baggage too. He certainly had the experience – even his old man would attest to that. Jake was just fourteen years old when Albie took him to sea for the first time.

The old man's boat was *The Banchory Thistle*, and she'd been trawling out of North Shields port for almost as long as Albie had been her skipper, which was twenty years. All those years being battered by the North Sea had left her looking like a boxer who had been in too many fights, but then all the Tyne fleet looked like that, and all the skippers looked like Albie and had done for centuries. Jake never bothered to wonder if he would have ended up the same had he followed his old man and the six generations of Moores before him on to the boats. He had seen those long-dead men in the sepia photographs, and the dark eyes staring out of their weatherbeaten faces were his own. So he knew that, when Albie first took him out on *The Banchory* at the age of fourteen, it was not to give him a taste of adventure – it was to show him his destiny.

Shortly before ten o'clock, a gleaming blue police car came bumping down the track from the direction of the highway and two uniformed officers climbed out. One of them identified himself as Chief Inspector Oliver Mugo of Malindi police. He was an imposing, broad-chested man of forty who stood nearly six feet tall in his patent-leather riding boots and who deliberately exaggerated his physique by wearing his police uniform one size too small and his belt three notches too tight. His head was shaved to the bone, but a luxuriant black moustache streaked with shafts of distinguished grey compensated for this. A single gold tooth completed the image of a man who meant business, and whose business relied heavily upon the careful cultivation of his own image.

'Myself and Constable Lokuru are here on a visitation of reassurance,' he said grandly, gesturing at the second officer whose tunic, in contrast to his own, appeared to be two sizes too big.

Jake and Harry exchanged glances, but Mugo was only just beginning.

'You will be aware, I am sure, of the most unfortunate incident which took place recently involving a fishing-boat captain from Flamingo Creek named Mr Dennis Bentley?'

'Dennis, yes,' Harry said. Harry usually took the role of Flamingo Creek's spokesman, usually when the boat tax officials from Mombasa came calling or the customs department decided to spring one of their periodical surprise visits.

Mugo beamed at him. 'Well, it is my pleasure to reassure you and all of the fine residents of Flamingo Creek that the incident has been thoroughly investigated by detectives from Malindi police, under the strict auspices of myself, Chief Inspector Oliver Mugo.'

Jake narrowed his eyes. 'That's reassuring to know. And what are your conclusions so far?'

Mugo looked at him quizzically. 'So far? No, you do not understand, sir. The case is *solved.*'

There was a collective murmur of surprise from Suki's regulars.

'Solved?' Harry nodded approvingly. 'That's quick work, Chief Inspector.'

Mugo's smile broadened. 'We at Malindi police pride ourselves on the efficacious resolution of criminal matters to the satisfaction of all concerned!'

'So what happened?'

'It was a tragic accident,' Mugo said with finality.

'That's it?'

The policeman regarded Jake with surprise, as if someone questioning his conclusions was a possibility he had never considered.

'Our investigations have been thorough, Mr—'

'Moore.'

'So!'

'Have you found Dennis's body?'

Now Mugo's eyes bulged. 'It is highly unlikely that a body will be found after—'

'What about wreckage? Have you had the wreckage analysed?'

'Mr Moore, I appreciate your concerns, but you are not a policeman and are therefore not experienced in the techniques of detection. Rest assured that we at Malindi police have assessed all available information and that our conclusions are safe.'

Jake was about to say something, but Harry put a hand on his shoulder.

'Thank you, Chief Inspector,' he said obsequiously. 'It's a great comfort to know that you and your officers are looking after our interests.'

Mugo smiled primly and clicked the heels of his boots together.

'Very well, gentlemen,' he said. 'I can see that you are busy. If there are any other matters which you feel may require our services, please do not hesitate to contact one of our experienced officers.'

With that, Mugo and Constable Lokuru climbed back into the squad car and were gone in a cloud of dust.

'Unbelievable,' Jake said.

'Forget it, Jake,' Harry said.

But when Jake looked at him, Harry knew from his expression that his partner intended to do nothing of the sort.

Chapter Thirteen

In the basement of Mombasa Hospital is a small, square, windowless room whose only light comes from three fluorescent tubes on the ceiling that, like the walls, is entirely covered in white tiles. The floor is unusual, consisting of a fine metal mesh resting on a concave concrete foundation. Embedded into the concrete is a network of broad ceramic channels, which in turn slope into a centrally positioned outlet. Above this drain, resting on the mesh, is a thin metal table with grooves and outlets of its own. When the room is to be used, a team of three hospital cleaning staff spend as long as it takes to ensure it is completely clean and sterilised. The job can be arduous sometimes; every piece of matter and dried fluid has to be scrubbed clean, even from the grouting on the ceramic tiles. But the cleaners know that, if Mr Christie sees even so much as a speck of dirt, they will all be fired on the spot.

Mr Christie frightens the cleaners. They sometimes joke under their breath as they scrub that even the dead bodies, the poor lifeless *mizoga*, are scared of him.

It is not just Mr Christie's temper that scares

them, though. It is the things that he does to the bodies in that white-tiled room. They have heard the English doctor has a huge collection of glinting knives with which he slices and cuts through flesh; that he saws through bones until they are powder; that he rips out organs with his bare hands and places them on silver plates. They have heard that, when Mr Christie is at work, the blood flows like a river along those ceramic channels.

They call him *bweha* – the Jackal.

Jouma knew of Christie's reputation among the terrified cleaning staff of Mombasa Hospital, and, privately, he thought the pathologist thoroughly deserved it.

A tall stooped sallow-faced man of about his own age, Christie looked as if he left the gloomy basement mortuary each night and went home to sleep in a coffin. He was good at his job, of that there could be no doubt, but it unnerved Jouma to see Christie work. The Englishman seemed to have an almost complete disinterest in the fact that the body upon which he was working was once a living, breathing human being. Flesh and blood were merely impediments to be cut and drained away; hearts and brains – the very essence of a man – merely physical evidence with which to pinpoint cause of death.

Something else that bothered Jouma about Christie was his apparent immunity to horror. During their fifteen-year professional relationship, the detective had deposited some quite unspeakable-looking corpses on the pathologist's narrow metal table, bodies that to Jouma no longer looked human, or indeed as if they had ever been human. Jouma had been around and seen many things, but it never ceased to amaze him quite how fragile a man was

71

compared to metal, fire or savage animals.

To Christie, it was all in a day's work.

The object on Christie's table now had once been a human being, but, as he watched it being unzipped from the black rubber bodybag, it looked to Jouma like something you might find in the ashes several days after the Feast Day of St Zaccharius. He grimaced behind his mask and shifted further into the corner of the room, gripping a metal shelf for support.

Christie stood over the corpse and scratched the bridge of his nose with one rubber-gloved finger. 'Where did you say it was found?'

'On the beach at Bara Hoyo.'

'When?'

'This morning.'

'Mmm.' Christie scrutinised the remains, and offered Jouma a running commentary of his findings. 'Negroid male, possibly aged thirty to forty. Skin shows signs of severe burning and also of prolonged exposure to salt water and marine life. The right thigh appears to have been eaten by an animal of some description.'

'The woman who found the body has a wild boar,' Jouma said.

'Then we're lucky there's anything left at all,' the pathologist remarked. He leaned over and carefully dabbed the torso with his finger. The rubber glove came back with a black stain. 'There is also a coating of a viscous black residue, which would appear to be oil of some sort. Abdomen violently severed just above the pelvis, most of the lower internal organs missing; right and left arms severed; left leg missing; head and neck relatively intact. Do you know who it is?'

Jouma was pretty sure he did, but said nothing.

Christie reached for his tools. He snapped opened the sternum and examined the chest cavity with deft probing hands. Presently, he said, 'It didn't drown.'

'Ah,' Jouma said quietly. *It* didn't drown. Typical Christie.

'There is sea water in the lungs, but it hasn't been actively inspired,' Christie explained, holding up what looked to Jouma like a rotten sweet potato. 'When it has, the mixture of air and water produces a distinctive fluid. This is just plain flooding.' He tossed the lung into a silver dish.

'You have lost me.'

'I'd say it was dead before it hit the water.'

'Cause of death?'

The pathologist shrugged. 'It's an interesting one, to be sure, Jouma. The fish and the wild boar have had a feast all right, but they weren't responsible for all this damage. And the injuries are not consistent with propeller contact. Last time I saw something like this was in Angola in the 70s. UNITA put a bomb under a judge's car. You haven't had any car bombings lately, have you? No. Stupid question. The weapons of choice round here are machetes.'

It *was* a stupid question and, as far as Jouma was concerned, a highly insensitive one. But the detective had a theory and he wanted it confirmed.

'How long has the body been in the water?'

'Always difficult to say with any degree of certainty – but judging by the state of decomposition I would suggest no longer than three or four days.'

'Thank you, Mr Christie,' Jouma said. He removed his mask and gratefully headed for the door.

'What do you want me to do with this?' the pathol-

73

ogist called after him, gesturing with a crooked finger at the body on the table.

Jouma turned. 'Send me your report when you are finished.'

Chapter Fourteen

Very few things upset Detective Sergeant Nyami –
but people helping themselves to his strawberry jam
was one of them. The arse was falling out of his
hand-me-down polyester suit; his one-room apartment had rats and cockroaches; and he was
grievously underpaid and overworked – but none of
that bothered him. What did bother him were the
thieving dogs of Mama Ngina Drive dipping their
knives into his precious pot of jam, a single pot
purloined each month from a consignment of
comestibles bound for the rich hotels on the coast.

*Tiptree strawberry jam from Essex, England, no
less! The coat of arms on the label proving that it
was used by the Queen of England herself!*

It was the only thing in his whole miserable life
that he could call a luxury.

'Have you been using my jam?' he demanded
when Jouma returned to the office.

Jouma, deep in thought, stopped in the middle of
the room and slowly turned his head. 'I beg your
pardon, Sergeant?'

'My strawberry jam – have you been using it?'

'I have no idea what you are talking about. But I

would advise you to remember who you are talking *to.*'

Nyami stood up at his desk and thrust the open pot accusingly in Jouma's face. A single deep stab wound had pierced the smooth dark-red surface.

'Look!' he said.

'Sometimes I think you are losing your mind, Nyami,' Jouma said and continued to his desk on the other side of the room. 'What are you working on at this moment?'

'The overnight crime sheet.'

'And?'

Nyami glanced at the sheet in front of him. 'Twenty-two car break-ins. A woman who claims her husband plans to assassinate the president. A man who claims his dog has been possessed by the devil—'

'Well, forget about that. I want you to get me the file on that fishing boat that went missing off Watamu the other day.'

Nyami looked surprised. 'I thought Malindi police were investigating that case.'

'Just do as I ask, Sergeant.'

When Nyami had shuffled petulantly out of the room, Jouma went across to a large dog-eared map of the Kenyan coast that was thumbtacked to the wall beside the sink. Then he picked up the telephone and dialled the Mombasa coastguard.

'Robert – this is Daniel. You recall that fishing boat that disappeared the other day off Watamu? The white skipper and the boy from Jalawi? Yes. Where was the wreckage sighted?' He waited for several minutes. 'I see. Thank you. Good day, Robert.'

Jouma hung up and returned to the map, massaging his chin between two fingers. Then he returned to his desk and dialled the local meteorological office.

'Harriet – Daniel Jouma here. What was the direction of the prevailing wind during the storm last night?' Another pause. 'I see. Thank you, Harriet.'

Once again he returned to the map, and then to his desk.

Nyami came back with a two-page print-out from the central police computer.

'This is it?' Jouma said.

'Malindi police have closed the case.'

'Closed the case?'

Nyami shrugged and sat down. He was more concerned with whoever had been helping themselves to his jar of Tiptree jam. All the way along the corridor, he had been systematically eliminating suspects, until now just one name remained. *Constable Walu! It had to be!* Nyami could just picture the fat-faced front-desk man now, sneaking into the CID office during the night shift, opening drawers, ferreting around with his sausage fingers, drooling uncontrollably as he discovered the unopened pot nestling between the stapler and the hole-punch . . .

Jouma read the two-page report from Malindi Police, then read it again with a growing sense of disbelief. As far as Chief Inspector Oliver Mugo was concerned, it was an open-and-shut case after an investigation lasting just three days. The bodies of Dennis Bentley and his bait boy had not been recovered and, in Mugo's opinion, were unlikely to be. Technicalities such as the cause of the explosion had been dismissed due to 'lack of available evidence'. In other words, the fat fool hadn't bothered to send the wreckage away for forensic analysis, if indeed he had bothered to have it collected in the first place. In conclusion, *Martha B* had simply blown up. It was most probably a terrible accident. The report was signed and dated in Mugo's typically flamboyant hand.

Jouma threw it in his out-tray in disgust.

'Nyami – do you have the file on George Malewe?'

The sergeant looked up irritably. 'What of it?'

'How old was he?'

Nyami opened the manila folder. 'Thirty-two years.'

'Pass me the file.'

'I don't know why you are wasting your time on this man!' Nyami grumbled.

'Just give me the file, Sergeant.'

George Malewe's criminal record was a document of several pages dating back more than twenty years. The mug shot attached to it had clearly been taken when he was drunk. His slack lips hung open and his eyes were half-closed, as if the shutter had caught him in mid-blink. But it was a face that was unmistakable.

Jouma sighed and closed the file. He looked up to find Nyami staring at him across the room. The sergeant was clearly agitated.

'For the last time, Nyami, I don't know anything about your jam!'

What he did know was that, unlike the case of the exploding boat, both George Malewe's disappearance and the body washed up at Bara Hoyo fell under his jurisdiction – and that now there was a very strong possibility that all three were linked.

Chapter Fifteen

'George Malewe? Exploding boat?' Superintendent Teshete exclaimed. 'What are you talking about, Daniel?'

'I am convinced that Malewe's body was washed up at Bara Hoyo this morning, and that he was on board the boat that exploded off Watamu,' Jouma said.

Teshete looked at him blankly, and Jouma wondered how, when it took him so inordinately long to register even the simplest theory, his boss had managed to scale the ladder to the heady rank of Superintendent.

But then of course he knew the answer.

Teshete was *Kikuyu*, right down to his hand-stitched leather shoes, and when you were a member of the most populous and historically dominant of Kenya's forty-two tribes – the same tribe that had produced two of the republic's three presidents – then ability to do the job came fairly low down on the list of priorities for any high-ranking position. Jouma, by contrast, was of the *Embu* tribe. His people were peace-loving livestock farmers from the fertile slopes of Mount Kenya who throughout history had spent much of their time defending their lands against other more rapacious tribes. Since becoming a policeman, it often struck Jouma how little things had changed.

For a second time, the inspector carefully explained his reasoning, using the information he had gleaned from the conclusions of Christie's post-mortem examination on the body at Bara Hoyo, the missing persons investigation into the whereabouts of George Malewe, and the coastguard and the weather office reports in relation to sea currents and their effect on floating wreckage in the last twenty-four hours.

'So you're saying Malewe was on the boat?' Teshete said presently, like a dumb child grasping a simple mathematical equation.

Jouma put his hand in his pocket and clenched it until his nails dug painfully into the flesh. 'Yes, sir.'

'Why would he be on the boat?'

'That is something I intend to investigate.'

'But it makes no sense, Daniel.'

'I know, sir.'

Teshete lit a cigarette and went to his window, which afforded a splendid view of the ocean as opposed to Jouma's office window, which looked out directly at the security fencing that surrounded the police headquarters compound.

'I thought the boat incident was being investigated by Malindi,' he said.

'It was, sir. They have closed the case.'

Teshete nodded appreciatively. 'Quick work.'

'But I believe the fate of that boat now has a direct bearing on the disappearance of George Malewe – a case which, if you recall, you yourself ordered me to investigate, sir.'

'So I did, Daniel. So I did.' The superintendent turned. 'Well, if that is what you believe, then you must follow your instincts.'

'Thank you, sir. I will.'

With that, Jouma sprang to his feet and hurried to the door before Teshete could ask him to explain his reasoning for a third time.

When he had gone, Teshete sat down behind his desk and sucked contemplatively at his cigarette. Then, after several minutes, he reached for his telephone and pressed a three-digit extension number. A message needed to be sent at once, and Teshete – a man who prided himself on his relationship with the detectives in his department – knew the very man to deliver it.

Chapter Sixteen

According to its own glossy publicity, the Marlin Bay Hotel was *the* premier hotel on the Kenyan coast. And, while the blurb was most probably right, it did not stop Jake Moore from thinking he'd rather spend a night in the flyblown jungle than a single second in one of its five-star suites. The Marlin Bay was a sprawling holiday complex occupying several acres of beachside real estate in Shanzu, just a few miles north of the city. The compound had been designed in the style of a traditional African village, although the only native Africans allowed on site were ancillary staff. The clientele were wealthy white tourists willing to spend upwards of a thousand bucks each for the privilege of staying in a luxury chalet with a whitewashed adobe exterior and a thickly manicured palm thatch, with access to an Olympic-sized swimming pool, tennis courts, private cinema, fully equipped health spa and marina. There was even a half-mile stretch of private beach, patrolled by security guards to keep undesirables away. After all, you did not spend a thousand bucks to be pestered by locals.

The chalets surrounded a large central atrium

containing restaurants and bars beneath a vast fibrous roof. It was into this cool air-conditioned oasis, through sliding smoked-glass doors, that Jake now strode in his sandals, rugby shorts and salt-caked T-shirt. He could almost hear the stunned intake of breath from the uniformed staff manning the onyx reception counter and prowling the marble-floored lobby. It amused him no end that they were all black Africans, yet all had been trained to be as tight-assed and white as if they were working at the Dorchester or the Savoy.

One of them, a young man in the embroidered purple and green livery of a concierge, scurried across from his desk near the doors. 'Can I help you, sir?' he demanded. The name etched on his enamel lapel badge was LOFTUS KIGALI.

'I'm here to pick up a fishing party, Loftus,' Jake said with as much insouciance as he could muster. 'Name of Halloran.'

'Yes, well, if you would care to wait at the marina, Mr Halloran, I will let them know you are here.'

'Halloran is the party. My name is Moore, from Britannia Fishing Trips at Flamingo Creek. I was supposed to meet them at the marina an hour ago.'

The concierge stared at him from beneath a furrowed brow as the information registered. 'Wait here, please,' he said presently.

'By all means.'

Loftus scurried to the main desk and was soon engaged in earnest conversation with one of the receptionists. Jake stuffed his hands into the pockets of his shorts and sauntered across to the other side of the atrium, where a vast plate-glass window looked out over the swimming pool. Like most of the tourist trade, the Marlin Bay had been affected by the

83

bloody tribal unrest that had broken out across Kenya. But everything was relative, and some businesses had been hit harder than others. The Marlin Bay was, by its very nature, accustomed to having as little as possible to do with the world beyond its compound gates. It had been designed to be a bubble of white privilege beneath the endless Kenyan sky, and it would take more than a raging civil war to prick it. Jake had heard – and had no reason to disbelieve it – that the biggest crisis to affect the hotel during those bloody days and weeks was a shortage of tonic for the guests' gin.

He gazed out at them, lounging like lizards under thatched parasols, their slack and mottled skin toasted butterscotch brown except for where it was criss-crossed by livid white hip-replacement and triple-bypass scars. Sure, their numbers would be down slightly on previous years – but then that was to be expected. In the scheme of things, it would make no difference to the profitability of the Marlin Bay. The rich would always come back, and they would always spend their bucks. The only problem was, that made them too good a resource to waste.

'Mr Moore?' Loftus had returned from the reception desk. He looked agitated. 'I am informed by my colleagues that the Halloran party left to go fishing at nine o'clock this morning.'

'Nine?' Jake looked at his watch. 'But they booked the boat for midday.'

Loftus wrung his hands and began to stammer some sort of explanation – but Jake waved him away. He knew damn well what had happened. He strode across to reception where the head desk clerk, a haughty-looking woman of about twenty-five, was primly stapling bar bills to invoices.

'Who did they go with?' Jake demanded, slapping his hand down on the cold stone.

'I beg your pardon, sir?' said the desk clerk.

'The Halloran party. Who picked them up this morning?'

'I don't know, sir.'

'Don't give me that bullshit.'

'Is there a problem, Elizabeth?'

A tall well-groomed white man in an expensive linen suit and with an even more expensive hair weave had materialised like a ghost behind Jake. His name was Conrad Getty, and he was the owner of the Marlin Bay Hotel. Jake knew him well enough to know that he was the reason behind the sudden change of heart of the Halloran party.

'What the hell are you playing at, Getty?' he said. 'You know damn well the Halloran party was booked with us.'

Getty shrugged. 'It's a free country, Mr Moore. They obviously decided to take their custom elsewhere.'

'Don't tell me: to one of your pals.'

'Like all our guests, Dick Halloran expects the very best when he stays at the Marlin Bay. When he told me he was considering a game-fishing trip, I thought it only appropriate to ensure he was fully informed about the wide range of options available to him. I think he was pleasantly surprised at what he saw.'

Jake could have swung for him then, a haymaker right between the eyes that would have done absolutely nothing to solve his problems but nevertheless cheered him up no end.

But Getty was already sweeping obsequiously towards the doors, where a wizened old couple with more than a dozen Louis Vuitton suitcases had just arrived on the exclusive hotel minibus from Moi Airport.

Son of a fucking bitch, he thought as he stalked towards the marina, his mood black enough to kick any one of the lounging lizards out of their chairs and into the crystal-clear, thermostatically controlled water of the swimming pool. But then what did he expect? Conrad Getty was renowned for shafting independent game-boat operators in favour of his chums in the fishing business. To Getty, outfits like Britannia Fishing Trips were no better than the hawkers who pestered his hotel guests. His skippers might cost fifty dollars an hour more, but standards had to be maintained. Especially in times of national crisis.

The lizards, already anaesthetised on gin rickeys, eyed him dozily as he passed. They most probably thought he was the pool attendant. And in the scheme of things here at the Marlin Bay he might well have been.

Chapter Seventeen

'Would you care for some refreshment, Sergeant Nyami?' Jacob Omu asked politely. 'Some tea, perhaps? Some Coca-Cola?'

'No thank you, Mr Omu,' Nyami said.

What Nyami wanted most of all was to get the hell out of Michael Kili's office. Away from Omu. Omu frightened him.

'How is your wife?' Omu asked.

'She is very well.'

'Jemima, isn't it?'

'Yes.'

'A delightful name. Are you sure you wouldn't like some tea?'

'No, thank you.'

From his position deep within the busted springs of the sofa that rested against one wall of Kili's office above the Baobab Club, Nyami watched nervously as Omu carefully watered a pot plant balanced on a filing cabinet on the other side of the room.

'*Citrus calamondin*,' Omu said, cradling one of the plant's bulbous orange fruits in the palm of his hand. 'They make delicious marmalade. Do you like marmalade, Sergeant Nyami?'

Nyami cleared his dry throat. 'I prefer jam.'

'Ah!' Omu exclaimed. 'Quince? Damson?'

'Strawberry is my favourite.'

'Strawberry is good, but I find the manufacturers tend to add too much sugar to the mixture. Sugar is very bad for the teeth and gums.'

In one fluid movement, Omu had crossed the room and now stood over Nyami. To his horror, Nyami saw that in Omu's hand was a thin-bladed knife.

'You should always look after your teeth and gums, Sergeant Nyami,' Omu said. The tip of knife was now pressing lightly against Nyami's bottom lip. 'Let me see.'

Nyami began to hyperventilate as he felt his lips being prised apart.

'There is nothing to worry about, Sergeant,' Omu said softly, peering into Nyami's gaping mouth. 'Open wide.'

Nyami heard the *tak tak* of polished steel against the enamel of his molars as Omu explored the furthest recesses of his mouth. He almost gagged as the blade caressed the back of his tongue.

'When was the last time you visited a dentist, Sergeant Nyami?'

'*Aaawwhh-gghh.*'

'I am no expert, but there are clearly signs of gum disease here and here.'

Nyami squawked in agony as Omu jabbed the point of the blade between one of his back teeth and the gum wall. Then, abruptly, Omu removed the knife and wiped it on the sleeve of Nyami's suit.

'You really should visit a dentist,' Omu concluded, as he stood up and moved across to Kili's desk. 'Look after your teeth and your teeth will look after you.'

Nyami massaged his throbbing gum with his tongue and tasted coppery blood. 'I will. Thank you, Mr Omu,' he muttered.

'Now what was it you were sent here to tell me?'

Nyami used the seeping blood from his gum to lubricate his throat. 'A – a body was found at Bara Hoyo this morning.'

'So?' Omu said coldly.

'It had been washed up on the beach by the storm.'

'So?'

Nyami reached into an inside pocket of his jacket and handed Omu a folded piece of paper, a Xeroxed copy of the incident report, and a photograph of the corpse. Omu scanned both items carefully.

'Like a bad penny,' he mused. Then he said, 'You say Jouma is investigating this case?'

Nyami nodded.

'And where is he now?'

'I believe he has returned to the mortuary.'

'And then?'

'I – I don't know.'

'Then keep me informed, Nyami,' Omu said smoothly. 'Of every development.'

Nyami flinched as Omu's thin hand reached once again towards his *khanzu* – but, instead of the knife, he produced a plain envelope that he handed to the terrified detective. Inside were five US dollars.

'Buy your wife a new hat, Nyami,' he said. 'And get yourself some dental treatment before it is too late.'

Chapter Eighteen

Missy Meredith had a yard up at Flamingo Creek that was patrolled by six of the meanest guard dogs imaginable. Missy herself could tear a strip off anyone who got on her bad side, but that was usually her younger brother Walton. Most of the time she loved playing mother hen to the game-boat skippers who brought their boats to be fixed, and all the skippers loved Missy because she happened to be the best boat mechanic on the Kenyan seaboard and had been for forty years. She was hard not to love. In her denim overalls and baseball cap, she cut an unmistakable figure as she stomped around the workshop and the dry dock with the energy of a woman half her sixty years, yelling abuse at Walton, who she employed only because 'he's a useless son of a bitch who would sit on his arse all day if I wasn't around to kick it'. A more prosaic reason was the fact that Walton was whippet-thin and was therefore able to access even the most narrow crawl spaces on a boat.

Poor Walton was getting it in the neck that morning as Jake nosed *Yellowfin* round the headland and steered the launch up to the jetty.

'Useless son of a bitch went all the way to town to

get me some fuse boxes – comes back with the wrong sort,' Missy explained. 'I'd send him back, 'cept the useless son of a bitch would still get the wrong sort. I ask you, Jake, why our dear departed mother didn't drown him at birth I will never know.'

Almost in the same breath she turned to Sammy, who was mooring the launch, and demanded a hug. The bait boy obliged with a huge smile, and was promptly clasped to Missy's substantial bosom.

'You run along to the office and help yourself to some lemonade, understand?' she said, pecking him on the top of the head like a chicken feeding on grits.

They watched him go and Missy shook her head. 'Poor little bugger. How is he coping?'

'Better than I would,' Jake admitted. 'He still thinks Tigi will walk through the door.'

'Yeah well, he just might. He just . . .' Her voice trailed away momentarily. 'Anyway, what can I do for you? Don't tell me that hydraulic line is playing up again.'

'Actually it's Dennis I wanted to talk about.'

They walked along the jetty, past the compound where Missy kept her dogs. She silenced their crazed barking with a single sharp command, and Jake told her about the visit from Chief Inspector Oliver Mugo that morning.

'Mugo is a useless son of a bitch,' Missy growled.

'Tug Viljoen reckons it could have been a cigarette dropping on to a leaky fuel line.'

'Tug Viljoen? What would that reptile-lover know about anything?'

'I heard Dennis was finding it hard to make ends meet,' Jake said.

Missy laughed harshly. 'Who isn't round here?'

'I mean, to the extent that he couldn't afford to

91

keep his boat serviced properly.'

'Who told you that?'

'Rumours have been flying around. You know what the crowd at Suki Lo's is like.'

'Yeah. I know what that crowd are like all right.' She stopped and looked into Jake's face with clear blue eyes. 'Let me tell you something, Jake, and this is what I told that useless son of a bitch from Malindi police. There was nothing wrong with *Martha B*, and there was nothing wrong with Dennis Bentley's bank account. Those fuel lines were six weeks old and cost ten thousand dollars. I should know, because I fitted them myself and Dennis paid for them in cash. What happened out there was no accident. If a cigarette caused that boat to blow up, then it's because some son of a bitch lit it with a stick of dynamite.'

Chapter Nineteen

It was all very strange, Inspector Jouma thought, and not a little unpleasant. In fact, as he sat in the shade of a palm tree in the walled compound of Fort Jesus, he felt quite unable to eat his simple snack of goat's cheese and half a tomato. He had always been a bird-like eater, but this whole affair had suddenly made him lose his appetite completely. He placed his food on the bench beside him and stood up.

Jouma liked to come to the fort. Positioned on a vast coral outcrop overlooking the Old Town on one side and the ocean on the other, it was one of the few places of quietude in a city that he found increasingly hectic and suffocating. Within its thick walls, Jouma could be alone with his thoughts – a rare pleasure when one shared an office with Sergeant Nyami. But today, as he watched the sunlight glinting on the battery of Portuguese cannon still pointing out to sea after four hundred years, Jouma felt as though his thoughts were stalking him like the muggers who lurked in the city after dark.

Until today his casebook had been frustrating but straightforward. A sheaf of petty offences to filter through the law courts, an English fishing-boat

93

skipper who still thought he was a detective in the Metropolitan Police, and an Old Town ne'er-do-well called George Malewe who had failed to turn up to his son's birthday party.

The body washed up by the storm had changed all that.

He reached in his jacket pocket and removed a small wooden bead. The bead was hand carved, with a zigzag pattern around its circumference. It was part of a necklace that belonged to Agnes Malewe. An hour earlier, Agnes had been methodically wrapping and unwrapping the beads around her fingers as she waited at the hospital mortuary to identify the remains of her missing husband. As the black rubber bag had been carefully unzipped to reveal George Malewe's ravaged face, the necklace had suddenly snapped in her hands, spilling beads on to the linoleum floor.

Jouma heard shrill laughter and looked up to see a white woman tourist posing for a photograph on the ramparts. She was wearing a red vest with a slogan across the chest that read FCUK. The slogan meant nothing to Jouma, but then he could never understand the need of Europeans to have writing all over their clothes. Why, when they had invented the suit, they chose to dress like vagrants when they came abroad was something he could never fathom. Jouma's own suit had been made in Jermyn Street in London, a fact of which he was inordinately proud – although, of course, it had been through at least six owners before it had reached his back.

As he watched the woman, it galled him to think that the vest and its slogan was probably worth more money than Agnes Malewe and little Benjamin would ever see in their lifetime. Especially now George was

94

dead. George the breadwinner. Poor deluded George, who thought himself a *tausi* – a strutting peacock – like Michael Kili, the man who pocketed all but a pittance of the money George conned for Agnes and Benjamin.

Slain, Agnes had said that day in the office. *My husband is slain.*

Yes. But where, and by whom, and why?

These were fundamental questions that every detective was trained to ask. But what happened when the answers made no sense at all?

Day Five

Chapter Twenty

The Capitoline in Rome had always been one of Whitestone's favourite European museums. Housed within two Renaissance palaces, overlooking the ruins of the ancient Forum and dwarfed by the marble obscenity that was the Vittorio Emanuele II monument, it seemed to sum up the very essence of the Italian nation: proud and all-conquering, yet schizophrenic and vainglorious.

The flight from Amsterdam had not suffered the delays he had anticipated, so he was early for his meeting. That was good. His trip so far had been frenetic. He needed a little down time, and where better than Rome? He followed the crowds meandering along the Via Sacra and climbed the Capitoline Hill itself. Two thousand years of pilfering and neglect, allied with incompetent nineteenth- and early-twentieth-century archaeology, had left little but pockmarked columns, empty shells and random piles of ancient debris of what had once been the very centre of the known world. Yet, as he paused at the top of the Capitoline and gazed back towards the Colosseum, Whitestone did not find it hard to imagine what this place must have looked like in its prime: the temples and the triumphal arches gleaming in the sunshine, the Forum packed with people of all nations, a glorious mish-mash of cultures drawn to Rome like moths to a flame.

At the top of the hill, he crossed the piazza, skirting the bronze replica of Marcus Aurelius astride his horse, and paid for a ticket to the Palazzo dei Conservatori. For a blissful hour he wandered through ornate high-ceilinged rooms filled with ostentatious Bernini sculptures, vast frescoes depicting Rome's history, and brooding religious canvases by Caravaggio, Tintoretto and Titian. Then he crossed the piazza once again and entered the Palazzo Nuovo. This second part of the museum housed many hundreds of statues and busts, some recognisable as Roman emperors and leading figures of the ancient world, others whose names and lives had been forgotten in the centuries that had passed since their death.

Whitestone checked his watch and sat down on a bench opposite a room that was lined with the heads of ancient philosophers. Presently, a man sat down beside him. He was heavyset, with steel-grey hair and thick-framed spectacles. When he spoke it was with the insistent tone of someone who wanted to be heard, but not overheard.

'I've been hearing good reports about you,' the man said, getting straight down to business. 'The organisation are particularly impressed with your dealings with our Russian clients.'

'I was concerned I might be stepping on somebody's toes,' Whitestone said, disguising his pleasure.

'Don't worry about other people's toes; just worry about keeping on yours. I heard about Barclay.'

'I felt I had no choice.'

'Of course not. You did the right thing. English prick. Remind me to sign you up as a partner next time there's a golf day. By all accounts you've got a good swing.'

The man laughed perfunctorily, and Whitestone smiled.

'In any case,' the man continued, 'that sector is a busted flush. Too many people are asking too many questions, and too many people are opening their mouths. Nobody knows the meaning of the word discretion in southern Europe any more.'

'I had noticed.'

The man nodded. 'That's why we need to keep pushing our routes to the east. The Russian – what's his name?'

'Dzasokhov.'

'Yes. The organisation are very pleased that you managed to hook him.'

'I just think he appreciates customer care, that's all.'

'Well, he's not the only one.'

Whitestone's ears pricked up.

'Dzasokhov has got some pretty high-powered friends who have expressed an interest in our East African product. And we are talking blue chip-clients here. How quickly can you get a shipment organised?'

'Everything is in place,' Whitestone said quickly. 'Two, three days.'

There was a pause as a couple of sightseers edged their way around the display before exiting back into the main hallway.

'I heard there had been a problem in Kenya,' Whitestone's contact said.

Damn. 'A little local difficulty, that's all. A courier who went off-message. The team down there are highly experienced. They already have a replacement.'

'Good – because this order comes right from the top. And I want you to take personal charge of it.'

'Of course. Do you have the details?'

The man handed Whitestone an envelope. Whitestone always thought it touching that, in these technological times, the organisation still preferred good old pen and paper. He opened the envelope and digested the contents. But, as he read, his face registered surprise.

'Twenty. Is that all?'

'It's just a taster. I have no doubt you'll make sure they are of the very highest quality.'

'That will not be a problem. I'll arrange a meeting with Kanga at once.'

'OK,' the man said. Then he smiled paternally. 'This could be the leg-up you've been waiting for. Do it right and this job's yours.'

'I wouldn't—'

'Nah, don't be so modest. You deserve the recognition. Me? I'm getting out just as soon as I can recommend a replacement. So don't fuck this up, d'you hear?'

'I won't,' Whitestone said.

The man stared thoughtfully at the rows of sightless busts. 'You think, if I ask nicely, they'll do me one of these when I retire? It would look much nicer on my mantelpiece than a carriage clock.'

Chapter Twenty-One

One hour after she heard her father was missing, presumed dead, Martha Bentley had hauled Lloyd Jasper into her office overlooking Battery Park and fired his ass on the spot.

Lloyd's first reaction had been to laugh. After all, he was a senior vice president of Rubinstein Zeigler, a man with more than forty years' experience of high-profile corporate legal representation; a man who, furthermore, was brokering deals on Wall Street when Martha Bentley was still on the goddamned *teat*.

When Martha pointed out that he had also been systematically creaming off high-number percentage points from those deals, Lloyd had really lost his cool. How long had she been with the company? Five minutes? What the fuck did *she* know about how things worked around here? If there was anything to discuss, then he would discuss it with Carl Rubinstein and not some snot-nosed pup from Yale.

At which point Martha informed him that she had graduated *summa cum laude* from Michigan State, and secondly that it was Carl Rubinstein who had instructed her to fire him.

Lloyd's face had turned as grey as his bouffant hair then.

The typing pool was in tears at the news, and so were some of the longer-serving staff. The others just glared at her through the glass walls of her office with a mixture of fear and hostility, as if she were some poison-fanged snake in a box.

Martha couldn't have cared less what they thought. Lloyd Jasper might have been Mr Popular in the office, but he was also a crook. The worst kind of crook, too. The kind who actually thought he wasn't. When Lloyd took his hush money from the conglomerates, he believed it was OK because back-handers had been greasing the wheels of industry since forever. It didn't matter to Lloyd that some-where down the line some small business or hard-pressed individual was going to the wall as a result. Out of sight was out of mind, even for a nice guy like Lloyd who gave handsomely to the Christmas collection every year and who sponsored a war orphan in Afghanistan.

No, Martha wouldn't be shedding a tear for Lloyd Jasper, even if he was just a few months off retire-ment.

But then Martha wasn't the type who shed a tear easily.

The news that her father was most probably dead had numbed her, but only in the way the death of anyone familiar derails the senses. At no stage did she feel the overwhelming grief of a bereaved daugh-ter. She wasn't even sure how a bereaved daughter was supposed to act.

Even Patrick assumed she was suffering from some sort of post-traumatic shock, and that her grief needed coaxing out.

'It's OK, honey,' he had soothed her on the morning of her long-haul flight to Nairobi, as they lay together in the bedroom of her apartment on the Upper East Side. 'Let it go.'

But the truth was, there was nothing *to* let go. Even as she stared down at the Tarmac from her seat in First Class, waiting for the flight to depart JFK, she felt only a pragmatic *lawyerish* need to put her father's affairs in order. It was only after the 747 took off and climbed away from the mainland that Martha felt the cold talons of Manhattan gradually loosening their grip. Eighteen hours later, when she stepped out of the aircraft and breathed in Kenya's warm thick air, she knew she was home, and that she was destined to have her heart broken in the very country where it still belonged.

Chapter Twenty-Two

Conrad Getty's imported Porsche Cayenne swept regally up to the reception of the Marlin Bay Hotel. Almost before it had come to a halt, a uniformed porter sprang forward to open the driver's side door. Getty eased his spare frame out of the seat and jumped down from the vehicle without acknowledgement. He was about to make his way into the hotel when he noticed something hanging from the bull bars. He grimaced as he saw what looked like blood spatters and fragments of skin and flesh adhered to the chromium.

Fucking wild dogs, he thought angrily, vaguely recalling bumping something on the highway as he changed the disc in the CD player.

'Get that cleaned up,' he barked at the porter, who nodded eagerly and with barely concealed fear.

Getty strode through the smoked-glass doors and into the reception atrium. 'Is the lady here?' he snapped at the duty concierge.

'She is in the cocktail lounge, Mr Getty,' Loftus said.

'Have you taken her bags to her suite?'

'Yessir,' Loftus said.

Getty peered round the doorframe into the open-plan bar, and grunted with approval at what he saw. The new arrival was petite and blonde, her lightly tanned skin contrasting pleasingly with the crisp white linen of her outfit. She fitted in perfectly and elegantly with her surroundings, reminding him of some sophisticated debutante from the colonial 1920s.

Getty paused in front of a wall mirror in order to smooth his augmented silver hair across his skull and liberally spray his tongue with peppermint breath-freshener. Then, straightening the pockets of his tropical jacket, he smiled and entered the bar.

'Conrad Getty,' he said smoothly, extending a hand and fixing his eyes greedily on the girl. 'I'm the owner of the Marlin Bay. So sorry I couldn't be here to greet you in person, Miss Bentley.'

The girl sat forward attentively. 'That's perfectly all right,' she smiled. 'And please – call me Martha.'

An unusual accent: mid-Atlantic, but with the slightest detectible residue of Kenyan, perhaps? Not unpleasant. Indeed strangely alluring. In fact, her voice, and the way she took his hand with such a delicate touch, sent a delicious shiver down Getty's spine. What was she? Early twenties? Dennis Bentley's daughter, he concluded, really was quite exquisite.

'I *do* hope you haven't been waiting long,' he said.

'Not at all.'

'And your flight from New York?'

'I slept most of the way.'

'Good. Good.' With that, Getty switched instantly and effortlessly into concerned patrician mode. 'On behalf of myself and all of the staff here at the Marlin Bay, may I offer my sincere condolences on your tragic loss.'

'Thank you.'

'If there is anything, *anything* that I can do . . .'

'You've been more than kind by putting me up at such short notice, Mr Getty.'

'The very least I could do. And please – call me Conrad.' He placed a hand on Martha's elbow and left it there. 'I'm sure you'd like to freshen up after your long journey. Let me show you to your suite.'

They walked through the air-conditioned atrium and out into the hotel grounds. To their right a dozen or so guests lay sunbathing around the Olympic pool. To the left, the Indian Ocean smashed against a low restraining wall, sending gouts of spray and seaweed high into the air. A fresh breeze scudded in off the sea and through the leaves of the palm trees with a noise like radio static.

'I heard about everything that's been happening here,' Martha said. 'It must have been terrifying.'

Getty shrugged. 'Oh, that! Just a little local difficulty, that's all.'

Martha looked up at him. 'But I read that hundreds of people were killed. One story I saw said that thirty men, women and children were burned to death in a church. That doesn't sound like a little local difficulty to me, Mr Getty.'

It was a stinging blow, but Getty recovered like a prizefighter. 'Oh, of course, across in Nairobi and the Rift Valley things were *dreadful*, simply *terrifying*,' he said. 'I thought you meant *here*, in Mombasa. There were one or two minor disturbances, but all in all we got away pretty lightly. Thank heavens.'

Martha said nothing and they walked on, past the pool, in the direction of the suites.

'Did you know my father, Mr Getty?' she asked suddenly.

This time Getty was prepared for the question. He smiled winsomely. 'Dennis? Everybody knew Dennis. He was a legend round these parts. A real gentleman. We were great friends. Lord only knows how such a tragedy could have occurred. It's shocking. Truly shocking.'

'The man from the embassy said the police were working on the theory it might have been a faulty fuel line that caused the explosion.'

'I fear we may never know the truth,' Getty said. 'How long do you think you might be staying?'

'That depends on Kenyan bureaucracy,' Martha said archly. 'If the wheels turn as slowly as they do in New York, then I could be here for a while.'

'It's a painful business,' Getty nodded. 'Rest assured we are at your service for as long as it takes.'

'That's nice of you to say so,' Martha said. She paused and looked out to sea. 'I understand his boat-yard was at a place called Flamingo Creek. Is that far from here?'

'North of here,' Getty told her. 'Five, ten miles as the crow flies.'

'Where can I hire a car?'

The hotel owner looked aghast. 'Kenya is not the kind of place a young lady should be driving alone. In any case, it will be far quicker by boat. Just let me know when you wish to go and one of the Marlin Bay fleet will be waiting at your convenience.'

She began to protest, but Getty waved her away magnanimously. 'At a time like this, it is the very *least* I can do.'

Martha watched from the window of her suite as Getty stalked back across the pool area towards the main building. She always prided herself on the

109

accuracy of her first impressions, and her first impression of the owner of the Marlin Bay made her skin crawl. Conrad Getty was from the same blue-print as every other white hotelier she had ever met in Africa, right down to the buffed fingernails, nylon rug and the ill-concealed waft of hard liquor on his breath.

In other words, a first-class asshole.

But at least his hotel had all the right amenities. She had the feeling that her stay in Kenya was going to involve the sort of bureaucratic nightmare that would require some five-star pampering in return. She slipped out of her clothes and stepped into the stone-flagged shower; the jet was powerful and deli-ciously lukewarm, and in an instant she could feel the grime of her journey from New York being blasted from her pores.

Wrapping a towel around herself, she padded back into the sitting room and unzipped one of her cases. She removed her clothes and transferred them to hangers in the bedroom wardrobe. Then she took her cell phone from her handbag and tapped in an auto-dial number. She heard the beeps and twangs of the long-distance connection, then a voice answered.

'Hi, it's me,' she said.

'What time is it?' the voice said blearily.

'Just after eleven.'

'Christ – it's four a.m. here.'

'I love you too.'

Laughter. 'I'm sorry, babe. You know what a pain in the ass I am when I'm woken up in the middle of the night. Where are you?'

'At the hotel.'

'How is it?'

'It's OK – but the boss is even more of a pain in

110

the ass than you are.'

More laughter. Then the voice said, 'Just abuse the facilities, honey. It'll make you feel better.'

'I intend to.'

'You OK?'

'Yeah.'

'You sound tired.'

'I'm OK. I miss you, though.'

'Yeah, I miss you too.'

'Is Chico missing me?'

'Chico's a cat, honey. Cats don't give a shit.'

'Chico does.'

'Then maybe Chico's about to have an unfortunate run-in with a New York City garbage disposal truck.'

Martha gasped. 'Don't you dare, you bastard!'

'These things happen, baby. But don't worry. I know a great pet cemetery out in Jersey where—'

'Patrick, you son of a bitch.'

'You know I'm only joking. Chico will dine on smoked salmon tonight while I make do with pizza. They give you a nice room?'

She looked around and smiled. 'It would be better if you were here.'

'I could get a flight.'

'No – I'm just being stupid. I can get this done quicker by myself.'

'You sure? How long do you think it will take?'

'That depends on Kenyan red tape.'

'See you next January, then.'

'Don't joke about it.'

'I love you, baby.'

'I love you too.'

The connection went dead. Martha threw the phone on the bed and went to the window again. Outside, the ocean thrashed and boiled against the

111

sea wall, generating a fine mist of salt spray that hung almost invisibly in the air. Beyond, on the ocean itself, a fleet of flimsy lateens bobbed up and down like seagulls on the swell, and for the first time Martha felt the first terrible pangs of sorrow, as she knew she would.

What happened out there, Daddy? What terrible thing could have possibly happened to you?

Chapter Twenty-Three

Jake was alerted by the sound of Harry shouting from the jetty, and gratefully heaved himself out of a deck service hatch that accessed a crawl space inch-deep with bilge water and sump oil. His vest and shorts were black and sodden, and there were small lacerations on his arms and knees where they had bumped up against jagged metal in the darkness. As he closed the hatch, he concluded that Walton Meredith was worth his weight in gold – even if it amounted to a little over eight stone.

But beggars could not be choosers. He might not be as thin as Walton, but at least he could still squeeze under *Yellowfin*'s deck. And, in terms of personal vanity, his trim waistline was a vast improvement on the belly he'd brought over from England. Back then, puffed up on a diet of best bitter and junk food, crawling around in *Yellowfin*'s bowels would have been a physical impossibility. But his midriff was not the only difference in his appearance. His pallid London-sky skin had turned a deep chestnut brown, the sun had bleached his short mousy hair and there was definition in the flaccid muscles of his upper body that he'd not seen since he was a teenager. He often fantasised about walking back into the lounge bar of the Cheapside Club, the favoured watering hole of the Flying Squad, just to see if any of the old lags would recognise him.

'Jake!'

He swung up to the flying bridge to check the fluid gauges.

'Jake! You stuck in there? We've got company.'

'Coming, for Christ's sake!'

He looked across to the bank where a dust-streaked Fiat Panda was parked on the roadside near the workshop. Next to it stood Harry, and beside him a diminutive African wearing an ill-fitting three-piece suit.

Jouma?

He jumped down into the launch and crossed the narrow channel of water to the jetty.

'Ah, Jake,' Harry said. 'Good of you to join us.' He smiled wolfishly. 'I told the inspector that I haven't let you out of my sight since your little adventure the other day – but it seems he's not interested in you this time.'

Jake wiped his oily hands on a rag. 'What's up?'

Jouma opened his mouth to speak, but Harry interrupted. 'He's trying to get to Dennis Bentley's place.'

The Mombasa policeman nodded sheepishly.

'I fully appreciate if you are busy, Mr Moore,' he said quickly.

Harry wafted his arms. 'No, we're not busy.'

Jake glared at him, but knew he was right. For a third day running, the bookings ledger was empty.

'I'd take you myself, Inspector, except I've got an appointment this afternoon.'

Jake looked at Harry suspiciously. 'You didn't

mention anything about an appointment.'

'Extraordinary General Meeting of the Elephant Club,' Harry explained. 'The knotty problem of women members has raised its ugly head once again.'

Jouma glanced from one to the other, bewilderment on his face.

'Then I suppose the hydraulics will have to wait,' Jake said.

Chapter Twenty-Four

In a part of Mombasa's Old Town that the tourist guidebooks do not mention, a sixteen-year-old girl called Mary Olunbiye was about to have her throat cut. Later her body, weighed down with chains, would be dumped fifty miles out to sea from the side of a Panamanian-registered freighter that was due to leave Kilindini port with a cargo of peanut oil later that night.

For now, though, Mary was doing what she knew best: performing fellatio on the man who planned shortly to end her life.

Mary's crime – the reason she had to die – was straightforward. Two nights before in a nearby alleyway, she had done the same thing to an American backpacker called Todd Fellowes. Todd, who was nineteen and taking a year out of college in order to broaden his mind, came in Mary's mouth then zippered up his jeans and gave her ten bucks. It was eight dollars more than the fee they had agreed on the street, but the American suddenly felt a pang of guilt about what he had done. He wished her good luck and left hurriedly.

At that moment, Todd was in a three-dollar-a-night

hostel in Nairobi, sweating and worrying himself
sick about the AIDS virus. Mary, meanwhile, was
about to die because, instead of handing over the
American's money to Michael Kili, she had kept
three dollars for herself in order to buy food and
clothing for her mother and her six-month-old
daughter.

That Mary had to die was a shame, Kili reflected,
because she still had many good years left in her. For
her, though, it would be a blessing – because even
Ugandan sailors wouldn't fuck whores with slashed
faces and amputated hands, the traditional punish-
ment for girls who did not pay their dues to the
Mombasa gangster.

No, Kili thought as he gazed down on her small
bobbing head, he would be doing Mary a favour by
killing her. And, just to show that there were no hard
feelings, he would even give her mother a few
dollars out of his own pocket. Just so she and the
child didn't go short.

That was the thing few people knew about Michael
Kili: beneath the necessarily ruthless exterior, he was
capable of great acts of mercy. It was, he always
thought, what set him apart from his rivals, what
made him such a great man. He could demand
obedience while at the same time cultivating loyalty.

'That's good, Mary,' he grunted.

And she *was* good. One of the best in Mombasa.
Which made it doubly unfortunate she had to die.
But, Kili consoled himself, by teaching her a lesson
he taught them *all* a lesson. And business was business.

He reached into the lining of his leather jacket and
removed a short-bladed kukri knife. He was
approaching climax now, the moment when he would

117

yank Mary's head backwards and slash her exposed throat – but then the cell phone in his pocket began to trill the theme from *Rocky*. Cursing, the moment fading, he pocketed the knife, pushed Mary further into his crotch, and answered the phone.

'Jouma is at Flamingo Creek.'

The voice was so quiet that it took him a moment to realise that it belonged to Jacob Omu.

'Jouma? Why?'

'He is on his way to Dennis Bentley's boatyard,' Omu informed him.

'Who?'

'The fishing-boat skipper.'

Kili shook his head irritably. '*Why?*'

'Because of George Malewe. Because he has a suspicious mind.'

'*Dah!* Jouma knows nothing.'

'Perhaps not. But it may be wise to act now, before he *does* know something.'

'What are you saying, Jacob?'

'It would be very easy to have him taken off the Malewe case. It could be done very discreetly. It could be done today with one telephone call.'

Kili could feel his cock wilting in Mary Olunbiye's mouth, in direct contrast to his rising temper.

'Then do it, Jacob!' he exclaimed. 'It's what I pay you for, isn't it?'

'Very well, Michael.'

Scowling, Kili put away his phone. '*Very well, Michael.*' There was something about Omu's deference that irritated the gangster beyond measure. Everything had to be so *discreet*, so *smooth*. The man could walk on sand without leaving footprints. And yet there was something in that quietly spoken manner that was ever so slightly *condescending*, as if Omu privately regarded him as some sort of idiot. What he failed to understand was that Michael Kili had created his Mombasa empire long before Omu had come along. And he had done it the hard way, with brute force and fear, not by whispering in people's ears and sliding envelopes full of American dollars into their pockets.

Kili felt another pulse of fury and retrieved the knife from his pocket. Then, after a moment's reflection, he put the blade away again. On second thoughts, perhaps he should not be so hasty. Mary *was* undeniably skilled, and to kill her ... No, he decided, withdrawing his flaccid member and shoving it into his tracksuit bottoms, perhaps a beating would suffice this time. But later. For now it was time to show Jacob Omu just who was the boss. There would be no discreet phone calls. Kili had always subscribed to the idea that, if a wasp was annoying you, you crushed it. You didn't open a window and hope it would simply fly away.

Kili looked down at Mary Olunbiye and smiled. 'I have business to attend to now, Mary,' he said, putting on his sunglasses. 'But I will be back.'

Chapter Twenty-Five

Jouma hated the ocean. There was something about its sheer incomprehensible *size* that unnerved him. Down at Kilindini port, the freighters loomed up over the warehouses and oil containers like huge rusting giants, bigger than any building in downtown Mombasa, bigger than anything Jouma had ever seen; yet compared to the ocean beyond the harbour they were just specks of insignificance. The sea could swallow them up in an instant and no one would be any the wiser. Even now, chugging along Flamingo Creek, a benign shallow channel of muddy water no more than half a mile across, the inspector felt vulnerable. The only thing that belonged in the water, he concluded, were fish.

'So what's this all about, Inspector?' Jake said presently. They were out of sight of the boatyard now, and Jake figured that now was the time for whatever it was Jouma had to say. 'You're working the Bentley case all of a sudden?'

Jouma pursed his lips. 'Not in an official capacity,' he said. 'But there are aspects which interest me.'

'Your friend from Malindi police is telling anyone

who'll listen that it's solved. It was all a terrible accident, apparently.'

'That would be Chief Inspector Mugo,' Jouma said, nodding. 'Well, if he says the case is solved, then it most certainly is.'

Jake chuckled. 'I take it you don't subscribe to his theory.'

'There is nothing wrong with the theory, Mr Moore,' Jouma said diplomatically. 'But perhaps I am a little uncomfortable at the speed with which it has been accepted as fact.'

There was silence between them for a few moments, then Jake said, 'OK. I'll bite. If you don't think it was an accident, what *do* you think?'

'I don't know what to think,' Jouma admitted.

'Me neither,' Jake said. His gaze was fixed on the river ahead, his thoughts racing behind his impassive expression.

Dennis Bentley's boatyard was situated on a shallow inlet at the mouth of Flamingo Creek. As *Yellowfin* anchored up, Jake stared across at the peeling wooden superstructure of the workshop, the cheap slabs of scabby breezeblock that made up the office and the scattered fuel drums and empty provisions boxes littering the ground outside.

'There it is, Inspector.'

Jouma scratched the side of his nose thoughtfully. 'Thank you, Mr Moore.'

Jake could tell from the tone of his voice that, like himself, the Mombasa detective could smell decay on the thick bug-laden air. DENNIS BENTLEY FISHING had once been painted in proud two-foot-high letters on the corrugated-iron roof of the workshop; now the legend, like the rest of the premises, had faded to obscurity. Even from a distance, it was clear that the cancerous recession eating into the livelihoods of all the independent skippers had reached a terminal stage here.

Yet both men knew the evidence suggested otherwise.

Just six weeks ago, Jake had informed the detective, Dennis had spent ten grand in cash on a new set of fuel lines for *Martha B*. In return Jouma revealed that four cash deposits of twenty-five thousand dollars had been made into the Kenyan skipper's bank account in the last eight months. Astonishingly, on the day he disappeared, Dennis Bentley was sitting on over ninety grand – and with that sort of money he could have afforded a new boatyard and a hefty down-payment on a new boat.

Jake was stunned. But Jouma had further revelations for him, about a petty thief from Mombasa called George Malewe whose mangled body had been spat up on Bara Hoyo beach the previous day. How all the pathology suggested that Malewe had been on *Martha B* when it blew up – despite the fact that the only other person supposed to be on Dennis Bentley's boat that day was a thirteen-year-old bait boy called Tigi Eruwa.

'I see pieces of a puzzle, Mr Moore,' the detective said. 'But I don't know where to begin fitting them together.'

'I'll get the launch ready,' Jake said. 'Let's see what we can find.'

On an average month, Jouma's detective's wage was enough to pay the rent on his flat in Mombasa and provide his wife Winifred with housekeeping so that they could eat. He knew that he could easily treble it with backhanders and sweeteners, and he knew that there were those at Mama Ngina Drive who regarded him with suspicion because he didn't. The fact was, Jouma didn't care for money. As far as he was concerned, it was simply a necessary evil. Allow it to dictate the way you lived your life, and your life would no longer be worth living.

What part had money played in the life and death of Dennis Bentley? Now *there* was a question. Wandering around the decrepit boatyard, Jouma thought about the pile of bank statements he had meticulously examined the previous evening, and the bald columns of dwindling numbers that described more vividly than words how Bentley's business was heading for oblivion – until eight months ago, that is, when it had suddenly risen from the dead with an injection of twenty-five thousand dollars in cash. Twenty-five thousand that soon became fifty, then a hundred.

The money was the key to everything. But, maddeningly, there was no indication of where it had come from.

For the best part of an hour, Jouma and Jake systematically turned Bentley's office and workshop upside down looking for log books, customer receipts, bookings ledgers – anything that might lead them to the missing skipper's mystery benefactor.

But even as they did so it was clear they were too late.

'Everything's gone,' Jake said, kicking over a chair in exasperation. 'There's not even a diesel receipt.'

'It is as I expected, Mr Moore. I was afraid our trip may have been a wasted one.'

'Mugo?'

123

'He has been more thorough than I thought.'

'Can't you request the paperwork from him? Aren't there official channels? How does it work in Kenya?'

'Not like England,' Jouma said sadly. 'Mugo will regard this investigation as a personal triumph. If he has Mr Bentley's paperwork, he will be guarding it as if it was gold bullion, just in case someone tries to steal his glory.'

'There must be *something*.'

Had it been Nyami, Jouma would indeed have told him to check again. But he trusted Jake's thoroughness. More importantly, he knew the Englishman was just as frustrated as he was. They had shared information, but the puzzle remained out of their reach. Yet, in the short time it had taken to travel to the mouth of Flamingo Creek, solving it had hooked them both like marlin on a line.

'I'm going to take another look in the workshop,' Jake said.

Jouma did not mind admitting that Jake Moore fascinated him. Until the baby-snatching incident in Mombasa, he had not been aware of any English skippers operating out of Flamingo Creek – and certainly none whose file contained a commendation from the Commissioner of the Metropolitan Police in London. Perhaps that was why the duty officer at the British consulate in Mombasa had been less than co-operative when Jouma had asked for Moore's details to be faxed across. It was most irregular, he had said, with a tone that suggested that he regarded any official request from the Kenyan police as a damn cheek.

In typically obtuse official language, the commendation told the story of a promising career stopped abruptly by a bullet. Moore was twenty-nine, a detective sergeant in the Flying Squad. The commendation described a botched armed robbery in some London suburb that Jouma had never heard of, and how the young officer had been shot in the line of duty. It went on to state how his selfless actions and bravery had helped prevent more bloodshed and, eventually, put a gang of criminals behind bars. But the detail was tantalisingly sketchy. There was no indication of Moore's motives for quitting the police six months later. No suggestion of why he should withdraw his pension and his life savings and jump on a plane to Kenya. All Jouma knew of Moore's life afterwards was what he had been able to piece together from the wearying compendium of game-fishing licences, registration documents, banking details and insurance certificates contained in his consulate file. In other words, nothing of any significance whatsoever other than the fact that the finances of Britannia Fishing Trips Ltd were as bad as Dennis Bentley Fishing's had been before its mysterious cash injections.

Jouma sat down in a grubby office chair and rested his elbows on Dennis Bentley's desk. There was a notice board on the wall in front of him, but even this had been stripped. All that remained were some grimy squares where Bentley had once collected – what? Invoices? Reminders? Photographs of loved ones? It struck him then that everything that Dennis Bentley had ever been had been ruthlessly erased. The day he disappeared was the day he had ceased to ever exist.

Mugo did not do this, he thought to himself. *Mugo would never have been so thorough.*

'Inspector.' Jake was in the doorway of the office. 'We've got company.'

125

Chapter Twenty-Six

Tug Viljoen took a long pull from a tarnished silver hip flask, belched effusively and said, 'One thing you must always remember about crocs, Harry: there are twenty-three species, they're all bastards, and every single one of them can outrun you.'

Harry Philliskirk peered through a wire-mesh fence into the murk of a freshwater lagoon and raised an eyebrow. He could see a dozen or so reptiles either wallowing in the brown water or basking peacefully on flat protruding rocks. 'I'll bear that in mind,' he said.

'Another thing worth remembering is that the bastards don't care,' Viljoen added, raising his arm so that the pallid scar tissue on his tanned skin stood out like fat on a joint of beef. 'They'll have fights and tear each other's limbs and tails off, but they don't care. They go off and sulk for a while and then they come back. I've seen 'em fighting with their jaws ripped off. *They just don't care.* Maybe that's why they've lasted sixty-five million years.'

Viljoen certainly talked a good game, Harry conceded. But, from what he'd seen so far of Croc World, the biggest danger to any unsuspecting visitor to the South African's reptile park was death through boredom. There were two man-made lagoons, and maybe twenty turdlike crocs playing statues in the water. The only other entertainment as far as he could see was a decrepit children's play area and a boarded-up wooden concession stand with a chalkboard menu that included Croc Burgers, Croc Ice and Croc-a-Cola.

Not for the first time, he wondered why Viljoen had arranged this meeting. *More to the point, why he had agreed to it.* The South African was the kind of person you wouldn't care to meet in a sunlit meadow let alone a swamp filled with man-eating reptiles. The fact that Viljoen had insisted on secrecy just made Harry's sense of dangerous isolation even more acute. He was beginning to regret not telling Jake the truth about where he was going now. The fucking *Elephant Club*? What sort of bullshit excuse was that? The Elephant Club had rescinded his membership six months ago for non-payment of subs.

'Just want to test the water, Harry,' Viljoen had said, cornering him in the toilets at Suki Lo's the previous night. 'A little business deal that could be mutually beneficial for all concerned.'

Well, Harry wasn't above a mutually beneficial business deal, especially in his current financial predicament. But the longer he stayed here, the uneasier he felt.

'You get many visitors, Tug?'

'Average about a hundred a day – although obviously it's close-season at the moment,' Viljoen said breezily and, Harry surmised, untruthfully.

'That's good.'

'Yeah, well – it's early days. There's plenty of scope for expansion.'

The park was situated about five miles south of Flamingo Creek, accessed from the highway by a dirt track which zigzagged through an oppressive mangrove swamp in the direction of the coast. It was set in a man-made clearing surrounded by a wire perimeter fence, and consisted of the lagoons and a concrete yard and a collection of ugly asphalt maintenance sheds in one corner of the compound. It had all the appeal of a concentration camp.

Tug took another swill from his flask. Enthusiast that he was, even Harry could tell that Viljoen had been giving it some hammer. Even if you couldn't smell the booze that oozed from his pores, the pouched red eyes and sallow skin were a dead giveaway.

'Over there I'm building a visitor centre,' he boasted, pointing with a thick finger to where a JCB digger sat marooned in half-dug foundations. 'You'll be able to see slide shows, buy souvenirs . . .'

'Shoes and handbags?'

Viljoen looked at him through narrowed eyes, then smiled and clapped him on the back. 'I like you, Harry. I like your English sense of humour.'

To prove the point, he handed him the hip flask. Harry felt the roar of cheap rum against the back of his throat.

'Why crocs, Tug?'

'Crocs. Fish. It's all fucking business at the end of the day. What counts is what you make of it. This might not look much to you, Harry, but, I'm telling you, one of these days it's going to make big buckaroos.'

At that moment it dawned on Harry what this was all about. Tug was looking for *money*! A big fat cash injection to kick new life into Croc World! He actually thought Harry might have a nest egg squirrelled away. He cursed himself for not realising sooner, and hoped that Tug would understand that circumstances had changed. *Actually, Tug, old man, I literally don't have two beans to rub together. In fact, if Jake and I don't get our own cash injection pronto, we're going to have to fold the business and sell the boat.*

But Tug did not launch into a sales pitch. Instead, he lifted the hip flask to his lips and took a deep swallow.

'I heard you had a run-in with the Arab the other day.'

Harry was not surprised that the news was out. The Arab had a mouth like Mombasa harbour. He shrugged and took a contemplative drag on the fat reefer that he had brought with him from the boatyard.

'A little misunderstanding, Tug, old man. It will be rectified, as these things always are. We just have to indulge the Arab his tiresome period of gloating, that's all.'

They had now moved to what Viljoen called his site office, but what was in fact a salvaged caravan parked up by the maintenance sheds. Viljoen stretched his skinny legs along a length of banquette and began peevishly picking at the foam rubber that spilled from its frayed upholstery.

'You know what pisses me off about oil?' he said. 'Those greasy Arab fucks own ninety per cent of it.'

'It does seem to be something of a bone of contention with the rest of the world,' Harry agreed.

He wondered where this was leading. He'd been here an hour and Tug had still given no explanation for the meeting. But he didn't like to push the matter; the South African seemed highly strung as it was.

129

'Of all the fucking people, the most valuable resource in the world goes to the ones who still stone their wives and wipe their arses with their bare hands. You're an educated man, Harry – if it wasn't for their oil, who would give a shit about them?'

'Fair point.'

Tug's eyes were blazing as he warmed to his theme. In his increasingly energised state, it seemed to Harry as if they might pop out of his head at any moment.

'I mean, what have they ever given the world apart from fucking grief?' Tug was saying now. 'Look at poor Dennis Bentley. Twenty-five years he works his balls off to earn a decent retirement, only to get fucked over by the Arabs. First they frighten off all his customers by flying planes into the World Trade Center, then, just when he's getting back on an even keel, they put up the oil prices so he can't afford to buy fuel for his boat without cutting back on servicing costs. Result? Well, we both know the fucking result, Harry. And he won't be the last, mark my words. Don't tell me you and Jake aren't feeling the pinch.'

'I don't intend going up in a blue flame just yet, Tug,' Harry said.

'No – you'll be out of business long before then, my friend.'

Viljoen snatched the joint from Harry's fingers and inhaled sharply. For a moment the effect of the strong weed seemed to knock the wind out of his sails, like a tranquilliser dart fired at a frenzied rhino.

'You know, there is a way we can help each other, Harry,' he said presently.

Here it comes. 'If you're asking for investors, Tug—'

'Nah – I'm not talking about this fucking place.

Croc World is a work in progress. I'm talking about a way to make fast bucks. And lots of them.'

Harry raised an eyebrow. 'Well, you know me, Tug. Game for anything.'

'Are you, Harry? Are you really?'

'It depends what it is, of course.'

'One job. And I won't lie to you, it ain't pretty. But put it this way – if you get a taste for it, you won't be beholden to fucks like the Arab any more.'

'I owe it to Jake to get us out of the shit we're in,' Harry admitted. 'What sort of money are we talking about?'

'Twenty-five thousand dollars.'

'Holy *shit*!' Harry said, but, despite the cheap rum and the dope, he knew immediately that a sum so obscenely large could only involve some sort of illegal activity. Still, there was no harm in playing along. 'Tell me more.'

'Can't do that, Harry. Not until you're one hundred per cent sure you want in.'

'You could tell me but you'd have to kill me, right?' Harry said conspiratorially, reclaiming the spliff then taking a deep draw of its harsh smoke.

Tug looked at him strangely. 'Something like that, Harry. Something like that.'

Chapter Twenty-Seven

As the twin-turbo Fountain speedboat scudded north towards Flamingo Creek, Martha found the journey helped take her mind off things. A frustrating morning trying to get paperwork sent through from her father's accountant in Mombasa, for one. The oleaginous Conrad Getty for another. It seemed that, wherever she turned in the hotel since her arrival, its owner was over her like a rash.

She was sitting low on the rear passenger banquette, both hands gripping the bolster seat in front of her, the sleek-nosed vessel hanging in mid-air as its hull skimmed another swell. After what seemed an improbably long time, it crashed down into the water again, sending spumes of snow-white spray high into the blue sky.

She felt the wind in her hair and she smiled for the first time that day. *God, this was therapy.* To Martha, the ocean was like home, even after so many years living in the high-rise city. Those long seemingly endless days with her father – when they could go from dawn to dusk without seeing another soul – had engendered a deep respect for its moods, its vastness and above all its power. One of the first lessons he had ever taught her was that those who the ocean claimed with the most relish were those who claimed to have mastered her.

The Fountain belonged to the Marlin Bay, and its pilot was a dour-faced employee of Getty's called Harold, a white Kenyan who seemed to regard the sheer exhilaration of the speedboat as an occupational hazard. He had barely said a word since they'd set off from the hotel's private marina, and any approach of civility on her behalf had been met with a grunt. Still, Martha noted, Harold was good at his job even if he didn't enjoy it. He handled the powerful boat expertly through the swells, and seemed to know the treacherous reefs and the sandbars as if they were old friends.

But now the engine note was changing as Harold throttled back. Ahead was the wide untidy mouth of Flamingo Creek, the muddy river current staining the sea where the freshwater met the salt. And now Martha felt a pang of apprehension, a sudden breathlessness accompanied by the thud of blood pulsing in her neck. The boat swept in a shallow arc into the navigation channel and she closed her fists so that her fingernails dug into her palms.

After a few moments, Harold gestured away to the left bank. 'That's it, Missy,' he said.

Martha looked across at what looked like a pathetic collection of shanty buildings huddled around a ramshackle wooden jetty, and she felt the prickling of tears once again.

Oh, Daddy . . .

'Friends of yours, Mr Moore?' Jouma asked as the Fountain eased back on the throttle and coasted into the inlet.

133

'I was going to ask you the same thing.'

The detective shook his head sadly. 'I'm afraid none of my friends have expensive speedboats.'

'Mine neither,' Jake said grimly. It crossed his mind that these days the going rate for a fifteen-year-old tub like *Yellowfin* would be about as much as one of the Fountain's turbo engines.

The boat idled up to the jetty and Jake caught the mooring rope. The pilot looked familiar to him, but only because he *looked* like a pilot. He had the same implacable, weather-beaten look of one of Suki Lo's regulars.

The same could not be said of his passenger.

With her honey-blonde hair tucked into a baseball cap and her eyes hidden behind expensive-looking sunglasses, she exuded metropolitan cool. He was therefore surprised when she ignored his outstretched hand and vaulted lithely and expertly on to the jetty.

'Good afternoon,' she said, landing lightly on the balls of her feet. She was smiling, but Jake could detect no friendliness there. It was the hard uncompromising expression of someone whose first instinct is mistrust. 'My name is Martha Bentley. This is my father's boatyard.'

Jake was stunned. Dennis had a daughter?

'Might I ask what you're doing here?' the girl asked.

Jouma cleared his throat and introduced himself.

'I was told the police had completed their investigation,' Martha said sharply.

'That would be Malindi Police, Miss Bentley,' Jouma told her. 'I am from Coast Province CID.'

'And you?'

'I'm just the transport,' Jake said, gesturing at *Yellowfin*.

134

'Yeah?' Martha said. 'Well, if the two of you have finished snooping around, I'd appreciate a little privacy.'

'Of course.' Jouma nodded, grateful that the grilling was over. He turned towards Jake. 'Perhaps it is time that we returned, Mr Moore. I would like to get back to Mombasa before dark.'

But Jake was not listening. His attention had fixed on the low-slung lines of a second speedboat, a red-painted Chris Craft, which had turned into the creek and was now making rapid, but erratic progress along the river towards the inlet.

'Are you expecting company, Miss Bentley?' he said.

There were two black men in the boat wearing leather jackets and baseball caps – but it was not until they were almost on top of them that Jake saw that one had what looked like an Uzi machine pistol in his hand.

'*Get down!*' he yelled, a split second before a burst of automatic gunfire danced across the brackish water towards them.

Jake leaped across the jetty, arms extended, and in one movement tackled Jouma and Martha to the ground, as bullets raked the dock, sending splinters of tinder-dry wood cartwheeling into the air. The flimsy structure shook as they landed, and Jake thought it might even collapse under them.

'Anybody hit?' he called out.

There was a groaned expletive from the pilot, who was sprawled in the front seat of the Fountain with blood streaming from a head wound. But the fact he was still very much alive suggested that a flying fragment from the jetty rather than a bullet had struck him. On the jetty itself, Martha and Jouma appeared to be unscathed.

'What's happening?' Martha said, staring with almost childlike fascination at a piece of planking which had been chewed in half barely six inches from where she now sat.

Jake knew there was no time to figure out the whys and wherefores. He looked up to see the Chris Craft executing a shallow hairpin turn a hundred yards upriver. The pilot was no expert, and the boat was an old model that had clearly seen better days – but, even so, he calculated that they had only a few seconds before the vessel made a second, deadly pass.

'Get into the workshop,' Jake ordered. 'Now!'

But there were fifty yards between the jetty and the workshop, fifty long excruciatingly exposed yards with nothing but scrub and discarded oil drums for cover. The triggerman in the Chris Craft was no sharpshooter, but with an Uzi you didn't have to be. All you had to do was aim in the general direction and six hundred rounds a minute usually did the rest. As Martha and Jouma began running, Jake cursed as he realised that they would be in range long before they reached shelter.

He jumped down into the Fountain and, after dragging the blood-soaked pilot out of the driver's seat and into the footwell, started the engine. The turbos exploded into life immediately and, having jettisoned the mooring rope from its cleat on the bow, he manoeuvred the boat in a tight one-eighty so that it now pointed out of the inlet towards the river.

The Chris Craft was careering towards the boatyard again, the gunman standing in the rear of the boat with one foot braced against the guard rail, baseball cap pulled down low, brandishing the Uzi in one gloved hand. Jake jammed the throttles forward and, with a furious roar of boiling water, the Fountain shot outwards into the navigation channel. He wrenched on the wheel and brought the bow directly in line with the Chris Craft, then gunned the powerful engines until even they whined in protest.

Up ahead, the pilot of the second boat stared wide-eyed as the Fountain headed towards him on a direct collision course. As the two boats reached the moment of impact, he swerved his vessel to the left, just as the gunman behind him drew a bead on Jake's head with the Uzi. The gunman was sent reeling backwards and Jake heard a ripping sound as the weapon spat out its magazine of bullets.

Then he was out in open water again, zigzagging against the roiling wake of the Chris Craft. He swivelled in his seat and saw the other boat was now out of control and heading at speed for the far bank. The pilot was slumped against the steering wheel with what appeared to be half his head shot away, while the gunman was desperately attempting to extricate himself from the floor of the cockpit where he had become wedged between the rear couch and the pilot's seat. His head popped up just as the boat ploughed into a submerged sandbank, flipped end over end as if it was made from balsa wood, and then smashed against a palm trunk and burst into flames.

'Jesus fuckin' Christ Almighty.' Harold, his face latticed with blood, pulled himself up on to the rear banquette and stared across at the inferno. 'What the fuck was all that about?'

'I have no idea,' Jake said. But, as he swung the boat round and headed back to Dennis Bentley's boatyard, he was going to make damn sure that he found out.

137

Chapter Twenty-Eight

There was something about crocodiles that filled Tug Viljoen with an overwhelming sense of inadequacy. Perhaps it was their hypnotic calm, the self-awareness of the power and terrible savagery of which they were capable – yet unleashed only when necessary. He marvelled at such self-control, studied it intensely, tried to learn from it, because he knew that it was a characteristic he himself lacked and that, no matter how hard he tried, he could never achieve.

Still, he was able to console himself with the fact that crocs might have been around for sixty-five million years, but there was only one dominant species on this fucking planet right now.

For three days now, Viljoen had been watching a twelve-footer in the south lagoon. It basked, muscular and arrogant, on its rock, its mouth permanently twisted into a knowing smile, and it goaded Viljoen from behind the fencing. The other crocs in the lagoon behaved as they should; they got the few visitors who came to Croc World excited by wrestling and thrashing their tails in the water when he tossed chunks of raw meat at them. But not this one. This one – exquisitely powerful, implacably dangerous –

clearly thought itself above the circus routine.

Which was why, in a yard up behind the maintenance sheds far from the prying eyes of the public, it
now hung by its tail from a steel gibbet.

Trapping it had not been easy. The croc was too
big and powerful to be simply chain-lassoed.
Instead, Viljoen had to prepare a noose trap, a sturdy
metal frame dug into the ground at the edge of the
lagoon and baited with freshly killed reedbuck. It
had taken time, but finally the succulent carcass had
proved too much of a temptation for the croc and it
had lunged for it. The spring mechanism popped,
snaring the monster by its front and back legs.
Viljoen had then dragged the croc slowly up and
down the path between the lagoons, chained and
muzzled and hooked to the back of a quad bike,
before taking it to the yard. The object was to humil-
iate it, to show the other crocs who was boss.

Certainly, the big croc was not so arrogant now,
Viljoen noted with some satisfaction as he slipped a
stiff leather glove on to his right fist and adorned it
with a brass knuckleduster. For more than an hour, it
had thrashed frantically against its bindings, smashing its armour against the steel post, trying to gain
purchase on the metal chains around its tail with its
long jaws. It had been strong all right. But now it
hung exhausted and motionless, its jaws slightly
agape, its dwarfish legs spread-eagled and useless.

Viljoen approached it, flexing his fingers in the
confines of the glove, feeling the brass pinching
across his knuckles. The first punch sank deep into
the croc's unprotected abdomen, doubling the creature up. As the jaws snacked blindly at him, Viljoen
punched and punched again until his rhythm was
metronomic and he was barely conscious of anything

139

other than the sound of his fist against the leathery underbelly.

Only when the creature was dead did he stop, staring with fascination at the wounds he had created with his own hands and the cold reptilian blood he had spilled over his own bare chest, arms and face.

Now he felt better.

For the last two days, Viljoen's mood had been Stygian, thanks largely to an unexpected visit from some uppity bitch from Customs & Excise in Mombasa wanting to see details of his livestock transactions as part of an investigation into wildlife poaching. She had got right up his nose with her hectoring. Who the hell did she think she was coming down here and telling him what to do? *What did she know about anything?* Had *she* spent fourteen years in the South African army? There was a big difference between swanning around with a clipboard and providing the thin white line between civilisation and *kaffir* anarchy in Jo'burg.

No, there were too many pen-pushers like her pulling rank these days, Viljoen thought acidly. She was no different to the brassnecks who had taken over South Africa in the bleak years following Mandela's release, the accession of *kaffir* rule and the formation of the laughable Rainbow Nation. They didn't have a clue about the real world either; all they cared about was tokenism and looking good.

But then they weren't up in Gauteng five years after the great revolution, when a thousand screaming *kaffirs* were smashing windows, torching cars, looting shops and throwing bricks at anyone with a white face.

He had been there. Sergeant First Class P. T. Viljoen and the rest of the thin white line. Ninety-six

140

of his men had ended up in hospital that day, one on life-support. CCTV caught Viljoen beating one *kaffir* looter with his rifle butt outside a burning electrical shop.

Guess who felt the wrath of the Rainbow Nation!

'Sorry, Viljoen,' the brassnecks had told him, 'but they've got the tape. It could be embarrassing.'

And that was it: fourteen years of loyal service to the military down the pan, just like that.

There'd been a sop, of course. Just to soften the blow a little. Somebody knew a friend of a friend who had a rundown croc park that, with a little bit of military-style organisation, could be something of an earner. Oh, and one other thing: the croc park was in Kenya. Was he interested?

Did he have a choice? The only alternative employment for white South African soldiers was bodyguarding *kaffirs* in suits, and that was one irony too far as far as Viljoen was concerned. No, he was interested all right. He'd go to Kenya, run the croc park and fuck the lot of them.

After the Customs bitch had left, Viljoen had gone through his five-strong workforce like a dose of salts, making their lives even more miserable for the rest of the day. After that, he had gone to a whorehouse on Mbaraki Road in Malindi and drunk a bottle of Pusser's Navy Rum, while some scrawny mulatto with a Caesarean scar tried in vain to give him a hard-on. Hitting her hadn't made him feel any better. He'd lain awake all night in his caravan, seething about the injustices in his life.

His mood had just gone downhill from then, exacerbated by a dull thump in the back of his head that wouldn't go away. It didn't help either that a dozen of the crocs were showing signs of skin disease, or that two of his staff had run off while he'd been in Malindi. Strung out on Tylenol and copious mugs of strong coffee laced with rum, Viljoen had nearly lost it on two occasions with the three that remained. He'd had one of them – a rabbit-eyed teenager whose job was to paint the sheds – up against a wall by the throat. His fist had been cocked and it was only the pathetic entreaties of the two other staff that had prevented him pulling the trigger and knocking the boy's head off.

The visit of Harry Philliskirk that morning had provided a pleasant enough diversion, and he thought real progress had been made regarding the pressing business to which he had to attend. But the banter and the wacky baccy hadn't changed his mind about killing the arrogant croc once Harry had left.

Only now that it was done, Viljoen noted with satisfaction, had his headache finally subsided.

Yes. He most definitely felt better now.

But his good mood would not last for long.

As he walked back to his caravan to change out of his bloody clothes, the holstered cell phone attached to his belt began ringing. He answered it with a bad-tempered grunt.

'I take it you've heard what your trained monkeys have done!' the caller said in a voice that was nudging the shrill upper reaches of hysteria.

'What the fuck are you talking about, Captain?'

'They've only gone and taken pot-shots at some fucking Mombasa policeman!'

Viljoen stopped walking and grimaced with irritation. 'Like I said: what the *fuck* are you talking about?'

'A detective. Name of Jouma. Snooping around this morning up at Dennis Bentley's yard. Two of your monkeys with machine guns turned up in a speedboat and opened fire. I just heard from the Malindi cops.'

'Is he dead?'

'No.'

'Too bad.'

'But the monkeys are. They drove their boat straight into a tree. Burned to a crisp.'

'Then what's the problem?'

There was an audible gasp as the caller sucked air into his lungs. 'The *problem*? Jesus Christ, Viljoen – apart from the fact there is now a detective wondering why someone wants him dead, Bentley's *daughter* was there!'

'So what?'

'What if your monkeys had killed her? She's an American citizen, for God's sake! You're talking about an international incident! The last thing we want is the FBI and the CIA crawling over everything.'

'*My* monkeys?' Viljoen snapped. ''Scuse my ignorance, Captain – but why do you keep calling them *my* monkeys?'

'They worked for Kili. And Kili works for you, right?'

Viljoen paused. 'I don't know anything about this.'

'Well, you'd damn well better find out and do something about it pronto.'

'Are you threatening me, Captain?' Viljoen said menacingly.

There was a bark of laughter. 'What difference does it make? If things go belly up round here, then we're all dead men. *All* of us, Viljoen. Including you.'

'You worry too much.'

143

'Do I? Well, for your information, our friend Whitestone has just been in touch. He wants us to arrange another shipment.'

This took Viljoen by surprise. 'But the next one isn't due until next month.'

'Yes – well, this one has to go in two *days*.'

'Shit.'

'You said it. How are you getting on with Bentley's replacement?'

'It's in hand, Captain.'

'Will he be ready in time?'

'He needs working on – but I'll make sure of it.'

'You'd damn well better.'

Viljoen thought about the croc on the hook, and how satisfying it had felt to pummel the creature to death. There were plenty of people he would enjoy dispensing the same treatment to – and right now the man on the end of the phone was one of them.

The caller began to say something, but Viljoen cut him off. As he did so, he noticed a thin corona of reptile blood trapped beneath the ragged nail of his thumb. He sucked it absently as he entered another number into the cell.

'*Salaam*, Abdul,' he said when it was answered. 'Sorry to bother you, but I need you to do me a little favour.'

Chapter Twenty-Nine

Flamingo Creek was forty miles south of Malindi. But as far as Chief Inspector Oliver Mugo was concerned, the Dennis Bentley case, and anything related to it, belonged exclusively to him. He was not about to let the small matter of jurisdiction prise it from his grasp.

For two hours, Jake and Jouma had watched Mugo and a dozen Malindi police officers umm-ing and ahh-ing over the charcoaled remains in the carbonised Chris Craft, standing on the evidence, prodding the bodies with sticks, failing to carry out even the most basic crime-scene protocols. On the north bank a scrum of spectators jostled for position around the remains of the boat. It had begun with just a few quizzical locals, but several had not seen each other for many days and had taken the opportunity to catch up on the latest news. Now there were more than forty of them. There were some half-hearted efforts to shoo them away, but for the most part Mugo and his acolytes seemed more interested in being photographed beside the bodies and impressing on Jouma that *they* were in charge of the case, even if the Mombasa detective had actually been present at the shooting. Eventually, some low-ranking officer had taken a cursory statement and said they were free to go. They had needed no second bidding.

Now the two men were back on *Yellowfin*'s flying bridge, heading back upriver towards the boatyard and the inspector's car.

'Mugo seems to think that it was attempted robbery,' Jouma said, no trace of irony in his voice. 'Apparently, there have been a number of similar unprovoked attacks in the area in recent months. Local gangs targeting tourists.'

'With Uzis and speedboats? That's bullshit,' Jake retorted. He turned his head to get one last look at the barrel-chested Malindi policeman stomping about officiously. 'I don't know why our two friends wanted us dead, but it wasn't for our jewellery. You want my opinion, Inspector? We should be asking *her* what she thinks. They turned up pretty sharpish once she arrived.'

He pointed down to the cockpit, where Martha Bentley sat alone in the fighting chair, a blanket draped over her shoulders. She was staring downriver to her father's boatyard, where just a few minutes earlier a team of paramedics in a helicopter had airlifted Harold the pilot to hospital.

'I don't know about you, but I don't believe in coincidences,' Jake said, his voice low so it did not carry over the sound of *Yellowfin*'s engines.

Jouma said nothing. He was thinking about the two men in the boat. Men who were now incinerated corpses. Unrecognisable as human beings. Yet, in that split second in which time stands still, *he had recognised them*. To anyone who knew Mombasa lowlife like Jouma did, they were unmistakable.

146

He looked at Jake. 'The driver of the boat was Stanley Sandara,' he said. 'The man with the gun was called Joshua Punda. It was me they were trying to kill, Mr Moore. Not Miss Bentley.'

Down in the cockpit, Martha watched her father's tumbledown boatyard disappear around a bend in the river. In a moment, all that could be seen was a faint swathe of black smoke hanging above the trees on the opposite bank.

Again she fought back tears and again she found herself unable to do so. *The Queen Bitch of Manhattan is well and truly history*, she thought, and laughed hollowly through her tears.

'Life's a big, unfriendly ocean, kid,' her father had once told her. 'But you're a Bentley. Bentleys always beat the current.'

Bentleys always beat the current. It was a maxim she had carried with her like a precious heirloom. But now she had seen it tarnished before her very eyes, in the rusting metal and eroded concrete of the buildings, the warped and coated wood of the dock, and the faded whitewash letters of her father's name on the roof.

Why hadn't he told her? Why did she have to find out now, when he was dead? When she could do nothing to help him?

It was this, more than anything, which was the knife through Martha's heart. There had never been secrets between them. From that very first time they'd gone out together on the water – her father lifting her up on to his knee so that she could steer the boat he named after her – they had shared a unique bond.

She thought back to the last time they'd spoken on

the phone, no more than three weeks ago, and how he'd made her laugh as he always did with his sarcastic comments about her Wall Street boyfriends and her high-flying lifestyle, before telling her that he was proud of her and loved her more than anything in the world.

'I love you too, Daddy,' she'd said, but then she'd had to go because there was a client she had to see on the other side of the island.

And, on the other side of the world, this is what her father had been reduced to: a desperate last stand on a godforsaken river.

'Sandara and Punda were hired thugs,' Jouma said. 'They worked for a criminal in Mombasa called Michael Kili.'

'I don't get the connection.'

'George Malewe also worked for Michael Kili. When Malewe was reported missing, I went to see Kili. He denied any knowledge of the man.'

Jake emitted a low whistle. 'Then Kili sends his goons to kill you. Looks like you might have touched a nerve, Inspector.'

'So it would seem.'

'And if you're right, and Malewe was on *Martha B*, then there's a link between Dennis Bentley and a Mombasa gangster.'

'It's a link that might explain the money in Mr Bentley's account,' Jouma said solemnly. 'Kili's preferred line of business is prostitution, racketeering, gun-running, illegal alcohol distribution, drugs trafficking ... anything you can think of, Mr Moore. His empire is worth millions of dollars. But he always needs reliable staff, even if they are contractors.'

148

It made sense, Jake thought. Any racketeer was only as good as his runners, and when it came to knowledge of the Kenyan seaboard there were few better operators than Dennis Bentley. A man with Dennis's expertise could easily charge twenty-five grand for his services, and it sounded like Michael Kili could afford to pay the going rate.

Again he looked down at Martha Bentley, and again he wondered what her connection was in all this. A grieving daughter, come to pay her last respects? Or an associate ensuring that all the loose ends were tied?

This was turning into one hell of a fucking jigsaw.

Chapter Thirty

At the precise moment he was knocked out of his chair by a punch to the jaw, Harry was dreaming about holing the winning putt of the British Open at Carnoustie. It was this, rather than the sustained beating that followed, that annoyed him most. For the last ten years Harry's dreams, by and large, had involved Juliet and the boys, the big house they had once shared in England and his six-figure salary which damn near became seven once you took into account performance bonuses and annual dividends. They were dreams that began as happy, smiling family snapshots – before inevitably turning into the same relentless nightmare about that dark night when Juliet, driving the boys back from a school play because Harry was working late, was hit head-on by some little prick stoned on cannabis and behind the wheel of his daddy's expensive sports car on the wrong side of the road.

One split-second. Three lives obliterated. Four, if you counted Harry's.

His disintegration had been swift and spectacular. After less than a year, with the job gone and the house sold, a tide of drink and guilt had washed him up in the one place left in the world where the only memories were good ones. Kenya, where he had lived as a boy with his diplomat parents. It had taken many years but, just recently, Harry had begun to dream about something else.

But the Arab was not known for his consideration. Especially when it came to unpaid debts.

'Wakey, wakey, Mr Philliskirk!' he'd crooned as one of his goons set about Harry's kidneys with steel-capped rigger boots.

'Is that you, Abdul?' Harry grunted from the cement floor of the boatyard office. 'All you had to do was knock.'

'I did – but you were fast asleep. Snoring like a pig. You should stop drinking so much at lunchtime; it impairs your productivity. Oh, but I forgot – you need diesel fuel to be productive in your line of business.'

The Arab began humming a lullaby as a boot connected with Harry's mouth and he felt his bottom lip explode against his teeth. Then he heard the Arab say something and the next thing he knew he was being dragged up from the floor and thrown into his chair. Supernovas exploded against his retinas for a moment, and when they cleared he found that his arms were tied behind his back and the Arab's sweating face was positioned an inch away from his own.

'Do you have the money you owe me, Mr Philliskirk?'

'Don't be ridiculous,' Harry told him with as much indignation as he could muster. 'You said I had five days at twelve per cent interest.'

'Yes. But then I suddenly grew weary of the excuses I would have to endure when five days were up and you still couldn't pay me. So, I will ask you one more time. *Do you have the seventeen thousand dollars you owe me?*'

'No.'

The Arab nodded and straightened. 'This is what I thought,' he said.

Harry girded himself for the next flurry of blows, or even the cold caress of a pistol barrel against his forehead. Instead, he opened his eyes to see the Arab planting one oversized buttock on the desk in front of him.

'I will tell you a story about when I was a young man living in Yemen,' he began.

Harry groaned. 'I'd rather you just killed me, Abdul.'

The goon's meaty paw fizzed through the air and sank into Harry's solar plexus.

'I will tell you a story about when I was a young man living in Yemen,' the Arab repeated over the sound of guttural retching. 'It involves a cousin of mine called Kareem. Now Kareem owned a number of stalls in the marketplace in Sanaa, selling vegetables and spices. It was a profitable business. It made a comfortable living for him and his family. We were all pleased with him.'

'Please, Abdul . . . No more.'

'One day, Kareem came to me and asked if he could borrow my car to visit friends in the next town. "Of course," I said. "Even though my car is a German-made BMW, you are my cousin, Kareem, and what's mine is yours." Sadly, Kareem was involved in an accident – and, although he was unharmed, the car was declared a write-off. Kareem was most apologetic, and promised to pay me back a hundred rials every month until the debt was settled. But I said to him, "Kareem, even if you pay me back a thousand rials a month, it would take years for you to settle the debt." So you know what I did, Mr Philliskirk?'

'I'm sure you're going to tell me.'

'I took his business and I sold it to his rival. Even though he was my cousin, I did this to Kareem because it taught him a most valuable lesson about the importance of being able to pay one's debts in full.'

'I hope you beat him up as well, Abdul,' Harry said. 'Just to emphasise the point.'

The Arab smiled. 'Kareem was family. You, Mr Philliskirk, are not. There is a difference.'

He nodded sharply and the goon standing behind Harry began raining down punches. When he had finished, Harry's nose was broken and his left eye was all but closed up.

'Now,' the Arab continued, 'to business. You owe me seventeen thousand dollars, yes? Your boat must be worth far more than seventeen thousand dollars. Maybe fifty, even in its advanced state of decrepitude. But I am a reasonable man. I will take your boat, and I will give you ten per cent of anything I can sell it for – minus, of course, the interest you have already accrued on your debt. Agreed?'

'You can fuck off,' Harry said.

The Arab wafted his hands. 'I thought you would say this. But it is already arranged. I have a buyer in Malindi.'

'Your buyer can fuck off as well. *Yellowfin* is not for sale.'

Abdul rolled his eyes, like a teacher confronted with a particularly dim pupil. 'But it is *arranged*, Mr Philliskirk. I have shaken on the deal and I am a man of my word. Now – I presume your partner Mr

153

Moore is out at sea at the moment. When do you expect him back?'

'I'll get the money.'

The Arab tutted. 'This is what you keep telling me—'

'I said I'll get it.'

'When?'

'Give me a week.'

'And then what? "Give me another week"? I am a businessman, Mr Philliskirk. Not a fool. And I have run out of patience.'

'I'll get you the bloody money. All of it. Listen – there's two grand in the floor safe, and the keys to the Land Rover are over there. Think of it as a deposit.'

The Arab glared at him from beneath huge furry eyebrows. 'This is your last chance, Mr Philliskirk. Be in no doubt that if you do not honour this agreement I will have you killed.'

Chapter Thirty-One

It was getting dark by the time *Yellowfin* anchored at the boatyard, except on the north shore of the creek where the lights of the new marina complex were jarringly bright. The three of them said little as they climbed into the launch, each of them lost in separate thought about the events of the last few hours.

The lights were off on the jetty and Jake silently cursed Harry as he manoeuvred the launch towards the pilings. He cursed him even more when he saw that the boatyard was in darkness too, and that the door to the workshop was standing wide open. There wasn't much of value inside, but they needed every last thing they had. His partner had clearly forgotten to lock up before setting off for his liquid lunch with the expat crowd at the Elephant Club. It was just as well Jake had come back: these beanos had a habit of continuing long into the next day.

'Wait here,' he said, leaving Jouma and Martha waiting on the jetty as he went across to the workshop. He fumbled blindly for a few moments until his hand brushed the handle of the generator and the garish strip lighting blinked to life overhead. A quick glance told him that nothing appeared to have been stolen, but he noticed that the office door was open. A more thorough examination of the premises would have to wait.

He went outside, where the jetty was now illuminated by the string of bulbs. Jouma and the girl were walking towards the inspector's car.

'The Marlin Bay Hotel is not far from here,' Jouma said. 'I can drop Miss Bentley off on my way back to Mombasa.'

'You sure?'

'It's fine,' Martha said. She looked washed out, almost dead on her feet.

'OK.' There was an awkward pause, then Jake said, 'Listen – if it makes any difference at all, I'm really sorry about your dad.'

She nodded. 'Thank you, Mr Moore. And thank you for what you did today. It was very brave of you.'

She climbed into the passenger seat of the Panda.

'What now?' Jake asked Jouma.

The inspector shrugged. 'I think I had better pay Michael Kili another visit.'

'You want me to come along?'

'No. I think this is a matter I can best deal with myself.'

'Then be careful, Inspector.'

Jake meant it. In the short time he had known Jouma, he had warmed to the diminutive Mombasa detective.

'I will, Mr Moore,' Jouma said, offering his hand. 'And thank you.'

'I think after today you can probably call me Jake.'

Jouma smiled. 'Thank you – Jake.' Then he

gripped the Englishman's forearm urgently. 'The pieces *will* come together,' he said.

When the Panda's tail lights had disappeared into the gloom, Jake went back into the workshop. Fatigue washed over him now, and all he wanted was a shower and something to eat. He had hoped Harry would be waiting to give him a lift up to Suki Lo's, but he was gone and so was the Land Rover. That meant a fucking treacherous walk in the dark and, worse, an even more fucking treacherous walk back.
For Christ's sake, Harry!
Just then, he heard a noise from the office and in an instant his hand had closed around a foot-long monkey wrench on the workbench beside him. Slowly, he moved forward until he was pressed against the concrete wall beside the door jamb. Then, in a single movement, he burst open the door with his shoulder and hit the light switch.

He was not sure what he was expecting to find, but it was certainly not Harry lying in a bloody heap on the floor beneath the desk.

His partner's eyes flickered open and he looked up through puffy purple slits.

'Jake,' he said. 'You're back.' And a thick gout of scarlet-coloured mucus splashed on to the floor from his ruined mouth.

Chapter Thirty-Two

In the members' dining room of the Kenyatta Yacht
Club, Conrad Getty had enjoyed a convivial lunch-
eon of gulls' egg soup, followed by terrine of veal
and Roquefort, charcoaled mallard with tamarind
chutney and a timbale of seared vegetables with
guava bark ambrosia, washed down with two bottles
of Veuve Cliquot. Now, back at the hotel and with
the clock on his office wall showing the time was
shortly after seven in the evening, the owner of the
Marlin Bay was on his hands and knees retching
what was left of it into an empty wastepaper bin
under the desk.

Groaning, he wiped his mouth with the back of his
hand and used the corner of the desk to lever himself to
his feet. In the porthole mirror on the wall, he checked
his shirt, tie and blazer for spatters of vomit.

Jesus Christ, he thought. *This fucking ulcer was
going to be the death of him. Unless he was already
dead first, of course. And that was now a distinct
possibility.*

There was an urgent knock at the door and Loftus
the concierge entered, the usual expression of utter
terror on his face.

'What do you want?' Getty demanded, staring at his reflection in the mirror with as much composure as he could muster.

'The lady – Miss Bentley – '

Getty spun round to face him. '*Yes?*'

'She has returned, sir.'

The hotel owner felt a spasm of relief pass through his body that was almost as powerful as the nausea earlier.

Then Loftus said, 'She is with a policeman from Mombasa' – and Getty's ulcer almost bent him double again.

'Are you all right, sir?'

'Get out of the way,' Getty snapped, pushing past Loftus to hurry downstairs to the floor of the hotel atrium with the concierge following him like a scolded puppy.

Thank God! he thought, vigorously spraying his mouth with peppermint. He'd been expecting to find Martha Bentley dishevelled, bloodstained and damn near hysterical – but instead she was standing at the reception desk, looking tired but nevertheless calmly waiting for her room key. Next to her was a small black man in an ill-fitting suit who was gawping at the atrium like a small child in a sweet shop.

'Miss Bentley!' he exclaimed, almost breaking into a run. 'I got a call from the police. They told me what happened!'

Martha looked up. 'Good evening, Mr Getty. This is Inspector Jouma from Mombasa police. He gave me a lift back.'

Getty shook Jouma's hand almost as an afterthought. 'Thank God you're all right.'

'We're fine,' Martha said. 'How's Harold? It looked like a nasty head wound.'

'He'll live,' Getty said, then, realising how dismissive he must have sounded, added, 'He's receiving the very best treatment as we speak. But I simply can't believe this has happened! That you should be caught up in an attempted robbery!'

'Sadly it is becoming all too common,' the policeman said. 'Once lawlessness becomes widespread, certain people believe it is common practice.'

Getty snorted. 'Well, they got their comeuppance, at least! Of course, as soon as I learned what had happened, I immediately sent one of our boats up to Flamingo Creek to collect you, Miss Bentley. I assumed – But, anyway, the important thing is you're back safely. Perhaps you would care to join me at my table for dinner tonight. It's the least I can do.'

'That's very kind of you, Mr Getty,' Martha said. She took her key from the girl behind the reception desk. 'But I'm pretty bushed, so, if you don't mind, I think I'll go straight to my room.'

She thanked Jouma for the lift and Getty watched impotently as she headed for the doors.

'Are you all right, Mr Getty?' the policeman was saying. 'You really don't look at all well.'

There were three missed calls on Martha's cell, and she tensed when she saw the number. Patrick had also left voicemail, asking her to call him. By the third message, Martha could detect the hurt in his voice and she could imagine him staring at his phone, wondering what he had done to upset her. Her lover was worldly wise in so many ways, and yet in others he was like a little boy in need of constant maternal reassurance.

He was also fiercely protective. Martha knew this – which was why she decided not to call him right

160

away. Not until she'd had time to think about what she was going to tell him. *Not until she'd got her own head round what had happened.* She stripped off and showered, then lay on the bed in the knee-length cotton T-shirt he had brought her from one of his trips to Europe. Only then did she dial his number.

'Where have you been, baby?' Patrick asked her.

'I got back late from Dad's boatyard.'

'Are you OK? You sound kind of tense. Why didn't you call me?'

'It's been one of those days.'

'*Martha.* I know that voice. Tell me what happened.'

She told him. And, when a long time passed and he still hadn't spoken, she said his name.

'Jesus,' he said. 'Are you OK?'

'I'm fine.'

'I'm coming out there.'

'No, Patrick – there's no need. It was just some spaced-out guys.'

'Dammit, Martha! These guys had *guns!*'

'They have guns in New York. Please, Patrick. The cops said they were ramped up on *chang'aa.*'

'What the hell is *chang'aa*?'

'The local brew. Like Scotch, but boosted with industrial methanol.'

'Jesus Christ.'

Again there was silence. She could picture his face, the way it seemed to darken when he was angry.

'And this guy with the boat,' he said. 'What about him?'

'He's just an English skipper who works out of the creek. He knew Dad.'

161

'Sounds like Captain America to me.'

'Are you jealous, Patrick?'

'Should I be?'

He laughed and Martha felt the tension ebb from her body.

'You sure you don't want me to come out there, honey? I'm worried about you.'

'I'm fine,' she said. 'Let me finish what I have to do. Anyway who's going to feed Chico?'

'I swear you think more of that goddamn cat than you do about me.'

'Chico's been on the scene a lot longer than you have.'

'Does Chico buy you tickets for U2? Does Chico take you to Sardi's on your birthday?'

'Does Chico leave his clothes scattered across the bedroom? Does Chico leave the toilet seat up after he's been for a pee?'

At the other end of the phone he laughed again.

'You think you're some Manhattan hotshot, Martha, but deep down you're just a typical woman.'

'And you're a smartass son of a bitch.'

'Yeah, well that may be so,' he said. 'But I'm the smartass son of a bitch who feeds your cat.'

He was still laughing as he ended the call. Martha was pleased. The last thing she wanted was Patrick to be brooding about her. Because if he brooded too much he was just as likely to get on the next flight to Kenya – and that was something Martha did not want. Patrick was a nice considerate guy; but he was also someone who, she had suddenly realised, was on the very periphery of her life. Even in the short time she had been in Kenya, Martha had felt a far deeper connection than she had with the superficialities of New York. For her,

162

this was a place of questions that needed answering.

And the more time passed, the more Patrick was just the guy who fed her cat.

Day Six

Chapter Thirty-Three

With its sweeping panorama over Lake Tanganyika and the Congo mountains beyond, Whitestone found the Presidential Suite of the Hotel Tanzania far too ostentatious for his tastes. He was not averse to luxury. Far from it. When you were brought up by parents who regarded numbing mediocrity as an achievement, you came to demand the finer things in life when they came within your reach. Had it been up to him, however, the breakfast meeting with Colonel Augustus Kanga would have taken place somewhere less obtrusive, where business could be discussed discreetly and without attracting unnecessary attention.

But discretion had never been Kanga's style. The fat Angolan seemed to wallow in the opulence of the Louis-Philippe furnishings and the spectacular view across the lake. Whitestone watched, mildly revolted, as he spooned Beluga caviar on to a wafer of toast and shovelled it into his large pink mouth, grunting with pleasure as he did so.

Caviar for breakfast. How crass could you get? Almost as crass as calling yourself Colonel when you hadn't been in the army for over a decade.

'So our Russian friend was pleased with his little appetiser,' Kanga said, his slow rumbling voice sounding even more imbecilic through a mouthful of food. 'That is good. And who are these friends of his who are so interested in our merchandise?'

'Only he can answer that,' Whitestone said.

It was typical of Kanga to ask such a stupid question, he thought. Even after all these years, he had yet to grasp the fundamental rule of the business he was in.

Kanga used his finger to scoop some caviar that had spilled on to the napkin he wore tucked in the collar of his shirt in order to protect his silk tie. He jammed the finger in his mouth and sucked greedily. Then he pushed away his plate and eased his bulk back against the plump cushions of the chaise longue. He looked, Whitestone thought, like a sated and debauched Roman emperor. All he needed was a toga instead of the tailored suit.

'I have studied your latest inventory,' Kanga said, swatting at a fly that had targeted the scraps on his plate. 'And I can't see any problems about procuring the relevant items.'

'Good. Then we need to discuss schedules. There is no time to lose.'

Kanga raised a hand. 'One moment, Mr Whitestone. Not so fast. There is the question of payment.'

Whitestone's eyes narrowed. 'The arrangements are the same as always.'

'I know, I know. But it strikes me that perhaps this *arrangement* is in need of updating.'

'What are you trying to say, Colonel?'

'What I'm trying to say, Mr Whitestone, is that perhaps the arrangement as it stands is loaded in your favour. After all, it is my people who are responsible for procuring the merchandise. As I see it, your job is merely to arrange distribution to our friends in Europe.'

Whitestone chuckled. 'Is that so?'

'That is so.' His breakfast over, Kanga lit a Cuban cigar and exhaled a plume of thick blue smoke in Whitestone's direction. 'Now I respect you, Mr Whitestone. But perhaps it is about time we *rationalised* our working relationship a little.'

'Go on.'

'I'm talking about a *partnership*. Fifty-fifty. I know that you are a good operator. The best. But, if truth be told, so am I. And, as things stand, our arrangement does not reflect this.'

Whitestone steepled his fingers and stared at the Angolan for several moments. 'Fifty-fifty, you say?'

'Fifty-fifty.'

'You know that is out of the question.'

Kanga exhaled smoke and raised his hands in resignation. 'You know, Mr Whitestone, I thought you would say that. And it breaks my heart. But, you see, I think that, without me and my people, you don't have a leg to stand on. A pimp is only as good as his whores, after all.'

Whitestone shrugged. 'So what do you propose?'

'I'm proposing to cut out the middleman,' Kanga said. 'Move the goods straight from the warehouse to the customer, if you take my meaning. And I'm sure our Russian friends would appreciate the significant saving in household expenditure.'

'I see.' Whitestone ran a hand through his hair, wondering just how many more strangled clichés he would have to endure before this interminable breakfast meeting drew to a close. 'You have a habit of

169

referring to my clients as *your* friends, Colonel Kanga.'

Kanga laughed. 'It's only a matter of time, isn't it? Listen, Mr Whitestone, I am offering you a chance to get in on the action first. After all, we go back a long way and I would hate to go behind your back.'

'I appreciate that.'

'More than anything else, Colonel Augustus Kanga is a man of honour. I respect my business associates.'

'Of course.'

'So I'll ask you again. A partnership. You and I. Fifty-fifty. What do you say?'

Whitestone smiled. 'You make a persuasive case, Colonel. But I will have to consult with my superiors.'

Kanga seemed surprised. He plucked the napkin from his collar and placed it next to his plate of caviar. 'I am delighted that you see things the way I do, Mr Whitestone. You know that I would never try to undermine you.'

'Heaven forbid.'

'Just to show you that I'm a man of my word, I shall get *my* people working on this latest inventory right away.' Kanga levered himself to his feet and proffered a hand. 'It remains a pleasure working with you, Mr Whitestone.'

Whitestone smiled back at him. 'The pleasure is all mine, Colonel.'

Chapter Thirty-Four

It was 10 a.m. and Harry had been licking his wounds at Suki Lo's for the best part of twelve hours. He was only marginally drunker than Jake. Last night, Jake had wanted to take Harry to the hospital, but Harry had insisted his injuries were superficial, and nothing that a couple of bottles of Jack Daniel's and a bowl of Suki's chilli noodles wouldn't cure. In any case, he added, they couldn't go to the hospital because the muggers who had beaten him up and taken two grand out of the safe had also driven off in his Land Rover.

'Mind you, they wouldn't get far in that old bus,' he said. 'There's a knack to driving without a clutch, you know.'

The stolen Land Rover had also provided them with a tenuous excuse to remain in Suki Lo's bar all night. With Harry's broken ribs and swollen knees, it had taken the two men nearly an hour to walk here. The prospect of walking back was just too terrible to contemplate for both of them.

'Still, who am I to complain?' Harry announced to Suki Lo, who had enthusiastically joined in the marathon drinking session and still, somehow,

171

looked bright as a button. 'My muggers were only armed with baseball bats. Jake here – his had fucking guns!'

'Fucking *Uzis*,' Jake pointed out.

'Well, there you go! So you see, Suki, my pet, everything is relative.'

'Sometime you talk shit, Harry,' Suki said, lighting her sixtieth cigarette since midnight. 'In fact, *all* time you talk shit.' She took a swill of Bacardi and Coke and tottered off to the kitchen.

'You should give the cops a description,' Jake said. 'Before you forget what they looked like.'

'No offence, old chap, because I know you're pally with that inspector from Mombasa, but I've never put much faith in the boys in blue. Especially not this lot. Besides, Chief Inspector Mugo would only say it was an accident.' Harry laughed, then winced with pain.

'You could always tell him that the bastards cleaned us out of every last penny we've got. Not to mention our only means of transport on dry land.' Jake stared mournfully into his glass. 'Admit it, Harry – it's over. We're finished.'

Harry glared at him across the table. 'Now you listen to me. Harry Philliskirk doesn't know the meaning of the word *finished*. This is our business, we've worked bloody hard at it, and I'll be damned to hell in a handcart if I'm going to watch it fold because of a pissing two grand and a clapped-out Land Rover.'

'We owe the Arab seventeen grand,' Jake pointed out. 'At twelve per cent interest.'

Suki appeared from the kitchen with an ice bucket and a concerned look on her face.

'Your eye really swollen now,' she clucked, her

172

thin fingers gently probing his swollen face. 'Aw –
they make a fuckin' mess of you, honey boy.'

'I think it gives me gravitas,' Harry said. 'I look
like Gentleman Jim Corbett.'

Jake grimaced. 'Did Gentleman Jim Corbett wash
dishes for a living?'

Suki looked at the two Englishmen with a puzzled
expression.

'You know, Suki,' Harry said, 'I don't think I ever
told you this, but Jake here was the only one who
answered my advert for a partner to run the boat
business. *The only one.* I remember when I first
brought him here from the airport. Showed him that
old shed and told him that one day we'd have a place
just like those swanky buggers in Malindi. Anybody
in their right mind would have turned straight round
and got back on the first plane back to Heathrow. But
Jake kept the faith. And I'll never forget that.'

'Jake is a good boy,' Suki said.

Harry looked at him. 'And that's why I'm asking
you to keep the faith one more time, old pal.'

'I will, Harry,' Jake said. 'But where the hell are
we going to get seventeen thousand dollars?'

Chapter Thirty-Five

That morning the air was gritty with dust blown overland from the vast expanse of the Masai Mara. In the heat and toil of Mombasa Old Town the tourists were hiding indoors, which for Kenneth Kariuku meant that business was slow to the extent that six of the eight shillings in his open guitar case were those that he'd tossed in earlier.

As he tugged on the tuning pegs of his five remaining guitar strings, ear cocked to the body of the battered instrument so he could hear above the roar of traffic, he silently cursed the parsimony of Mombasa's tourists. OK, he was no great shakes as a guitar player – but what did they want? At least his self-penned folk songs were more culturally valid than the tacky carved elephants and fake Rolex watches being peddled on every street corner.

No, Mombasa was not what he had expected at all when he'd arrived two days ago on the weekly *matatu* minibus from his home village in the Taru desert.

'Go to Mombasa and play your music, Kenneth,' his mother had told him. 'Within a week you will have made your fortune!'

How wrong she was. In two days, he had made

precisely three shillings profit – barely enough to catch the next *matatu* home.

Well, Kenneth thought, if it was tourist tat they wanted, then that's what they would get. Tuned up, he slipped the guitar strap over his head and began to sing.

Kenya ni nchi nzuri, Hakuna matata.
Nchi ya kupendeza, Hakuna matata.
Nchi ya maajabu, Hakuna matata
Nchi yenye amani, Hakuna matata.

Yet, even as he sang, Kenneth's heart sank. Was this what he was reduced to? Popular ditties that appeared on a million and one cassette tapes of traditional Kenyan music? It was no good. Tomorrow he would head to Nairobi. He had heard talk of a club there whose owner actively encouraged young folk singers such as himself.

'That is a very nice song, boy.'

Kenneth ceased strumming. He'd been so wrapped up in his own frustration he had not noticed the two men watching his performance intently from the sidewalk. The man who had spoken was stocky, with mirror-lensed sunglasses and an expensive leather jacket. He was shorter by at least a foot than the second, bespectacled, man, whose slim body was draped in a white cotton *khanzu*.

Kenneth's heart pounded. He had heard about moments like this, when unknown singers were plucked from the street by passing record-company executives and turned overnight into superstars.

'Thank you, sir,' he said.

'*Hakuna matata*,' said the stocky man. '"There are no problems".'

175

'Most certainly not, sir!' Kenneth beamed.

'You are wrong, boy.'

Kenneth was taken aback. He knew the words to 'Jambo Bwana' backwards. His own mother used to sing them to him when he was a small child.

'Wrong?'

The man in the sunglasses raised a finger and pointed above Kenneth's head. 'You see that sign?'

Kenneth twisted his neck. There was a black metal-clad door behind him and, on the wall above it, a small unlit neon sign.

'Baobab Club,' he read aloud.

'I own the Baobab Club,' explained Michael Kili. 'And one thing I hate is when beggars play musical instruments outside my club without asking my permission. So, as you can see, the words of your song *are* wrong: there *is* a problem.'

Kenneth's bowels turned to mush. 'I – I apologise, sir, for my mistake,' he spluttered.

The man just smiled at him. 'Normally I would have you killed,' Kili said. 'But I am in a good mood today.'

He reached out and ripped Kenneth's guitar from its strap, then held it at arm's length and fired his right fist straight through the cheap boxwood body. Then he dropped it on the ground and stamped it to splinters with the fat foam sole of his Reebok training shoe.

'There now, Jacob,' Kili crowed as he and Omu climbed the stairs to his office. 'Not only did I allow Mary Olunbiye to live, but I have also spared a beggar his life. Does that not prove that I am a merciful man?'

'Merciful and wise,' Omu said respectfully,

176

reflecting that Mary Olunbiye would undoubtedly agree. Having one's little finger chopped off with a kukri knife was, after all, preferable to having one's throat slashed open with it.

Kili laughed. *'Merciful and wise.* You sound like a preacher, Jacob. A man of God.' He reached out and grabbed the folds of Omu's cotton *khanzu.* 'You dress like one, too. Really, Jacob, I don't know why you don't treat yourself to some nice clothes. Something modern! And that apartment you live in! Surrounded by dock rats. The whores on Hutambo Road live in more luxury!'

Omu smiled indulgently as they entered the first-floor office. But no sooner had they done this than both men stopped in their tracks.

Sitting in his chair, feet up on Kili's desk with a copy of *The Daily Nation* in his hands, was Tug Viljoen.

'Morning, gents,' the South African said, baring his teeth in an approximation of a smile. 'Wasn't sure how long you would be, so I thought I'd make myself comfortable.'

'What do you want?' Kili demanded, puffing out his chest like a territorial bird. 'Who let you into my office?'

'Don't worry about that. You see, we have a problem, Michael.'

'Problem?'

'You've been taking matters into your own hands again. Now you *know* what I said about taking matters into your own hands . . .'

Kili turned to Omu. 'Call Christopher and have him throw this dog out of my office,' he said insouciantly.

But Omu walked across to the desk and stood

177

beside Viljoen, his hands folded neatly behind his back.

'Jacob!' Kili exclaimed open-mouthed. 'What is the meaning of this?'

'I'm sorry,' Omu said respectfully, 'but I am afraid I must on this occasion side with Mr Viljoen.'

Kili's jaw dropped further. 'Have you lost your mind? What are you talking about?'

'He's trying to put it as politely as possible that you're a fucking liability, Michael,' Viljoen said. 'He's saying that he no longer wishes to be associated with anyone so fucking dumb as to send a hit squad to bump off a detective from Mombasa police in broad daylight.'

'But Joshua—'

'Joshua's dead. And so's the other monkey you sent to Flamingo Creek yesterday. And now I'm afraid the time has come to deal with the organ grinder.'

With a roar of anger, Kili strode towards the desk with his kukri knife clutched in his fist. But he had barely made two paces before Viljoen fired a silenced Glock automatic from behind the newspaper and shot him through the left eye.

'I take it you have dealt with any other indiscretions this prick may have left behind,' Viljoen said calmly, unscrewing the silencer and placing the gun into the waistband of his shorts.

Omu stared at the twitching body on the floor. 'Everything is in order, Mr Viljoen.'

'Good. Then get this mess cleared up pronto and maybe we can all lead a quieter life for a change.'

Chapter Thirty-Six

Five minutes later, Viljoen emerged from the Baobab Club and jumped into a dust-covered jeep parked illegally on the pavement outside. From the driver's seat of his Fiat Panda parked fifty yards further down the street, Jouma clucked to himself as he took the South African's photograph with an ancient Kodak Instamatic.

'Number eleven,' he said, checking his watch. 'Left the premises at ten-twelve precisely.' He removed the undeveloped photograph from the camera and placed it with the other twenty-two on the dashboard of the car.

Beside him, Sergeant Nyami pulled a face. 'He was most probably there to watch the rude dancers. Like all the others.'

'Just write down the licence-plate number, Sergeant,' Jouma said, winding on the film.

'How many more?' Nyami said impatiently, scribbling into a spiral-bound notebook.

'Nyami, did anyone ever tell you that surveillance is a basic and highly effective means of collecting information?'

'Of course! Do you think I am a fool?'

'Then you will also be aware that it can often be a long and arduous process, consisting of many hours of patient observation.'

'But who are we *looking* for?'

'That remains to be seen, Nyami,' Jouma said, confident that somewhere among the snaps and number plates he would find justification for the last two hours of sitting in the sweltering car.

'Look, Inspector!' Nyami hissed.

The door of the Baobab had opened once again, and this time the unmistakable figure of Jacob Omu emerged, carrying a leather attaché case in his hand. Kili's lieutenant glanced warily up and down the street, then set off towards them with wide precise strides.

'Get down, Nyami,' Jouma said calmly, and the two policemen shrank down in their seats as Omu passed by.

'He's gone,' Nyami said, peering over the dashboard, the relief evident in his voice. 'Can we go now?'

'On the contrary,' Jouma said brightly. 'We have been presented with a rare opportunity: a chance to talk to Michael Kili on his own.'

Nyami flinched and his face paled slightly. 'Talk to *Kili*? Are you mad? What will that achieve? He will say nothing!'

'Kili says nothing because Omu tells him to. With the cat away, perhaps the mouse will be more forthcoming.'

'But *why*? Surely this is not still to do with George Malewe? You are obsessed with that Likoni cockroach!'

'I have my reasons, Nyami. Now come along. We are policemen and we have a job to do.'

*

180

After straightening the creases in his buttoned rain-coat, Jouma knocked briskly on the metal-plated door of the Baobab Club. After a few moments, it opened a fraction and a pair of narrowed eyes peered out at him.

'What?' said a disembodied voice.

Jouma snapped open the leather wallet containing his badge and warrant card and thrust it an inch from the eyes. 'Open the door.'

Slowly the door swung back and Jouma saw that the eyes belonged to a thickset, crudely scalped bouncer wearing regulation bodybuilder's vest and tracksuit bottoms.

'Ah, good afternoon, Christopher. How is your mother?'

'She is very well, Inspector Jouma,' the big man said sheepishly.

'You must tell her that I am asking after her health.'

'I will, Inspector.'

'Good. Now be so kind as to take me to Mr Kili's office.'

Christopher's face froze. 'Mr Kili is not here.'

'I saw him enter the premises no more than thirty minutes ago,' Jouma said pleasantly. 'Perhaps he left through the window – but I doubt it.'

'But, Inspector Jouma—' Christopher wailed.

Jouma wagged a finger at him. 'Christopher Kalinki, if your poor mother knew the people with whom you associated she would have something to say about it – and we all know your mother stands for no nonsense, don't we?'

Christopher weighed up the no-win situation with growing despair.

'If anyone says anything to you, just tell them that

I insisted,' Jouma said, patting the abject bouncer on the arm.

He stepped inside, walked a couple of paces and turned round. 'Well – what are you waiting for, Nyami?' he said tersely.

Behind him on the street, Sergeant Nyami cleared his throat nervously and followed Jouma into the dimly lit interior of the club.

It truly was as Jouma imagined the waiting room of Hell. Not even ten-thirty in the morning and yet the booths were already full of seedy-looking Africans, Asians and Europeans being attended by frightened-looking young girls barely into their teenage years; tables of leering drunken men positioned in front of a tiny stage upon which an ageing, pock-marked whore was wearily removing her clothing to the thumping beat of unintelligible music. Not for the first time, Jouma felt a flush of shame at the depths to which the city of his birth had sunk. Parts of Mombasa needed to be burned to the ground and built again. Such was the way of dealing with vermin and infestation.

At the other side of the bar was a studded door covered with peeling leather. It was marked STRICTLY NO ENTRY. Jouma saw Christopher take a deep breath before he pushed it open.

'Thank you, Christopher. I think we know the way from here.'

Chapter Thirty-Seven

Omu's apartment on the waterfront near the dhow harbour was simply furnished: a single cot, a bedside table, a wardrobe, a sink and a copy of the Koran. Kili was forever berating him for leading such a parsimonious existence, but it suited perfectly a man of Jacob Omu's monkish requirements.

Material wealth did not interest Omu; it never had. He was a man who derived his pleasure from *control*. Its mechanics fascinated him – how action in one place led inevitably to reaction elsewhere, and how it was possible to manipulate that reaction to one's own ends. What also pleasured him greatly was the omniscience which total control required. The need for information was, for Omu, an addiction – receiving it a drug that gave him an unsurpassed high. That was why he had assiduously cultivated tendrils in all strata of Mombasa society, from the lowliest barfly to the society hotelier, from the street corner to the very corridors of power.

And that was why, until now, Michael Kili had been important to him. The gangster's multifarious criminal activities did not interest him in the slightest, but *controlling* them for him did; for Kili's position of power meant that Omu effectively controlled Mombasa.

But everything was temporary.

Omu felt no loyalty to Kili. Kili was stupid and he was greedy. Even before recent events, his future had been plain to see: he would get stupider and greedier, until, one day, he would make one mistake too many and someone would come up behind him and slit his throat.

Or shoot him through the eye.

Such was the fate of second-rate thugs who came to believe their own publicity. The only difference was that Kili's demise had come rather quicker than Omu had anticipated.

Fortunately, Omu had always believed in contingency plans. And he had been planning for this moment for some time.

He returned his attentions to the half-packed suitcase and neatly folded clothes on the bed. A few moments later, he locked the case and left the room. Down a flight of stone steps, Omu exited the apartment building by a back entrance that led by means of a rancid-smelling alleyway to the waterfront. When he'd first moved there, the alleyway had been home to a handful of scabrous beggars who one night had attempted a shambolic mugging. After Omu had killed two of them with his knife, the rest soon leached away into the shadows. They had obviously spread the word, as ever since the only vermin to be seen in the alley nowadays were water rats.

At the end of the alley was a fenced and padlocked wooden jetty. Moored to it was a Sea Ray 220 speedboat. Omu smiled as he looked at its sleek lines. It had cost him twenty thousand dollars, yet he planned to use it only once and then dispose of it. That was the kind of mindless consumerism that would have impressed Kili. How ironic.

Omu stashed the suitcase and the attaché case in a hold at the front of the boat, then retraced his steps to the apartment building and out on to the busy main street. He looked at his watch. There was one more onerous task to complete before he could depart. One last duty to perform for his former employer. There was no logical reason why one of Kili's henchmen could not be entrusted to dispose of the body – it was not as if they hadn't done it hundreds of times before. But without Omu to oversee proceedings there would always be a chance that things would not go to plan. Look what had happened when Kili had taken matters into his own hands yesterday.

No, if his work here was done, then Omu did not want a single thread left untied. For a man who thrived on control, that would be simply unacceptable.

Chapter Thirty-Eight

At first Jouma did not see Michael Kili. What he saw as he entered Kili's office was what he was expecting: the desk, the worn leather sofa against one wall, a grubby pawed poster of Anna Kournikova wearing leather underwear and holding the handle of a tennis racket suggestively between her finger and thumb, mismatched chairs, a threadbare rug, a coffee table, a grimy window overlooking the alleyway and, standing side by side, a metal filing cabinet and a cheap plywood stationery cupboard.

But then he saw the blood. A large dark pool of it in the centre of the carpet. Splashes of it on the ceiling. Spatters on the walls and the furniture.

And then he saw Kili.

'Close the door, Nyami,' he said quietly.

The gangster had been propped up in a sitting position in the narrow gap between the stationery cupboard and the filing cabinet. What was left of his shattered head was resting on his knees, his hands lying slackly at his sides.

'Nyami, close the door.'

When there was no response, he turned to find his sergeant backed up against the wall behind the desk, his eyes bulging, an expression of horror on his sweating face as he stared at the scene.

'*Nyami!*'

Nyami momentarily snapped out of his paralysis.

'Close the door, please,' Jouma told him.

Nyami moved to the door, but his gaze never wavered from Kili's body.

'Thank you,' Jouma said, attempting to remain as businesslike as possible, even though he was shaking. 'Now remember, Nyami, we are here on official police business. And, even though this is now a crime scene, we must not forget the reason for being here. I want you to check the desk drawers while I examine the filing cabinet.'

'We should go,' Nyami said.

'We are going nowhere, Sergeant.'

'But we need to tell someone about—'

'Tell who? The police? We *are* the police, Nyami! Now pull yourself together and do your job!'

Trying hard to keep his own wavering composure, Jouma went to the filing cabinet and pulled open every drawer. The cabinet was empty, and the skewed hanging files suggested it had been emptied in a hurry.

'There is nothing in the desk drawers,' Nyami reported.

'Keep looking.'

'What am I supposed to be looking for?'

'*Anything.*'

Anything that might prove that Michael Kili had ordered his assassination yesterday. Anything that might explain why Kili was now slumped on the floor with half of his head blown off.

Jouma thought about the attaché case that Omu was carrying as he left the Baobab Club, and cursed.

While he had been taking Polaroids of dirty old men, fifty yards away Michael Kili's Mombasa empire was in the process of being overthrown in a bloody coup. The evidence had been removed right from under his very nose! A sudden wave of impotent fury rose up inside him and he smashed his fist hard against the metal sides of the filing cabinet.

'Looking for something, Inspector?' a voice said from the doorway. 'As you can see, Mr Kili is indisposed. Perhaps I can help?'

Jacob Omu's demeanour was that of a polite librarian offering assistance in finding a book. He stood with his hands behind his back, resting lightly against the jamb.

'What is the meaning of this, Mr Omu?' Jouma demanded.

Omu seemed amused – and who could blame him, Jouma thought. To the man in the white cotton *khanzu*, he must have cut a pathetic figure standing there beside the emptied drawers of the filing cabinet, amid all the blood.

'The meaning?' Omu was saying. 'Of death, Inspector? Now that is a very esoteric question, even for an educated man such as yourself.'

Jouma gestured at Kili's body, although he could not bring himself to look at the corpse. 'Are you responsible for this?'

'Me? No.'

'Then who?'

'I have no idea.'

'Then I am placing you under arrest, Mr Omu.'

Omu casually pushed his spectacles along the bridge of his nose. 'With what am I charged?'

'Where do I begin?' Jouma said. 'Drug dealing, extortion, prostitution, smuggling, murder . . .'

188

'And do you have any evidence to back up these outrageous allegations, Inspector?' Omu said calmly.

'There are more than enough decent people in Mombasa who would be willing to testify to your illegal activities,' Jouma told him.

Omu saw through the emptiness of his threats and smiled again. 'Inspector, you and I both know that, if that were the case, you would have arrested me and Mr Kili long ago.'

'Nyami, handcuff the suspect please.'

'Might I suggest,' Omu said smoothly, 'that you both go back to Mama Ngina Drive and forget everything that has happened here?'

'Sergeant, did you hear me? *Sergeant!*'

But Nyami stood behind the desk, fidgeting, sweating, his eyes averted.

'Oh, Nyami,' Jouma sighed with genuine disappointment.

'You should not blame the sergeant,' said Omu. 'Nobody should be expected to uphold the law on the pittance Kenya police pays its officers.'

'I have always managed,' Jouma said quietly.

Omu shrugged. 'Then I will be doing you a favour by putting you out of your misery, Inspector.'

By the time Jouma saw the thin serrated knife that had appeared from the folds of the *khanzu*, Omu had crossed the room in a single catlike stride. Jouma felt no pain, just a dull impact as Omu drove the knife into his chest.

Chapter Thirty-Nine

Colonel Augustus Kanga had ordered many men killed in his time. During the war against the UNITA rebels in Angola, just one command could result in the liquidation of an entire village. Those were happy days, he reflected sadly. Things were so much simpler then.

Kanga was not ashamed to admit that he found the world a frustrating place these days. There was not a day went by that he did not wish he was putting on his crisply laundered army fatigues instead of a lambswool Italian suit, or that he was dealing with a regiment of disciplined soldiers instead of insolent businessmen motivated only by their own greed.

But his army days were ancient history now. These days Kanga had more pressing concerns.

The first was dealing with Whitestone. Even that was problematic compared to the days when he had any number of eager death squads at his disposal. No, in this frustrating world of business, assassins had to be hired, instructions had to be given, money had to be exchanged. There was none of the *spontaneity*, none of the *immediacy* that he had become accustomed to in the military.

In a way, Kanga was sorry that things had come to such a head. After all, it was Whitestone who had been instrumental in setting him up in business, and who had taught him the rudiments of the trade they were now in. Yes, there was no doubt that Kanga owed Whitestone a great deal.

But there was one lesson Kanga did not need to learn, and that was the importance of being ruthless. In offering Whitestone a fifty-fifty partnership, he had been more than generous; Whitestone's noncommittal response was, as far as Kanga was concerned, tantamount to a rejection.

So he was left with no choice. Whitestone had to be eliminated.

In the back seat of his chauffeur-driven limousine, Kanga jabbed a number into the satellite phone built into the leather upholstery beside him. As he waited for the connection, he marvelled at the technology that was literally at his fingertips. Had he been equipped with such a device when he was in the army, the war would have been over long before any talk of ceasefire.

Which was why he was now puzzled, not to say *irritated*, that for some reason the connection did not seem to be working.

He leaned forward and rapped on the glass screen separating him from the driver.

'Robert! The satellite phone is not working.'

Robert was a bullet-headed man who in a previous life had been Kanga's batman. When Kanga had quit the army, Robert had loyally followed him.

'Perhaps the area is not suitable for a signal, sir,' he said.

Kanga looked out of the window and saw that they were proceeding along a road that was framed on either side by low scrubby hills. Even so, he thought, this terrain should not affect the operation of the phone.

He was about to speak when the phone suddenly chirped to life.

'Finally!' Kanga exclaimed. He pushed the hands-free button. 'Djali, my friend! It is about time you checked your batteries. I have been trying to contact you.'

'I charged my batteries this morning, Colonel Kanga,' Whitestone's disembodied voice said through the speakers. 'Right after our meeting.'

Kanga masked his surprise. 'Mr Whitestone! How nice to hear from you. You have considered my offer?'

'I have,' Whitestone said. 'And I'm afraid the answer is no.'

'As I thought,' Kanga nodded. 'That is a great shame. I have enjoyed doing business with you. I trust you feel the same way.'

As he spoke, Kanga noticed that the limousine was slowing down and was now pulling into the side of the road. He leaned forward again and rapped on the glass, but it was as if Robert did not hear him.

'It's always a pity when a profitable business arrangement comes to an end,' Whitestone was saying. 'Especially through the pig-headed ignorance of one of the partners.'

Distracted, Kanga almost missed the insult. Now anger flooded through him. 'I trust you are talking about yourself, Mr Whitestone!'

Whitestone's laughter filled the car. 'Colonel, you're so dumb you don't even know who's on your side any more. You're probably wondering why Robert has stopped the car.'

192

Startled, Kanga shifted in his seat in order to look out of the rear window of the limousine, but the road was empty. Then came the heavy thud of the central locking being activated and when he turned round the driver was pointing a heavy-duty silenced automatic at him through a gap in the dividing screen.

'Robert?' he said. Then, angrily, 'You cannot kill me, Mr Whitestone. Where will you get your merchandise?'

'You seem to be under the misapprehension that you are the only supplier in Africa,' Whitestone said. 'In fact, I could replace you with ten others by this afternoon. It's the one lesson in business you never learned.'

The expression of fury was still frozen on Kanga's face when Robert pulled the trigger and blew his brains against the bullet-proof rear window.

'Thank you, Robert,' Whitestone said over the speakers. 'That can't have been easy.'

Robert said nothing as he replaced the gun in his holster and closed the screen. It had been surprisingly easy, as a matter of fact. But then what Whitestone had offered him was extremely generous. And, as Colonel Kanga had never ceased to remind him, they were no longer in the army.

Chapter Forty

The telephone in the office of Britannia Fishing Trips Ltd, which had steadfastly refused to ring for more than two days, was ringing.

'Well, I'll be damned,' Harry exclaimed. 'I was about to call out the engineers to see if it was broken.'

They were a hundred yards from the workshop, on the last leg of a marathon half-pissed trek back along the jungle path from Suki Lo's.

'Well, don't just stand there, old boy! Go and answer it!'

Jake gratefully unhooked Harry's arm from round his shoulders and ran to the phone.

'Fly like the wind!' Harry laughed, following at a snail's pace, his weight resting on the hickory handle of a furled umbrella.

Despite his bravado and the drink inside him, he was now forced to admit that he was in quite a bit of pain. He hadn't felt it necessary to go into all of the gory details of the beating he had received at the hands of the Arab's henchmen – or indeed that it was the Arab who had been responsible. The last thing he wanted was Jake embarking on another vigilante mission. A mugging would suffice until he could straighten this mess out. But he also knew, from the succession of dull aches and sharp pains that wracked his body, that his internal injuries were just as severe as the bruises and abrasions on his skin. It had been, without a doubt, one *hell* of a kicking. And maybe later, if things didn't abate, he would swallow his pride and pay a visit to Dr Markham on the far side of the river. At the very least the odious old quack might find it in his mercy to give him a few Paracetamol to dull the pain.

But that would have to wait. Because right now Harry had business to attend to. Business that might just *save* the business.

He was at the jetty now, and it was all he could manage to ease himself into the battered director's chair he kept there for his mid-afternoon nap. Across the water, *Yellowfin* bobbed lazily on the current. Harry looked at her with paternal pride, and an uncharacteristic irritation came over him when he thought about the Arab using her in some grubby deal with a buyer in Malindi. She might be knocking on a bit and her glory days might be behind her, but she was all he had left – and no one was going to sell her from under his nose.

Jake emerged from the workshop, wearing a quizzical expression.

'That was Cyril from Malindi,' he said. 'Says he's got a booking for us.'

Harry grunted with surprise. 'Cyril? Are you sure he had the right number? That little bastard deals exclusively with anyone who might give him a back-hander.'

'The Ernies asked for Britannia Fishing Trips specifically, he said.'

'What name?'

'Cruickshank,' Jake said.

He could see Harry racking his brain for anyone of that name who might have once appeared in the Forbes Rich List.

Eventually Harry shrugged. 'Buggered if I know,' he said. 'You'd better get up there before they change their minds.'

'OK,' Jake said. 'I'll get the beer and food loaded and drop by Sammy's on the way.'

'Good man. And, Jake, I would have a strong coffee first.'

Harry watched from the jetty until *Yellowfin* disappeared around the headland, then made a phone call of his own. Thirty minutes later, he limped off on foot along the dirt track that led eventually to the Mombasa highway. A journey that would have normally taken fifteen minutes took him nearer forty, but then that was what you got when you were half-crippled and you'd handed the keys of your Land Rover to the Arab in a desperate attempt to buy some time. Still, Harry thought, with any luck he might be about to cut a deal which would mean he could get rid of that heap of junk for good. OK, with Tug Viljoen involved, he would undoubtedly be selling his soul – but having worked in the City of London he was used to that. And how illegal could this scheme be?

As arranged, the jeep was parked up by the side of the road. Harry hobbled towards it and let himself in on the passenger side.

'Fucking hell, Harry,' Tug Viljoen said at once. 'What happened to your face?' The South African leaned across and peered with fascination at the contusions as Harry eased himself into the seat beside him.

'I had an unscheduled meeting with the Arab last night.'

'*Fuck*ing bastard!' Viljoen smacked a meaty fist into his palm.

'Yes, well. It was a strange day all round yesterday. I take it you heard about the excitement up at Dennis Bentley's place?'

'I heard,' Tug said grimly. 'Fucking *kaffirs* with Uzis! It's getting like Jo'burg round here. Still – they got what they deserved. Sounds like quite a cook-out.'

'Quite. Anyway, back to the Arab. You mentioned some sort of mutually beneficial financial arrangement you might be able to put my way. Something in the region of twenty-five thousand big ones?'

'You interested?'

Harry shrugged. 'My hand has been forced. What do you want me to do?'

Viljoen considered this for a moment. 'You tell anybody else about this?' he said presently.

'No.'

'You sure? You didn't tell Jake?'

'Not a soul, Tug. Just like you said.'

Viljoen stared at the road ahead for what seemed like a long time. Then, apparently satisfied, he nodded and pulled out on to the highway.

Chapter Forty-One

The Vasco da Gama Pillar is a large whitewashed edifice jutting from the rocky promontory at the southern end of Malindi harbour. It commemorates the great explorer's arrival there in 1498, when the local sultan greeted him with gifts of goats, oranges and sugar cane. What the sultan didn't know was that within a decade his sultanate would be overrun by Portuguese marketeers and European slavers, who would milk the town of its resources and strategic importance and, by the middle of the sixteenth century, abandon it for the more lucrative port of Mombasa sixty miles to the south. Today the Pillar is a landmark for game-fishing boats and tourist leisure cruisers, and the town itself has been overrun by a new set of invaders in the shape of Malindi's wealthy Italian ex-pat community.

The Ernies were waiting at the tourist information office on Beach Road, cool boxes and ghetto blasters stacked and ready to go. They were Americans. College boys by the look of them. Jake could hear the simian whoops and high-five slaps a hundred yards away on *Yellowfin*'s flying bridge.

'Looks like you'll have your work cut out today, Sammy,' he observed.

Down in the cockpit, Sammy smiled and continued slicing the baitfish into fillets; and once again the kid's demeanour made Jake feel ashamed and angry at his own self-absorption. It had been nearly a week, but Sammy still believed his brother was coming back. Jake was dreading the moment when he would have to tell him the truth. *Whatever the truth was.* Not for the first time that day, he wondered how Jouma was getting on with Michael Kili. And, not for the first time, he felt a twinge of annoyance that he was not there.

He made his way along the wharf, casting covetous glances at the gleaming luxury motor yachts anchored in the bay, some of them nearly two hundred feet long and resembling sleek floating hotels complete with five-star accommodation, restaurants, on-board cinemas and gymnasiums. Was it any wonder that businesses like his and Harry's were going to the wall when this was the opposition?

'The Cruickshank party?'

The Ernies looked at him with beery incomprehension.

'Whassat, buddy?' one of them said.

'I'm looking for the Cruickshank party. Booked up with Britannia Fishing Trips.'

'*Crockshank?* Whassat?'

'I heard-a *Shawshank.* You mean *Shawshank,* man?'

Jake smiled unconvincingly and backed away towards the tourist office, which was a grand name for a wooden box the size of an ice-cream kiosk, manned by a young African wearing an oversized peaked cap and a lapel badge that read CYRIL TAYARI.

'*Jambo*, Mr Moore!' he exclaimed with a grin. 'How the devil are you today?'

199

'I'm looking for my booking, Cyril. Name of Cruickshank. Party of six.'

Cyril frowned and ran his finger down a list of names scribbled on a ledger in front of him. *'Crook, Shank; Crook, Shank . . .'*

'You phoned the booking this morning,' Jake said testily. 'I answered the phone.'

'Of course, of course,' Cyril said, licking his lips nervously.

'It was me who made the booking, I'm afraid,' said a familiar voice, and to Jake's astonishment Martha Bentley appeared from behind the kiosk.

'Ah! Mrs Crook Shank!' Cyril clapped his hands. 'Now I remember!'

'Mrs Cruickshank, eh?' Jake said. He folded his arms and leaned against the kiosk. 'You appear to have lost the other five members of your party.'

Martha held up a wad of dollar bills secured by a silver clip. 'Don't worry,' she said. 'I made sure they paid up-front.'

Chapter Forty-Two

The man standing at the reception desk of the Marlin Bay Hotel had that swagger of youthful confidence born of good health, expensive education and too much money that Conrad Getty found hugely irritating, yet at the same time filled him with boiling envy. Dressed casually in Chinos and a linen shirt, and with a pair of aviator sunglasses pushed back against a full head of thick hair, he was everything Getty despised simply because he was everything the cadaverous, balding and sick-to-the-soul hotel owner wanted to be.

'What is his name?' he hissed, staring through narrowed eyes at the man across the hotel atrium.

'Mr Noonan, sir,' Loftus informed him.

'Is he a guest?'

'He checked in twenty minutes ago, sir.'

'Then what's his problem? Is there something wrong with his room?'

'No, sir. He says he was expecting to meet someone here, but he cannot find them on the premises.'

'Who, for God's sake? *Who*?'

'Miss Bentley, sir.'

Shit! Was this the moment he had dreaded? Had American investigators suddenly taken an interest in his little corner of Kenya? In the instant it took him to stride across the atrium, Getty's demeanour transformed from that of bitter hobgoblin to fawning host.

'Mr Noonan?'

The young man glanced up and smiled, revealing – as Getty had expected – a set of perfect white teeth.

'Patrick Noonan,' he said. 'Pleased to meet you.'

'Conrad Getty, owner of the Marlin Bay. My concierge tells me you have a problem?'

'No problem, Mr Getty. Just a little mystery, that's all.'

Getty's blood froze and, to his annoyance, a tic began fluttering in the corner of his eye.

Noonan lowered his voice. 'Between you and me, I've just flown in from New York to pay a surprise visit to my girlfriend. Martha Bentley? Your receptionist tells me she's been staying here, but I've looked everywhere for her and I can't find her. I was just wondering if you knew where she might be? If she left a message maybe?'

'Of course. Miss Bentley,' Getty said evenly, although the knowledge that this jumped-up piece of shit was Martha's boyfriend was only slightly less galling than if he'd been a CIA agent. An image of Noonan's sculpted buttocks pounding between Martha Bentley's thighs flitted briefly but unpleasantly through his mind. 'She went to Malindi this morning,' Getty said, relishing the surprise on Noonan's face.

'Malindi?'

'She took one of the hotel's boats there this morning. I believe she had some outstanding business regarding the estate of her late father.'

'OK. So can *I* get one of your boats? A fast one? I'd really like a fast one.'

Arrogant prick. 'Not a problem, Mr Noonan. If you would care to see our concierge, he will be delighted to arrange transport for you.'

'Thanks, buddy. I appreciate it.'

Buddy? 'No problem, sir. Enjoy your day. And I trust we will see you both for dinner this evening?'

'Count on it,' Noonan said, gesturing with his finger as if it was a pistol.

Getty could feel a patina of cold sweat materialising on his brow and, as Noonan sauntered away, he wondered how the hell he had let himself get involved in this industry, this *act*. As always, he knew the answer all too clearly.

His greed. His stupidity.

His cell phone rang.

'What?' he snapped, without bothering to check the number in the window.

'Captain!' the voice exclaimed at the other end. 'How are you!'

'*Jesus Christ!*' Getty scurried out of the atrium and upstairs to the landline in his office. 'Where the hell have you been? I've been trying to get hold of you for two days!'

'Bit difficult to talk now, Captain. I'm driving.'

'We *need* to talk.'

'Don't worry, we will.'

'*When, dammit?*'

'Sooner than you think. You in your office?'

'Yes.'

'Then take a look out of your window.'

Getty let the phone slip from his ear and hurried

to the window. His office was on the first floor of the hotel, and from here he could look out over the clear-glass reception portico and beyond to the main gates. A revoltingly unwashed jeep was barrelling along the Tarmac drive, making a mockery of the speed bumps and chewing up the edges of the mani-cured lawn that had cost Getty fifty dollars a square foot to import from Ireland.

He swore and grabbed the receiver. 'What the hell are you doing here?'

Below, the jeep had stopped directly outside the entrance to the reception and the driver was climbing out, cell phone still clamped to his ear.

'Do I leave the keys in the ignition or do I give them to the *kaffir*?' Tug Viljoen asked, peering up through the glass and waving at Getty.

'And who the *fuck* is that with you?' Getty demanded.

Viljoen's passenger was gingerly extricating himself from the vehicle with the aid of an umbrella. With his scruffy clothes and beaten-up face, he looked like the sort of down-and-out bum the secu-rity guards were forever moving from the hotel's private stretch of beach.

'This is Harry from Flamingo Creek,' Viljoen said. 'He's in the market for a little courier work.'

'Are you *fucking mad*?'

'Easy, Captain,' Viljoen said calmly, but his eyes were like lasers burning through the portico awning. 'I don't have to remind you that we are understaffed and up against a deadline.'

Getty watched Viljoen hand his keys dismissively to the African doorman. 'I'm sorry, I—'

'That's all right. Now why don't you put a call through to that bar manager of yours and tell him to

204

set the beers up. On second thoughts, tell him to
make one of them a large bourbon. Harry here is in
need of a hair of the dog.'

Chapter Forty-Three

In Jouma's locker at Mama Ngina Drive was a wooden box with a padlock. Inside the box was a .38 detective special handgun and six bullets. The weapon was standard issue to any officer of inspector rank or above, and Jouma had been given his ten years earlier. Ever since, it had remained in the box in the locker, because Jouma had believed that any policeman who felt it necessary to walk around with a pistol was no better than a common Mombasa hoodlum.

That morning, as he loaded the bullets into the chamber of the .38, the inspector concluded sadly that such high-minded nobility was nothing more than pitiful self-delusion. Yesterday, Michael Kili had despatched two men to kill him. They had failed. Kili would not make the same mistake again. Which was why Jouma had also taken the precaution of signing out a Zylon protective vest. The vest, designed to stop bullets, was bulky and uncomfortable. But under his Burberry raincoat, his pride and joy despite being two sizes too big, it was pretty well disguised.

As it turned out that day, Michael Kili had been the

victim of an assassin's bullet. But the Zylon vest had done its job. And so had the .38. Strangely, all Jouma could remember of that surreal moment in Kili's office was Omu staring quizzically at his own knife, the vicious tip bent out of shape as if it had been jabbed against a brick wall, then his eyes widening behind the spectacles as he looked down at the snub-nosed revolver that had appeared in Jouma's hand.

In the confines of Kili's office, the report from the .38 had been like a bomb going off. As Omu lunged for the door, the slug had ripped into the exposed flesh between the hem of his *khanzu* and his canvas sandal, spattering the wall with blood and shards of ankle bone. With a shriek of agony, Omu had pirouetted twice across the room before slumping to the floor beside Kili's body. Then Jouma had pointed the still-smoking gun at the stunned Nyami, who was cowering with his hands over his ears beneath the poster of Anna Kournikova.

'Well, Sergeant Nyami?' he'd said, trying hard to control his breathing and his shaking hand. 'Are you going to handcuff the prisoner, or do I have to shoot you as well?'

In his sickbed on a secure ward of Mombasa Hospital, Omu had listened patiently as Jouma detailed with great relish precisely what conditions would be like for an educated man thrown into one of Kenya's high-security prisons.

The inspector had described how, apart from the endemic shortages of food, clean water and clothing, the overcrowding and the non-existent medical care, every single one of them had an abysmal record of human-rights abuses including torture, rape and institutional murder.

207

'Are you trying to scare me, Inspector?' Omu had asked wearily, wincing as he attempted to wiggle the toes that poked from a large bandage around his shattered ankle.

'I am merely stating fact, Mr Omu,' Jouma said. 'These places exist, and you will be going to one of them very soon. How you are dealt with when you are there is a different matter.'

'I see. And, if I tell you everything I know, then I can expect preferential treatment – is that it?'

'You can expect *nothing*,' Jouma snapped. 'You forget that at the top of your extensive list of felonies is the attempted murder of a police officer.'

Omu waved his hand dismissively. 'Much is required for a charge to become a conviction, Inspector Jouma.'

'So you have judges as well as policemen on your payroll?'

'I am merely stating fact. Which reminds me – how is Detective Sergeant Nyami?'

'Helping us with our enquiries.'

Omu laughed. 'Nyami is so stupid he needs his wife to tie his shoelaces for him in the morning. I have known anything he has ever known, and I assure you that you are wasting your time and energy. Let him go, Jouma. Demote him to traffic duty, but do not punish him for being a traitor. He cannot help what he is.'

'That is very magnanimous of you, Mr Omu. I will be sure to pass your suggestions on to Superintendent Teshete.'

'Teshete!' Omu spat contemptuously. 'You look for reasons why Kenya is rotten to the core, then look no further than Teshete and the thousands like him all across this country. Idle, complacent, greedy, ignorant – it is because of people like Teshete that people like Michael Kili gain power.'

Jouma stared at him in disbelief. 'What is this? You are a great patriot all of a sudden? You disassociate yourself from Kili just like that? Like a snake shedding its skin?'

'Spare me the moral outrage, Inspector. Kili was a common street criminal who died like a dog. I am no more like him than you are, and you know it.'

'Never compare yourself to me,' Jouma said, his anger barely contained, jabbing a finger at the man in the bed in front of him. 'Never—'

'Why? Because you are a *policeman*? Because you have sworn to uphold the law and protect the people? Don't think so highly of your vocation, Jouma. You saw what happened when they gave the people ballot boxes. Chaos. Anarchy. Death. They are animals and should be treated as such. No, Inspector, Kenya is about one thing and one thing alone: survival of the fittest. It doesn't matter how you do it, as long as you do. You honestly think I had anything but utter contempt for Michael Kili? That I thought he was anything other than an *animal*? No – Kili was my means of survival, just as that badge you so proudly wear is yours.'

'Yes,' Jouma said, 'but I continue to survive.'

Omu shrugged. 'Perhaps. But for how long?'

Jouma realised then that it was pointless trying to extract information from Omu. A man like this would not talk unless it was beneficial to himself, and so far Jouma had nothing to offer him other than vague threats about prison. He would need something else, some other form of bait to dangle in front of him.

Jouma turned for the door.

'Inspector!'

'Mr Omu?'

'Could you ask the guard at the door to stop whistling, please? It is giving me a headache.'

After leaving the secure ward, the inspector went to Mombasa's downtown police station where Nyami was in custody.

Dressed only in his ragged underwear, Nyami had whimpered like a whipped dog and shrunk away to the corner of his cell, shivering, weeping and huddled into a foetal position against the wall.

'*Why*, Nyami?' Jouma had asked him. 'Was it the money? Is that why you betrayed me? Is that why you betrayed *yourself*?'

Nyami hung his head. 'I was scared. Omu said he would kill my wife if I didn't give him the information he wanted.'

'It was you who told Omu about my visit to Flamingo Creek yesterday?'

The sergeant nodded.

'Was it Omu who murdered Kili?'

'I don't know!' Nyami exclaimed. 'I swear I know nothing about that,' he said.

'No. I expect you don't.'

'What will happen to me, Inspector?'

Jouma shrugged. 'I really don't know, Nyami.'

On his return to the hospital, Jouma reported to a curtained cubicle in the emergency room where a somewhat haughty registrar prodded and poked him and concluded that no bones were broken.

'You'll have a nice bruise on your chest for a week or so,' he said, 'but things could be worse.'

Disturbingly, Jouma's next visitor was Christie.

'I heard you were in here,' the pathologist said with a smirk.

'You have been misinformed,' Jouma said, hurriedly climbing off the gurney and reaching for his shirt. 'I am not dead.'

'No,' Christie observed, peering at the patient's notes which were hanging from a lightbox on the wall. 'But if he'd gone for your throat you would have been.'

'Fortunate for me, then, that he did not.'

Jouma winced as he saw a jagged slash mark in his precious Burberry raincoat.

The pathologist shook his head. 'I don't know, Jouma. A man of your advanced years getting into knife-fights with hoodlums. What must you have been thinking?'

'I think he came off rather worse than I did,' Jouma said.

Christie grinned, and it was not a pleasant sight. 'Yes – I heard. Anyway, don't you think you should rest up for a while? You've been through a traumatic experience.'

'Thank you for your concern – but I have work to do.'

Christie nodded. 'So do I. There's a chap lying on my table with most of his head shot away.'

'Then it shouldn't take you long to deduce the cause of death.'

'Come on then, Inspector,' Christie sighed. 'I'll walk with you. And, should you expire on the way, I promise I shall be gentle with your remains.'

They left the emergency room and proceeded along a rabbit warren of corridors towards the secure ward where Omu was being held. It had been an hour; perhaps Kili's representative had changed his mind and was now prepared to talk. Jouma was not hopeful, however.

'All this murder and mayhem,' Christie said as they walked, 'I assume it's all related to that body washed up on the beach the other day?'

'Why do you assume that?'

'Call it an educated guess. That and the fact that, ever since it was found, the corpses have been piling up like nobody's business. My colleague Mr Gikonyo in Malindi had the onerous task of examining the remains of those two chaps who crashed their speedboat into a tree at Flamingo Creek yesterday. It seems that, wherever you go, Inspector, death and destruction follow. I may even be taking my life in my hands being this close to you.'

'Then please don't let me delay you any further.'

'Unfortunately for you, there is a shortcut to the mortuary through the isolation wards.'

They rounded a corner and in that instant Jouma's stomach turned to lead. The guard who had been posted outside Omu's room was nowhere to be seen. The inspector broke into a run but, when he saw the door was standing open, he knew for certain that it was too late.

'Oh no.'

'Good God, Jouma,' Christie said, pushing past him into the room. 'You really *are* a jinx.'

Omu's body was sprawled in a semi-sitting position by the side of his bed. One end of a length of fabric, torn from his *khanzu*, had been tied to the metal bars of the headrest. The other was wrapped tightly around the dead man's neck just beneath the jaw. The middle section, however, hung slackly against his shoulder.

It was this piece that Christie held up disparagingly with one forefinger. 'Pathetic,' he said, shaking his head and levering himself to a standing position on cracking knees. 'I would have thought even the dimmest murderer in Mombasa would have realised that the ligature needs to at least *appear* to be taut if the murder is to look like suicide.'

Jouma looked at him blankly.

'In order to asphyxiate himself with that length of ligature,' Christie explained, 'our man would have had to stand on his head and then, once dead, assume his present sitting position. Hardly feasible, Inspector – especially for a man with a rather large plaster cast on his foot.'

'What killed him?'

Christie indelicately prodded Omu's exposed eyeball. 'Oh, he was asphyxiated all right. And the marks on the neck suggest it was probably with that very same ligature. But my guess is he was on the bed when it happened, and didn't know much about it. Asleep, most probably. I'll find out, naturally.' He sighed. 'You go to all that trouble and then you use a ligature that's six inches too long. Schoolboy error.'

'Perhaps,' Jouma said.

Or perhaps not. It was obvious that Jacob Omu had not committed suicide – but then that was not the point.

The point was that they had got to him. And if they could get to Omu this easily . . .

Chapter Forty-Four

'*Cruickshank?*'

'It was my grandmother's maiden name,' Martha said.

'Why the subterfuge?'

'I didn't think you would come all the way out to Malindi for one paying guest.'

Jake laughed bitterly. 'The way things have been going lately I would go to Zanzibar if it meant a paying guest. What were you doing in Malindi?'

'There was a boatbuilder my dad used years ago. I was trying to track him down – I thought maybe he would have a few answers. But they turned his work-shop into a souvenir shop. So I thought, fuck it. I haven't been on a game boat for years.'

'There must be a hundred skippers in Malindi.'

'I figured you would be the only one that would let me drive the boat.'

Martha eased forward *Yellowfin*'s throttles and brought the boat around in a gentle arc so that the thin smudge of land on the horizon was now off the starboard bow. Beside her on the flying bridge, Jake observed the clean line of the wake and was impressed. The girl clearly knew how to pilot a thirty-footer – but then she should. From what he knew of her, she'd virtually grown up on fishing boats. His eye caught that of Sammy, who was down in the cockpit tending to the booms. The boy gave a nod of appreciation.

'The first time my dad let me drive one of these things unsupervised, I was nine years old,' she said. Then she giggled. 'He had this friend called Howard Miller, some sort of money man from Nairobi, and he was trying to sweet talk him into investing in a new boat. Anyway, poor old Howard was sitting on the stern rail talking business and I decided to find out just how fast a twin-engine thirty-footer will go if you give it both barrels. The next thing I know, my dad is yelling at me to stop and Howard Miller is in the water.'

'Did you get the investment?'

'Unfortunately, Howard didn't see the funny side.'

'Dennis must have been pissed off with you.'

'Dad never got pissed off with me. I was the daughter who could do no wrong.'

Off the port bow, a fleet of dhows made their way slowly southwards towards Mombasa, flecks of luminescent white against the rich blue of the sea.

'So what's your story?' she asked. 'How does an ex-cop from London end up fishing for marlin?' He looked at her with surprise, and she laughed. 'I'm a lawyer. I make it my business to dig dirt on people.'

'You mean Jouma told you.'

She shrugged coquettishly, and Jake could see all too clearly how Martha would be one hell of an operator among the alpha males of Manhattan. 'We had an hour to kill driving back to Mombasa the other night,' she said. 'And the local FM station sucks.'

'What else did he tell you about me?'

'Nothing much. He's a man of few words. It was like getting blood out of a stone to get him to tell me that much. But I'm intrigued. Cop to game-boat skipper – that's not what I'd call a natural career progression.'

'I wasn't always a cop,' Jake said. 'In fact, my old man was pretty pissed off when I decided not to follow in the family business.'

'Which was?'

'North Sea fishing. Drag-netting for herring, haddock and cod two hundred miles off the river Tyne. My old man was the skipper of a trawler. He had grand plans for me to take over from him one day.'

'Why didn't you?'

'Because I didn't like the idea of freezing my balls off for a living. And because I could see the way things were going. Quotas and restrictions. Cheap imports. The industry was fucked. I was twenty years old, and I knew I'd be on the scrapheap before I was thirty if I stayed where I was. The old man knew it too – he just didn't want to admit it was over. Who would, with six generations breathing down your neck? So, I took the easy way out. I joined the police and headed down to London.'

'That must have been hard on your dad.'

'He accused me of betraying the family. We never spoke again. A year later he was dead. Fifty-two years old. They said it was cirrhosis, but I reckon he just gave up the ghost.'

'Jesus.'

'Fathers and sons, eh? What are they like? Sounds like you didn't have the same problems with Dennis.'

'Mom died when I was eleven years old,' Martha said. 'Dad loved me, but he knew he couldn't raise me on his own. He sent me to live with Mom's sister in Michigan. It broke my heart.'

'But you never lost touch with him.'

'We were always close. Dad made sure of that. That's why—' She paused, then shook her head. 'You know, when I saw his boatyard the other day, I was so *angry*. Why didn't he *tell* me about the trouble he was in? Why did he just let it slide without ever asking for help?'

'Blokes are like that,' Jake said. 'God forbid we ever show any sign of weakness.'

But Martha shook her head. 'The times I spent with him on *Martha B* were the happiest of my life. Dad never wanted the big bad world to spoil those memories.'

Martha turned and Jake saw that, behind the designer sunglasses, she was fighting back her emotions.

'He was a good man and a good father, Jake,' she said. 'Now don't you think I've got a right to know what he'd got himself involved in?'

Chapter Forty-Five

Tug Viljoen watched Harry limp slowly out of the office.

'So? What do you think?'

Getty downed a whisky and ginger and pulled hard on a cigarette. 'Think? Think about what?'

'About *Harry*. Jesus H Christ, Captain – you're jumpier than a barrel of monkeys today. What the fuck's the matter?'

'Did you take care of our little problem?'

'Kili? Yeah.'

The hotel owner sighed. 'Thank God. How?'

'I killed him.'

Getty felt his ulcer switch to overdrive and it took a moment before he could be certain he was not about to throw up.

'You OK, Captain?' Viljoen asked. 'You've gone grey.'

'He's going to hear about all this. I just know it.'

'Who?'

'The fucking Pope!' Getty exclaimed. 'Who do you think? *Whitestone!*'

'So what?' Viljoen said, unconcerned. 'If I was Whitestone, I'd be impressed with our crisis-management skills.'

'Impressed? Your crisis-management skills seem to consist of killing everyone.'

'You worry too much, Captain. You'll give yourself an ulcer. Now – what do you think of Harry?'

Getty rubbed his eyes wearily. 'God, I don't know. What do *you* think?'

'I think he's got a boat. And I know he needs the money. As you can see, I arranged for his creditor to give him a little chivvy along last night.'

'Christ, Tug, I hope you're right. We don't want another Dennis Bentley on our hands. Not now.'

'Dah! Dennis just had a crisis of confidence, that's all. I wish you'd stop going on about him. Harry's an Englishman.' Viljoen chuckled. 'You don't get to run an empire without balls.'

Harry stood with his head resting on the cold marble of the toilet wall. Judging by the way it hurt when he pissed, and the blood flecks in his urine stream, the Arab's henchman had landed rather more blows to his kidneys than he had thought.

As he zipped up his pants, he thought about Tug Viljoen and Conrad Getty, and how the pair of them were perfectly suited: the loudmouth thug and the oleaginous spiv. Under normal circumstances, he wouldn't have given them the time of day.

But Harry was desperate. And they had offered him a way out.

One job. That was all. And, if the very thought of it made him feel sick to his stomach, he knew that at least afterwards their money worries would be over. Jake didn't need to know about it. He would arrange for Jake to be somewhere else when the time came. The deception would be simple enough to organise.

He stepped out of the toilet and made his way

along the corridor to Getty's office. James Last was playing discreetly in the background and there was a cloying smell of lavender. Up ahead, a small black girl in a nylon housecoat emerged from a laundry cupboard with a large pile of sheets in her arms. She could not help but stare as he approached, and Harry wondered if she found him as grotesque to look at as he felt inside. He wanted to reach out to her, to tell her that he wasn't really like this; but the girl averted her gaze and placed the sheets on a service trolley.

Back in the office, Viljoen and Getty ceased their conversation as Harry entered the room.

'Well, Harry,' Viljoen said. 'What's your answer?'

'I suppose I don't have a choice,' Harry said. 'I'll do it.'

Chapter Forty-Six

Martha listened in silence as Jake told her what he knew about her father. When he had finished, she thanked him in a firm controlled voice.

'For what?'

'For being honest with me. It can't have been easy for you.'

Jake rubbed a hand down his face. She was right. It hadn't been easy. It was never easy telling someone their dead father appeared to be up to his neck in organised crime, and had, in all probability, been killed for it. The only saving grace was that Martha wasn't stupid. She'd accessed the same bank statements as Jouma. And she'd already reached the same unpalatable conclusions.

'You never answered my question,' she said.

'What question?'

'How did you end up here?'

For a moment Jake thought about spinning her some yarn about taking a five-year sabbatical from the force. But he'd been honest with her so far; it seemed strangely pointless to start lying now.

'I got shot.'

'Jesus.'

'There was a robbery. A security-van heist in East London. The Canning Town Firm, they called themselves. They'd done a few jobs and thought they were indestructible. But we'd been watching them for weeks. When the day came, we were waiting for them. It should have been straightforward, but things went wrong. One of them got away and took a load of people hostage in a post office. Ronnie Cavanagh, his name was. I was sent in to talk to him while the armed response unit got set up. But he was just a kid. Scared out of his wits. I was *that* far away from talking him down – but something spooked him. He saw one of the marksmen outside, I think. Shot a woman in the head. Then he shot me. Then we shot Ronnie.'

Jake lifted up his T-shirt to reveal a puckered scar on the right side of his abdomen.

'I was lucky, I guess. Six weeks in hospital, but I survived. After that, though, I just didn't have the stomach for it any more. They say it happens, but I never believed them. I was like Ronnie Cavanagh. You think you're indestructible, until the day you find out you're not.'

For a long time after Jake finished talking, the only sound was the insistent *whup whup whup* of *Yellowfin*'s twin diesels and the occasional fizz of surf against her bows.

Then Martha said, 'And so here we all are in Kenya. The lost and the lonely. You must think I'm a nosy bitch, prying into your private life.'

'You are!' Jake laughed. 'But, like you said, it's your job so don't beat yourself up about it.'

'Sometimes it's good to have someone who listens.'

'Is that so? So who listens to you when you're in New York?'

'Chico, my cat. And Patrick, I guess.'

'Ah. The boyfriend.'

'Patrick's OK. A little self-absorbed, maybe – but he would probably say the same about me.'

'Should I disapprove of this man?'

'Now you sound like my father.' She laughed.

'What is he? Another high-flying lawyer?'

'International bonds trader.'

'Sounds grand.'

'It is if you like spending most of your life at thirty thousand feet. In the last two months I think we've spent four nights together.'

'Must be hard.'

She shrugged. 'We both like our own space. That makes it easier.'

'Trust me, staying single is easier,' Jake said.

'You never married?'

'Could never get anyone to put up with me long enough to pop the question. So how did you meet, you and this international jetsetter?'

Martha laughed. 'People don't meet in New York, they collide. Most of the time they bounce off each other, but sometimes they stick around in orbit for a while. I met him at a party. I kind of liked his smile.'

'His *smile*?'

She laughed again. 'Yeah. Have you got a problem with that?'

But Jake did not reply. Not at first. Then, in a low firm voice, he said, 'Get her up to full speed and keep her on this heading.'

Martha turned and looked beyond the stern rail, where a boat was smashing towards them from landward side, its massive engines spewing arcs of brilliant-white foam high into the air behind it.

Oh, God – not again! she thought, but her hand

was steady as she started easing forward the throttles.

Jake was already sliding down the ladder to the cockpit.

'Sammy, I want the booms in double quick. Then get up on the bridge.'

He looked back at the closing vessel one more time, then hurried into the cabin. As he did so, he heard *Yellowfin*'s diesels kick into life and he grabbed hold of a spar to stop himself toppling backwards. The surge, he knew, was deceptive. *Yellowfin*'s top speed was thirty knots; judging by its lines, the craft that was chasing them was a powerboat, and its top speed would be anything from seventy to a hundred. It would be on them in a flash.

There were stowage compartments under the cabin's banquettes. Jake ripped off the panelling and rummaged frantically through emergency flares, spare life preservers and coils of fishing line until he finally found what he was looking for: a stainless-steel harpoon gun with a foot-long double-barbed projectile. The weapon was a one-shot, compressed-air model designed for spearing fish at a range of thirty feet – fucking useless against someone with a real gun, but other than throwing beer bottles it was the only defence they had.

'Jake! It's gaining on us!'

You don't say . . .

Priming the compressed-air canister, Jake stepped out into the cockpit again.

The powerboat was now running parallel to *Yellowfin*, barely fifty yards off the starboard rail, and at this range Jake could see for the first time what a monster it was. From the tip of its stream-lined prow to its three five-hundred-horsepower engines, the craft must have been more than forty feet in length. A Sonic 45ss.

There was a man behind the wheel and he was waving to attract their attention.

'What should I do, Jake?' Martha called down from the flying bridge.

'Well, we're not going to outrun him,' Jake conceded. 'Let's see what he wants.'

But, as Martha throttled back and the Sonic closed in, he kept the harpoon gun gripped tightly and his finger poised on the trigger.

Yellowfin was idling now. The Sonic came alongside, the pilot skilfully manoeuvring it against the swell.

'Good afternoon,' he called out brightly. The accent was American, the smile as white as the boat's paintwork. 'The name's Noonan. Patrick Noonan. I'm looking for Martha Bentley.'

Chapter Forty-Seven

Word of Jacob Omu's demise had spread quickly among Mombasa's lowlife scum, as Jouma expected it would. Accompanied by two uniformed constables he knew he could trust, he went to Omu's apartment near the old harbour to find it had already been picked clean of every scrap of furniture and that the one remaining item, the leatherbound copy of the Koran, was being fought over by two men in beggars' rags. When they saw the uniforms, they scattered like rats; one out of the window on to the rooftops, the other attempting to follow but hampered by a rolled-up rug under his arm. Jouma grabbed him by the scruff of the neck and dragged him back into the room.

'Where is the briefcase?' he demanded.

The beggar shook his head.

Jouma despised any form of physical violence, especially when it was carried out by a police officer on a suspect. But these were trying times, and the detective was not in the mood to be patient. His open palm connected with the side of the beggar's thin face and a gobbet of saliva flew across the room.

'*The briefcase.*'

Like a whipped dog, the beggar led the policemen down to the alleyway and beyond to the waterfront where half a dozen of his emaciated cronies were systematically stripping Omu's speedboat of its upholstery and engine parts. They glanced up warily as Jouma passed, but felt sufficiently strong in number to ignore the detective and his two constables.

There was a narrow path connecting the tenement buildings. Further along was a rubble-strewn area where one of the buildings had either been demolished or collapsed of its own accord. Here, to Jouma's astonishment, the beggars had established a sprawling shanty community of hovels, jerry-built from chunks of masonry, metal, plastic sheeting and anything else they had been able to scavenge. To Jouma, it looked like some hellish vision, a place of wild dogs and rats and inhabitants who were more feral than human. He felt their eyes on him as he picked his way around the spilled garbage, the excrement, the detritus of what was laughably called civilisation.

Presently, they came to what at first glance appeared to be a discarded metal door dumped at forty-five degrees against a pile of bricks and masonry blocks. But, when the beggar tugged on the handle, the door opened outwards to reveal a short flight of steps cut straight out of the earth.

My God, Jouma thought as he followed the beggar down into a foul-smelling tunnel illuminated by tallow candles jammed into crevices in the mud walls. This was not so much another level of society, but a different species altogether! A burrowing subterranean creature so despised by the world outside that it had retreated to the very bowels of the earth!

227

In fact, the tunnel soon opened out into a series of connected concrete chambers, and Jouma realised that they must be in what had once been the basement of the ruined tenement building. Here there was even feeble electric lighting, which proved that whatever these people had become they were still perfectly able to work a generator.

'This way,' the beggar said, and led Jouma followed by the constables through another door into a spacious room that, had it not been for the stench of rotten food, damp and human decay, could have almost passed for habitable. The stone floors were covered with scraps of carpet and rugs, and it was furnished with an eclectic selection of old car seats, sprung settees, cushions and even a glass-topped coffee table.

At the far side of the room, sitting cross-legged on an oversized armchair and flanked on either side by two scrawny bare-breasted women, was a boy. He could not have been more than thirteen years old, and he was wearing what looked suspiciously like one of Jacob Omu's *khanzu* robes. The clothes were far too big for him and gave the boy a faintly comical appearance – but, compared to the rags worn by the rest of the encampment, his attire was the height of sartorial elegance.

The beggar and the boy communicated in a strange hybrid language that Jouma could not understand, then the beggar backed out of the room and closed the door behind him.

'Tabo says I may have something you desire, policeman,' the boy said in a voice that was harsh, almost sneering.

Jouma looked at him and with a shiver of revulsion realised that he had seen those fresh-faced features and heard that same derisive tone before, many years ago. Only then they had belonged to a boy called Michael Kili.

'Give me the case,' he said.

The boy smiled and lifted the slim leather case from the side of his chair. 'You mean this?'

'Yes.'

'The dog who it belonged to is dead, I hear. And now his briefcase is mine.'

'*Was* yours. Now it is mine.'

'Why should I give it to you?'

Jouma sighed. 'What is your name, boy?'

'Steven. Steven Kisauni.' The boy tossed his head arrogantly as he spoke.

'You seem very young to be speaking with such assurance, Steven.'

Steven shrugged. 'Age does not matter when you have power.'

He reached out to one of the women beside him and stroked her breast, his gaze never leaving Jouma's.

'Is that so?'

'In the kingdom of the blind, the one-eyed man is king.'

Jouma nodded appreciatively. 'This is true. But what makes you so special?'

'*Education.*' The boy smiled, tapping his forehead.

'Education?'

'I can both read and write. I learned at the orphanage in Likoni.'

'That is very admirable. With such knowledge you could go far, instead of sitting in a pestilence-filled hole in the ground, surrounded by the very dregs of humanity.'

Steven laughed, a high-pitched bark of derision.

'And do what? Become a policeman like you?'

'It is surely preferable.'

'I have *power*!' the boy exclaimed.

'So you say. But so do I – and my power is far greater than yours,' Jouma said.

'From what I hear, your power can be bought for a few dollars.'

'Well, in that case, Steven Kisauni, you are not as educated as you think.'

Jouma signalled to one of the uniformed officers, a burly man who had once played prop forward for the police rugby team in Nairobi. He grabbed the boy and slung him under his arm as easily as if he was a side of pork.

'Take him outside,' Jouma said, as he picked up the case and followed the two officers and the squealing, kicking boy back along the dimly lit tunnel. A wide-eyed crowd quickly gathered as the four of them emerged into the daylight.

'This young man says that policemen have no power,' Jouma announced, gesturing at the squirming boy. 'He says that because he can read and write he has somehow achieved greatness. And at such a tender age.'

Jouma turned and yanked up the boy's robe so that his skinny backside was exposed. There was a gasp of horror from the crowd.

'When I was at school,' Jouma continued, 'the likes of Steven Kisauni were regarded as bullies and braggarts, and my teacher, Mr Yalanu – a most wise and venerable man – had a simple but effective way of dealing with them.'

Without further ado, Jouma picked up a stick from the ground and administered six sharp blows to the boy's buttocks. When he had finished, Steven

Kisauni was snivelling and his backside was criss-crossed with a pattern of ugly red welts.

'Never forget who *really* has the power, boy,' Jouma hissed into his ear. 'I shall be keeping a very close eye on you in the future.'

Chapter Forty-Eight

Patrick Noonan did not need much encouragement to make himself at home on *Yellowfin*. It was just as well he had restocked the beer coolers, Jake reflected, because at the rate the American was working his way through the boat's supply of Tuskers they'd have been empty an hour ago.

'Tell Patrick what you and Harry call tourists,' Martha said.

'Jesus, Martha.'

Patrick leaned forward in the fighting chair. 'Tell me, Jake. I'm all ears.'

Martha rescued him. 'He calls them "Ernies". Because the doughboys all think they're Ernest Hemingway.'

Patrick laughed, exposing his perfect teeth. 'Ernies. That's nice, Jake.'

The way he said it made it sound like the lamest joke ever. Jake smiled weakly and went through to the cabin to get some more beer. He returned in time to see Patrick attempting to plant a kiss on Martha's mouth. She turned her face away from him self-consciously. It was symptomatic of the way she'd been acting ever since he had turned up unannounced in his fancy powerboat. Jake was surprised. He had been expecting her to be pleased to see him; instead, from the moment Patrick had stepped on board *Yellowfin*, Jake had been given the distinct impression that Martha viewed her New York lover boy as an unwelcome interloper.

He could not deny that it pleased him.

'That's a nice boat, Patrick,' he said, stepping out into the cockpit, and nodded at the Sonic that was now roped hard to *Yellowfin*'s port side.

'You think so?' Patrick threw up his hands. 'I don't know about boats. But I asked the guy at the hotel for the fastest one he had. Figured I'd need it if I was ever going to catch you guys.'

'I still don't understand how you knew where I was,' Martha said.

Patrick shrugged. 'The guy at the hotel said you went to Malindi. I went to Malindi and asked around. Trust me, honey, *everybody* remembered you. Especially the little guy in the booking hut. I think he had a thing for you. And he's not the only one.'

Again he leaned across to kiss her, only for her to pull away.

'You did well to find us,' Jake said, handing him another beer. 'It's a big ocean.'

Patrick nodded enthusiastically. 'You would not believe the tracker system they've fitted in that boat, man. It's like something from NASA. You just input the specs of the boat you're looking for and it gives you a read-out of every match in a hundred miles. It led me to you guys pretty much first time.'

'Neat toy.'

'I'll be recommending it to all my Ernie buddies, Jake.' There was a split-second when Patrick's eager smile seemed to harden, then it was gone. The American leaned back in the chair and stretched like a cat.

'You know, honey, I could get used to this. The speedboat is all very well, but we should think about maybe hiring one of these tubs when we go to Biscayne in the fall.' He yawned contentedly. 'Sitting here sure chills you out after the eighteen-hour flight from hell. You flown First Class lately, Jake? Man, standards have slipped.'

'I told you not to come here,' Martha said.

Jake detected a harshness to her voice that he had not heard before. He thought about what she had said about people in New York colliding with each other, and wondered if maybe Patrick had just shot out of her orbit.

'I was worried about you, baby,' Patrick said. He lifted his sunglasses and winked at Jake. 'She's pleased to see me now, Jake, but any minute she's going to remember her cat.'

'Chico!' she exclaimed. 'What have you done with him, Patrick?'

Again the easy laughter. 'Don't panic. Mrs Leibnitz is cat-sitting. She's not cheap, but she can be trusted.'

Patrick unbuttoned his linen shirt to reveal an expanse of sculpted torso.

'Martha told me about what happened yesterday, Jake. I guess I owe you a debt of gratitude.'

'It was one of those things,' Jake said.

'Do the cops know who these guys were?'

'They were just a couple of assholes,' Martha said. 'This kind of thing happens all the time. And it sure as hell happens in New York.'

'Jeez, and I always thought Kenya was the safest

234

country in Africa. Is that right, Jake? These guys were high on some local rocket fuel?'

'I guess so,' Jake said.

He hoped that would be an end to it, but Patrick said, 'You were up there with some cop from Mombasa, right?'

'That's right.'

'Why?'

'He needed a lift.'

Patrick smiled indulgently. 'I mean, why was the cop there?'

'Something to do with Dennis's disappearance,' Jake said cautiously, uncertain what Martha had told him. 'He didn't go into it.'

Patrick nodded, apparently satisfied. He finished his beer and tossed the bottle overboard. 'Could you get me another of those, honey?' he said.

'Sure.'

Martha padded into the cabin.

'One question, Jake,' he said when she was out of earshot. The sociable demeanour had evaporated. 'Why are you bullshitting me?'

'I don't know what you mean, Patrick.'

'This jungle juice and methanol crap. These guys were firing Uzis. What's going on?'

'I really don't know, Patrick. I'm just a guy who drives a fishing boat for a living.'

Patrick looked at him. Then abruptly the American smiled. 'Sure, Jake,' he said. 'I understand.'

He stood up as Martha returned and walked across to the starboard outrigger.

'When I was a kid I kind of had a thing for Hemingway. *The Old Man and The Sea*. Guess that makes me an Ernie for real, huh? You think I could catch me a big fish, Jake? A marlin, maybe?'

'You could try. But some people fish for a lifetime without ever catching one.'

'Yeah – well, I kind of feel lucky today. Let's try, shall we?'

'Come on, Patrick—' Martha said.

'Dammit, Martha, I want to catch a big fish,' Patrick snapped, and Martha visibly flinched. 'Sorry,' he said with a smile. 'Like I say – I'm feeling a little stressed out.'

Chapter Forty-Nine

Jouma lived with his wife Winifred in an apartment overlooking the Makupa Causeway on the north-west side of Mombasa island. The apartment packed a kitchen, sitting room and bedroom into a space that was barely larger than his office at police headquarters – yet his wife somehow managed to make it seem almost spacious. The furniture was spartan but homely, and the entire place was kept scrupulously clean.

Winifred Jouma was even smaller than her husband. She had to stand on tiptoe to stir the large metal pot on the stove in the corner of the kitchen, and the ladle she used to transfer the pungent meat and potato stew on to two plates was almost as big as her head. The first spicy mouthful, however, reinforced the detective's belief that his wife was the finest cook in Kenya.

They said little while they ate. In more than thirty years of marriage, Winifred had never once been interested in police business. Presently, she cleared away the dishes and went into the bedroom to do the ironing.

Jouma went into the sitting room and placed

Omu's case on the floor. The combination lock was still intact, although somebody had already tried to break into it by smashing it with a blunt instrument. Jouma picked the lock and opened the lid. Inside were some papers, neatly bundled with string and inserted into loose unmarked files. Beneath them was a large oxblood ledger. He removed all the items and placed them carefully to one side. Now all that remained in the case were a dozen or so evenly stacked piles of US dollar bills in denominations of one hundred, and a thick book of bearer bonds. As he counted the cash, Jouma whistled with amazement. It amounted to sixty thousand dollars, which was more money than Jouma had ever believed possible to see in one place. He calculated that, together with the bearer bonds, Omu had been carrying more than a million dollars in his case. The figure was breathtaking, but Jouma knew it represented but a fraction of what Michael Kili's criminal empire was worth.

He looked at the money and then he looked at the four walls of his five thousand-shilling-a-month flat. In the tiny bedroom Winifred was singing, her voice just audible above the noise of the traffic streaming relentlessly across the causeway to the Changamwe peninsula and onwards to Nairobi. *A million dollars*. How easy it would be simply to pocket the bills and disappear. With a million dollars they could go anywhere in the world, live what was left of their lives in luxury.

But no. Money was not the answer. It was never the answer.

He thought about Nyami. Shivering and weeping, his sergeant had presented a pitiful sight in the cells, and the beating he had received was truly shocking.

But what had sickened Jouma most of all was that the brutality was not a symbol of self-righteous outrage among honest police officers towards a Judas in their ranks – that he could have understood – but a purely cosmetic, cynical attempt to deflect guilt away from the guilty.

Jouma had always known there was corruption in Mombasa, but it was only as he analysed Jacob Omu's fastidiously maintained book-keeping that he realised its full extent. The documents detailed both regular and one-off payments made by Omu not only to police officers, but also to officials in virtually every sector and level of civic administration. With few exceptions, and on a sliding scale depending on their importance, Omu was systematically paying off anyone with influence in the coastal province, anyone with information, anyone who could turn a blind eye to Michael Kili's illegal activities.

The backhanders to Nyami barely registered on this scale; occasional pocket money compared to the healthy salaries others were claiming from Kili's crime empire. Compared to them, the amounts his sergeant had pocketed were so negligible as to make him almost innocent of corruption. In theory, of course, he was as guilty as the rest of them, and he deserved to be punished like the rest of them. Yet Jouma kept thinking back to the moment in Kili's office when Omu had produced the knife, and the tortured expression on Nyami's dumb face as the terrible consequence of his naive duplicity was suddenly made apparent to him.

It was this that had convinced Jouma that his sergeant would be of more use out of his cell than in it. He would certainly live longer.

Three hours earlier, as Jacob Omu's body was

239

being transported the short distance from his deathbed to Christie's white-tiled morgue, Jouma had freed Nyami. Babbling incoherently, it was clear his sergeant still expected to die, even when Jouma shoved him into the rear footwell of the Panda and drove him to Winifred's sister's flat in Mkomani district on the north shore. As a safehouse, it was hardly ideal, but it was the one place he could be sure Nyami would not be found in a hurry. As his sister-in-law tended Nyami's wounds, Jouma drove to Kilindini and picked up the sergeant's wife from their one-bedroom flat near the docks. Confused and tearful, Jemima Nyami had no idea what was happening or why. But that would be for her battered and bloodied husband to explain. One way or another, Nyami had a great deal of explaining to do.

After replacing the cash and the ledger in the attaché case, Jouma closed the lid. In the bathroom Winifred was performing her ablutions in readiness for bed. But Jouma would not be sleeping that night. There was much more reading ahead of him. Much to be learned. And none of it, he suspected, would be pleasant.

Chapter Fifty

They made love that night, but there was something mechanical about it as if her mind was elsewhere.

'I'm sorry,' she said.

Patrick rolled away. 'What is it, baby? Was it something I said?'

A warm sea breeze billowed the curtains and a shaft of pure white moonlight was cast across the bed.

'It's nothing,' she said. 'I'm just tired.'

He held her until her breathing became as regular and heavy as the waves crashing against the sea wall beyond the window. Then, gently so as not to wake her, he pulled the sheets up around her bare shoulders and eased out of bed. He dressed quickly in a pair of shorts and a T-shirt and then, after making sure she had not stirred, he opened the door and slipped out into the night.

When he had gone, Martha opened her eyes and stared at the shadows playing on the wall next to the bed. *What the hell is wrong with you?* she asked herself. Ever since Patrick had arrived, she had felt irritated with him being around, *embarrassed* almost by his dick-swinging behaviour. On the boat with

Jake he'd been like some overgrown frat boy trying to show off with his beer-drinking exploits and with the macho game-fishing routine. *I've got a bigger GPS tracker than you.* Yet it perplexed her, because in New York Patrick's childishness was what appealed to her most. It was a buffer between her and the superbitch world she had created for herself. So why was it different now? What had changed?

She knew one thing for certain. As they'd made love, she'd stared at the ceiling and waited for him to come so that the ordeal would be at an end.

On the other side of the hotel complex, Conrad Getty's ulcer was drowning in Scotch. He had not slept now for two days. Not since Viljoen's pet mobster, Kili, had decided to solve the Dennis Bentley problem in his own breathtakingly idiotic fashion. Viljoen seemed confident that everything was under control, but then he was just a pig-ignorant psychopath with ideas above his station. He always had been, ever since they'd met in boot camp back in 1969.

It wasn't Viljoen who dealt with Whitestone. It wasn't Viljoen whose head would be on the block if Whitestone found out what had been going on.

Whitestone. Even the very thought of the name sent another spasm of agony through his ruined stomach lining.

Getty had never seen Whitestone in the flesh. He had never even heard his voice. They communicated solely via cryptic emails. And maybe that was the problem. Like the bogeyman, he preyed on the hotel owner's imagination, twisting it into all sorts of fevered shapes, haunting his dreams and his waking hours and leaving him shaking and sweating with terror. Not for the first time, Getty wondered how the hell he had allowed himself to get involved in all this shit. The Kapok Hotel wasn't the biggest bed and breakfast establishment in Mombasa, nor was it the best; but it was serviceable and clean, and it had reasonably steady year-round custom. With a little time and effort, it could have been built up into something far more impressive. By now, it might even have been competing with some of the ritzier hotels in the city. He could have been respectable. He could have been *legitimate*, for Christ's sake!

But no – that wasn't the Conrad Getty way, was it? The Conrad Getty way was to get rich quick without so much as a second thought for the consequences. And when the opportunity had come along, he'd jumped straight in with both size twelves.

Viljoen! To think his fortunes would end up being so inextricably linked with that *animal*. Thirty years ago, Getty would have laughed in the face of anyone who suggested something so preposterous. But then thirty years ago he was Captain Getty of the South African Defence Force, and Viljoen was a conscripted street thug with little else to commend him other than an almost psychotic hatred of the coloured majority.

In the years that followed, all they'd had in common was that they had both profited out of apartheid and had been well and truly shafted when it collapsed. Viljoen had stayed in the military and made sergeant, but his uncompromising attitude to the blacks had been incompatible with the new regime and he had been booted out. Getty, meanwhile, watched in equally impotent fury as his lucrative post-military career as an orange trader in Bloemfontein was destroyed by labour reforms and

243

the sudden political correctness of his main business contacts in Europe and the US, who no longer thought it prudent to deal with someone associated with the apartheid regime.

It still seemed incredible to him that, after all he had given to his country, he should be forced to flee it like a refugee, his reputation and his Krugerrands virtually worthless in the world beyond its borders. And to Kenya of all places! A place whose corrupt wretchedness was living proof of the black man's inability to govern himself. Kenyatta? Nothing more than a Mau Mau terrorist. Arap Moi? A pocket-lining crook. And on it went. From the comfort of the Marlin Bay's residents-only bar, he had watched Kenya tear itself apart with self-righteous pleasure. As far as he was concerned, the election of December 2007 and the bloodbath that followed merely reinforced what he'd been telling everyone for years.

But beggars could not be choosers, and upon his arrival in Kenya all those years ago Getty was savvy enough to recognise the potential of a country blessed with seven-hundred square miles of inland game reserve and three hundred miles of coastline. So he invested what little money he had in the Kapok and waited for boom time. And while he waited he started drinking heavily, almost as heavily as he gambled, and it wasn't long before the only way to pay his debts was to sell up.

Which was why, when he bumped into his old comrade-in-arms Sergeant Viljoen one night in an Old Town strip joint called the Baobab Club, he was all ears to any suggestions, reasonable or otherwise.

And Viljoen, of course, had a suggestion.

An organisation specialising in very specific

import-export goods were looking to establish themselves in East Africa. They'd already recruited Viljoen as a footsoldier, and now they were looking for someone to manage the operation. And who better, Viljoen suggested, than his old army captain?

And, while the job sickened Conrad Getty to his very core, he had now reached the stage where he could no longer live *without* the money. The money had bought him the Marlin Bay, bought him his reputation in Shanzu, *bought him a new life*. Without the money, he was no one. He was dead.

It was midnight and the best part of a bottle of Glenfiddich before Getty left the hotel bar. He would have stayed longer, except that would have meant paying the barman overtime. Besides, he had a fresh bottle in his office that was just calling out for some love and attention.

First, he decided to take a stroll across the pool area, in the hope that the night air and the sea tang would stimulate him sufficiently to appreciate his nightcap. All it did was hit him like a brick wall. His legs turned to mush and he stumbled towards the pool in the darkness; his flailing arms grabbed the thick wooden post of a folded canvas parasol and he clung to it for dear life beside the still water before toppling backwards on to an empty sun lounger.

'Shit,' he said, wheezing hard, and above him the stars in the clear night sky spun alarmingly in his vision. He lay there for a moment, listening to the distant soothing crump of the ocean. As he did so, he became aware of a presence sitting opposite him in the darkness.

'Who's that?'

A voice he did not recognise said, 'You know, I

could stick a knife between the first two vertebrae of your neck and nobody would know you hadn't just fallen into the pool and drowned.'

Getty sat up with a start, his eyes blinking into the shadows. 'Who's there?' he said.

'Alternatively, I could take you out on to the beach and slit your throat and everyone would think you'd been mugged by a couple of hoods high on *chang'aa*. From what I hear it happens a lot round here.'

And then Getty said, 'Oh, Christ – *you*,' and he pissed himself, because, even though he had never heard Whitestone's voice, he knew it was him. *The bogeyman.*

'Who did you think it was?' Whitestone said, leaning forward slightly in his chair so that the moonlight cast his face in alabaster. '*Patrick*? The lovely Miss Bentley's *paramour*?'

Getty stared with horrified fascination, his booze-sodden brain overloading as he tried to reconcile what he was seeing with what he was hearing. The face of the bogeyman belonged to the clean-cut, all-American Patrick Noonan he recognised from the hotel atrium – yet the voice did not. The Ivy League twang had gone. The bogeyman had no discernible accent or human emotion in his voice. It was clipped and impersonal as the coded emails with which he communicated.

'My compliments to the chef, Conrad,' Whitestone said. 'Martha and I thought tonight's dinner was outstanding, although the swordfish steak was a little overdone for my tastes.'

'Listen,' Getty whispered. 'What happened the other day ... It was nothing to do with me, I swear, I—'

Whitestone brought a finger to his lips. 'Keep your voice down, Conrad. You don't want to wake the guests. They don't pay all that money to have their beauty sleep interrupted.'

'I swear to you that I had nothing to do with what happened up at Dennis Bentley's boatyard.'

'Ah yes. Dennis Bentley's boatyard. Now that wasn't good at all.' Whitestone paused to let his words sink in.

'Things got out of hand,' Getty admitted.

'Out of *hand*? I should say so, Conrad. Those trigger-happy niggers damn near blew my girlfriend away. Martha's a sweet girl. I've become very fond of her, and I wouldn't like anything to happen to her. After all, you've already killed her father.'

'I—'

'Oh, I appreciate that Dennis had become a liability. In fact, I was impressed with the speed with which you terminated his contract. The nigger's body floating back to shore was unfortunate – but these things happen. No, what worries me is when your men start shooting at policemen.'

'I swear—'

'I know, I know. It had nothing to do with you. But the fact is I pay you handsomely to make sure that *everything* that happens in this sector is to do with you. Do you understand that?'

'Yes. There's no excuse.'

'No, Conrad. There's not.'

Getty hung his head – yet, even as he waited to die, he felt a strange elation that at last it was all over.

'But let's not be too downcast,' Whitestone said.

Getty lifted his eyes, and saw that the bogeyman was actually smiling. But then he knew from long experience that killers often smiled just before they dealt the fatal blow.

Whitestone, however, sat back in his chair with his hands behind his head. Getty was struck by how *young* he was. The bogeyman could have been his own son.

'If it was anybody else, I might feel differently,' Whitestone said. 'But there is the question of this urgent shipment which needs to be attended to. Which is why I thought I'd better come down here to make sure nothing else goes wrong. How prepared are you?'

For the first time ever, Getty had cause to thank God for Tug Viljoen. 'Everything is in place.'

'What about the courier?'

'We have a replacement ready.'

Whitestone raised an eyebrow. 'I'm impressed, Conrad.'

'Just say the word, Mr Whitestone. We're ready to go.'

Whitestone gave him instructions and Getty memorised them as if they were military orders. Even as he did so, his mind was already working out the logistics. But then Getty had always been good at that. It was why he had been given the job in the first place.

'Very well,' Whitestone said. 'In that case I think I'll go to bed. It's been a long day. Room service at nine tomorrow morning, eh?'

'Of course.'

The bogeyman stood, and the expressionless face suddenly broke into a toothy grin.

'No more mistakes, or you die,' Patrick Noonan said, the forefinger of his right hand extended like the barrel of a pistol. '*Count on it.*'

248

Day Seven

Chapter Fifty-One

It was seven in the morning, and, considering he rarely stirred from his hammock in the workshop before eight, Harry was in an unfeasibly good mood. Jake, who slept on *Yellowfin* and had been up since just after dawn, regarded him with suspicion as he moored the launch and leaped ashore.

'You hollered?'

'Good news, old boy!'

'I hope so,' Jake said peevishly, wiping his oily hands on his vest. 'I've been trying to get those bloody hydraulics fixed for the last—'

'I've just got us a new radio!' Harry announced. His face still looked like pounded steak, but there was a discernible sparkle in his eye.

Jake looked at him suspiciously. 'I thought it wasn't due for another fortnight.'

'That's the *Nairobi* radio,' Harry said dismissively. 'I just got a call from Missy Meredith. Seems this chap she knows in Mazeras owes her a favour. And it just so happens he's got a secondhand ship-to-shore in his workshop, good as new. It's ours for fifty bucks if we can pick it up this afternoon.'

'Mazeras?' The township was west of Mombasa

along the main Nairobi highway. 'How the hell are we supposed to get to Mazeras? We don't have a car, remember?'

'*Initiative*, old boy,' Harry said, tapping his nose. Then, as if dispensing great wisdom, he said, 'Suki Lo's Honda.'

It took a moment for the full significance of his words to sink in. Then Jake backed away, his hands raised. 'No way! That old wreck is a death trap, and you're talking about a three-hour round trip on a good day.'

'Well, I'd go myself, but I'm hardly in a fit state to get behind the wheel of a car,' Harry said. 'The way my back is, I wouldn't get as far as the highway without medical assistance.' He shrugged. 'But it's up to you. If you're happy to wait two more weeks . . .'

Jake knew when he was beaten. 'Jesus, Harry.'

'I scribbled the address on the pad on the desk,' Harry said, grinning. 'There's a hundred bucks in the jar next to the phone. That should be more than enough to pay for the radio and for petrol there and back.'

'What are you going to do?'

'Paperwork, old boy. The system is long overdue for an overhaul. I sense there are good times ahead, and we must be ready to embrace them with open arms!'

Grumbling, Jake headed for the cool of the workshop and made his way to the office. An address in Mazeras was indeed scrawled on Harry's notepad, but as Jake had never been to the township before he was none the wiser. He ripped off the sheet of paper and folded it into the pocket of his shorts. Next to the phone was a brinjal pickle jar with a selection of mixed currency bills inside. Officially this was petty cash, but right now it was investment capital. Jake peeled off four twenty-dollar bills and replaced the rest of the money – which in the same currency came to a little over five hundred dollars – in the jar.

He was on his way out of the door when the phone rang.

'Who was that?' Harry asked as Jake emerged from the workshop a few minutes later.

'Somebody trying to sell me life insurance.'

'I trust you told them to fuck off.'

'I told them I was about to drive Suki Lo's Honda to Mazeras, and *they* told *me* to fuck off.'

Harry laughed. 'That's the spirit!'

'You think I'm joking?'

The two men said their goodbyes and Jake set off on foot along the track to Suki Lo's. Thirty minutes later, he returned along the same track in Suki's luminous-green Honda Civic, a relic which the bar owner had picked up for a couple of hundred dollars from a scrapyard in Kilifi and kept 'for emergencies' in a lean-to garage at the rear of the building. Its suspension was shot to hell and the brakes appeared to be working on a time-delay mechanism, and there were thick scabs of bird and monkey shit on its paint-work – but, as he skirted potholes en route to the highway, Jake was no longer thinking about the car and whether he would survive to hand the keys back.

He was thinking about the telephone call he had received in the boatyard office – and why it meant he wouldn't be driving to Mazeras township after all.

Chapter Fifty-Two

The Arturet was a thirty-six-year-old former Yugoslavian-registered grain freighter now transporting anything from grape nuts to secondhand-car parts – but mostly drugs – under a flag of convenience around the African coast. She had limped into Kilindini at dawn on her one functioning engine, ostensibly for mechanical repairs but primarily to offload a large consignment of cannabis resin she had picked up in Oran two weeks earlier.

The skipper was a bearded and bellicose Greek called Aristophenedes, who had once held a lucrative and prestigious position piloting Aristotle and Jackie Onassis around the Dodecanese in one of the billionaire's yachts, until he was sacked for downing two litres of retsina and attempting to grope Jackie.

Thanks to *The Arturet*, sailing under the influence of alcohol was no longer a problem for Aristophenedes; the freighter was such a lumbering piece of shit that he could easily manoeuvre it blindfold, let alone blind drunk – which he was most of the time. The Greek's only concern these days were his illicit cargoes – and, more specifically, offloading them. In the past, this had not been a problem. His regular stops – places like

254

Rabat, Libreville, Maputo and Quelimane – were generally patrolled by an official with a peaked cap and shiny badge who would allow you access to his own sister for a couple of US dollars. But that had all changed after September 11th and the war on terror. Now, even in these godforsaken places – perhaps because they *were* so godforsaken – it was commonplace within minutes of docking to find your vessel swarming with security goons in search of rocket launchers and al-Qaeda stowaways. On more than one occasion recently, Aristophenedes had looked out from the bridge to discover a reception committee waiting on the quay, and been forced to either dump the illicit cargo in the sea or else set it adrift in a lifeboat to be picked up later.

Mombasa, at least, was one place where he could breathe a little easier. If only, Aristophenedes reflected, someone like Michael Kili ran all African ports. Think of the *order* there would be, the refreshing lack of *harassment* for sailors such as himself just trying to get by in difficult times. Kili made it so simple: you pitched up at Kilindini and were free to unload whatever cargo you wished – as long as the gangster received twenty-five per cent of it. He would even provide dockhands to offload it for you. Twenty-five per cent was steep, but it was a hell of a better option than throwing the whole lot in the sea.

Aristophenedes had been looking forward to his stopover in Mombasa. Kili was not only a good businessman, but also a generous host and there was one whore in particular from his stable, a young girl called Mary, who gave the most exquisite oral pleasure. But now, as he stood in the temporary office belonging to the warehouse controller, waiting to put his name to the largely meaningless customs documentation, he felt his temper beginning to rise.

255

'But I don't understand, Pieter,' he barked. 'There is never usually a hold-up.'

The port supervisor, a white Kenyan called Pieter Sylvian, removed his cap and ran his fingers through thinning hair. 'What can I say, Nikos? These are difficult times for us all,' he said miserably.

'I have seven hundred kilos of cannabis resin in the hold of my ship!' the Greek shouted, his eyes bulging. 'That makes life *extra* difficult for me!'

Sylvian gestured for him to calm down and keep quiet, but Aristophenedes jabbed at him furiously with a thick tobacco-stained finger.

'Where is Kili? Let me speak to Kili!'

'Kili isn't here.'

'Then where the hell is he?'

'He is dead, Captain,' said a voice from behind him.

The Greek skipper turned and stared with bemusement at the besuited African standing in the cabin doorway.

'And who the hell are you?'

'My name is Detective Inspector Daniel Jouma of Coast Province CID.'

'Police?' Aristophenedes glared accusingly at Sylvian, who raised his hands abjectly.

'There was nothing I could do about it, Nikos.'

'I will see you in Hell,' hissed the Greek.

'About your cargo, Captain,' Jouma said.

The Greek smiled broadly. 'As I was explaining to the gentleman here, I had no idea these narcotics had been smuggled aboard my ship until I personally conducted an inventory of the cargo this morning. I—'

'Please do not insult my intelligence,' Jouma said. 'I have documentary evidence which proves that you have been regularly offloading drugs at Kilindini for the last two years. You know that in Kenya the penalty for trafficking marijuana is twenty years' imprisonment?'

Aristophenedes seemed to choke slightly behind his rictus grin. 'Perhaps we can work this out, Inspector,' he said smoothly. 'I'm sure I don't have to tell you how much twenty-five per cent of such a delivery would be worth to you.'

'I am not Michael Kili and I am not open to bribery, Captain,' Jouma snapped. 'Those days are over.'

At his desk, Sylvian put his head in his hands.

Aristophenedes, meanwhile, had abruptly dropped his blustering façade and was now pleading with Jouma. 'Why catch the sardine when you can land the whale?' he said. 'I myself hate drugs and all they stand for. I can give you names of those responsible for threatening me and my family to transport these evil substances—'

'Enough!' Jouma ordered.

Aristophenedes hung his head like a scolded child.

'Now listen to me carefully, Captain,' Jouma continued. 'You will get back on board your ship and you will leave Kilindini on the next tide and you will not return. Do you understand?'

The Greek's bushy eyebrows shot up. 'Of course, Inspector,' he said hurriedly.

'Mombasa may have been an easy touch in the past, but now things have changed. I repeat: *do you understand, Captain*?'

'Yes, Inspector.'

'Once out of Mombasa waters, you will ditch your cargo over the side. Understand?'

Aristophenedes flushed briefly with affront, but nodded.

'There is one more thing.'

'Yes, Inspector.'

'You will be taking two passengers with you.'

257

Chapter Fifty-Three

Had he actually been a bonds trader, Whitestone had no doubt he would have been good at it. After all, what was his true profession if not profiting from the transfer of saleable commodities across international borders? The only difference was what was perceived as legal and what was not. But that was of little importance anyway. Anyone who hoped to flourish in the real world knew that legality was just a word. What really counted were market forces.

Whitestone understood the market, which was why he had flourished. His sector was southern Europe, crucial both for its established client base and for export routes to the burgeoning markets in the north. To have been put in charge of such an important operation so young was an extraordinary achievement. Whitestone was just thirty-three, and there were many who saw him running the whole organisation before he was forty.

'Patrick, do you have the letter from Dad's insurance people?'

Whitestone slipped easily out his reverie and into the persona of Patrick Noonan. It was not difficult. As far as Whitestone was concerned, the American had the complexity of a barn door. He reached into the door pocket of the BMW X5. The car belonged to Marlin Bay Hotel's fleet of courtesy cars and was far too extravagant for their needs. But Conrad Getty had good reason to be generous, so Whitestone wasn't complaining.

'There you go, honey,' he said, handing her a foolscap envelope. 'You want me to come with you?'

Martha smiled thinly and climbed down from the passenger seat. 'No. But you can buy me lunch when I'm done.'

'Sure thing.'

He watched her jog smartly across the street to the offices of one of Mombasa's leading law firms and found himself admiring the tight lines of her figure silhouetted against the white linen of her suit. He grinned. If ever there was an example of the benefits of a hands-on approach to the job, then Martha was it. Had it not been for his insistence in running background checks on all of his network operatives, he would never have discovered that the daughter of one of his East Africa couriers was not only intelligent and beautiful, but also living in New York.

Another philosophy dear to Whitestone's heart was that work should never be to the exclusion of pleasure. And Whitestone took pleasure wherever and whenever he chose. Until now, he'd had no idea how long this particular relationship would last. Until he tired of it, he'd supposed, or until the inevitable question of commitment arose. It was just a shame that circumstances should have precipitated this unscheduled reunion. He thought about Martha's father and was gripped with a spasm of anger at the complete fuck-up the Mombasa cell had made of liquidating the old man. Once this latest valuable shipment was complete, he had plans for Conrad Getty and his team – and they were not pleasant.

There was a tapping at his tinted window and, when he lowered it, Whitestone found himself looking down into the melted-chocolate eyes of a small African girl who was standing on her tiptoes on the pavement beside the BMW.

'Excuse me, sir,' she said, 'but my ball has rolled underneath your car and I cannot reach it.'

'Then I'd better move my car,' he said, and the girl smiled – an angelic toothy smile that lit up her whole face. 'Stand back now,' he said, starting the engine and reversing a few feet along the kerb.

The girl picked up her ball and, with a wave of thanks, skipped happily away towards the apartment complex on the other side of the road. She could not have been more than eight or nine years old, yet she was truly exquisite, Whitestone thought, appraising her with the eye of a connoisseur.

He was certain there would be many others who would think the same way.

Chapter Fifty-Four

Jouma's beverage looked and tasted like water in which root vegetables had been boiled; but the toothless hag who owned this particular roadside refreshment stall did not serve English breakfast tea. Indeed, she seemed most put out that anyone should have the temerity to ask for a drink that she'd never heard of. 'Mama's Nectar' she called it, this insipid pondweed brew, and she claimed it was more beneficial to the innards than any English breakfast tea. Indeed, Jouma had to concede it was refreshing, but only in the way that splashing one's face in stagnant river water was refreshing.

The stall, which was little more than a trestle table laden with plastic bottles of warm cola, was situated at the northern end of Nyali Bridge, and was one of a number of similar stalls optimistically erected by traders hoping to make a few shillings from wide-eyed tourists on their way to the hotels and resorts further north along the coast.

It was not a salubrious spot. Every few minutes a huge pantechnicon would roar past with a noise like the bowels of the earth erupting and threaten to sweep up the traders and their flimsy stalls and deposit them in the river gorge a hundred feet below. Jouma checked his watch. Quarter to nine. He had been waiting here a little over ten minutes and his suit was already coated in a filthy film of dust that meant it would most certainly require professional cleaning.

Presently, a car approached the bridge from the north and swung off the road on to the dirt parking area adjacent to the stalls. It was a garish green colour and appeared to have more holes than body-work. The door squealed open and Jouma breathed a sigh of relief when Jake Moore levered himself out.

'It would have been no trouble to meet you in the city, Inspector,' Jake said, squinting uncertainly at his surroundings.

'Mombasa is not a good place right now,' Jouma said. 'Thank you for coming, Jake.'

'As I said on the phone, I was heading this way anyway,' Jake said.

Another eighteen-wheeler hammered past in the direction of Malindi, and Jouma was forced to grab hold of Jake's arm to stop himself being blown over by its draft.

'So what's going on?' Jake shouted over the din. 'It sounded pretty urgent over the phone.'

Jouma nodded and led Jake away from the highway to where his Panda was parked beside the refresh-ment stall. Once the two men were inside, Jouma held up a cell phone.

'I have never understood these devices. But this morning I bought this for five dollars from a trader in Jamhuri Park. He says it only has thirty minutes of credit before I have to throw it away, but I do not trust him.'

Jake laughed. 'Why the sudden quantum leap into the twenty-first century?'

'Because I suspect that the telephone in my office will soon be bugged – if it is not already.'

Jouma described the events of the previous day. When he reached the part where he'd stumbled across Michael Kili's body in the office above the Baobab Club, Jake blinked with surprise.

'Omu killed his boss?'

Jouma shook his head. 'I don't think so.' He described his surveillance of customers coming in and out of the club that morning. 'Most of them, to my shame, I have been able to identify as known members of the Mombasa community. The rest were tourists. Despicable as their intentions may have been, they all had legitimate reasons for being there. This man, however, interests me.'

He handed Jake a creased Polaroid. Although the subject was blurred and distant – Jouma was no photographer – Jake instantly recognised the barrel chest and the spindly legs.

'Tug Viljoen?' Jake exclaimed.

Jouma nodded. 'According to our records, Mr Viljoen runs a reptile park near Flamingo Creek. Do you know of it?'

'I know it all right. But you think Viljoen murdered Kili?'

'Supposition,' Jouma admitted. 'But the killing took place while Mr Viljoen was on the premises, and none of the staff in the club recalls him in the bar or the dancing areas.'

Jake was stunned. 'Tug's a nutcase, I'll agree – but a killer?'

Jouma passed Jake a sheet of Xeroxed paper. On it was what looked like the kind of previous-convictions charge sheet Jake remembered from the days when he was a young beat officer. But, instead of

263

burglary, breaking-and-entering and car theft, the list contained details of beatings, looting, drugs offences and conspiracies to murder stretching as far back as the early 1970s.

He whistled. 'This is all Tug's handiwork?'

Jouma nodded. 'A brief résumé of his years in the South African Army. Propitiously for him, at least, the regime was such in those days that he was allowed to get away with it. He was eventually discharged for hospitalising a protester during a public disturbance in Gauteng Province in 1999. Needless to say, the matter was swept under the carpet by the military authorities.'

'Jesus. But why would he murder Kili?'

'I was rather hoping you might be able to assist me with that.'

'How?'

'Believe me, Jake, I would not ask for your help if there was anyone else I could possibly turn to,' Jouma said apologetically. 'Anyone else I could *trust*. But—'

Jouma sighed and finished his story. And, when Jake had heard about Sergeant Nyami's treachery and Jacob Omu's murder, he said, 'Shit. What a mess.'

'Sadly, yes. That's why I need your help.'

'But what can I do?'

The car shook as another lorry thundered past in the direction of Mombasa.

'It is quite simple,' Jouma said. 'I need you to be a policeman again.'

Chapter Fifty-Five

At the Tamarind restaurant, overlooking Mombasa from the Nyali shore, Martha was eating cold lobster and wondering why Patrick kept looking at his Rolex.

'It's two minutes later than it was last time you looked,' she said irritably.

Patrick looked up and smiled. 'Sorry,' he said.

'You got to be somewhere?'

'I'm still getting used to the time difference,' Patrick said, which was one of the lamest excuses Martha had ever heard. But then Patrick had been acting as if he had ants in his pants ever since they'd arrived at the restaurant. OK, the place wasn't Sardi's and Mombasa wasn't Manhattan, but the food was good and—

'*Goddammit, Patrick, will you stop looking at your watch!*'

His face fell into that 'scolded little boy' expression that always made her melt, but now just got under her skin. She'd *told* him not to fly out. This wasn't a holiday. Sure, he'd had to wait two hours outside the lawyer's office, but *she'd* been the one wrangling with a man who in New York wouldn't even get a job as an ambulance chaser.

'I have to pee,' he said presently, and Martha was glad when he left the table. She reached across to his untouched plate and speared a shrimp that was the size and shape of a telephone receiver.

Conrad Getty had been expecting the call, but when the phone rang he still jumped out of his skin.

'Is everything on schedule?'

A sheen of cold sweat instantaneously formed on the hotel owner's forehead. 'The van is on its way, Mr Whitestone.'

'And the shipment?'

'It will be in position on the border.'

'Good. I don't have to remind you that this is a very important delivery, do I, Conrad?'

'No.'

'And I can't stress enough what will happen if anything goes wrong.'

'I understand, Mr Whitestone.'

'Then we have nothing to worry about, do we?'

Whitestone pressed the End button on his cell phone, then removed the SIM card from the handset and tossed it into the urinal trough. He unzipped himself and drove the chip along the trough and down the pipe with the force of his piss. Then he zipped himself up, fitted the handset with a new SIM, and went back outside to the restaurant. It was a precaution – some would say an unnecessary one, but Whitestone didn't care what other people said. If Augustus Kanga had taken precautions, he would never have got to the position where he trusted his driver so implicitly – and so fatally.

Ah, there she was, Whitestone thought as he approached his table. *His little Martha, scavenging from his plate of leftovers like a hungry dog.* Once he had found her pathological hatred of wasted food rather endearing. But now, like so many other things about her, Whitestone found her habit suddenly tiresome. It puzzled him why, and indeed how quickly, this feeling of indifference towards her had materialised. Perhaps it was because for the first time ever he was attempting to combine business *and* pleasure. Before, Martha had always been a welcome release from the stresses of his profession. He used to look forward to seeing her, being with her, making love to her; now that she was in such close proximity to his real life, well – she felt like more of a *hindrance*.

He sat down opposite and for a while they talked. Or rather Martha talked. Whitestone was thinking about the shipment and about the damnable truism of business that, no matter how hands-on you were, you could never be in two places at the same time.

And then it struck him that this whole situation was ridiculous. Why the hell was he sitting here listening to this shit about insurance documents when potentially the most important deal of his life was going down somewhere else? And the more he thought about it the angrier he became, and the angrier he became the more he needed a focus for his anger.

'Jesus Christ, Martha,' he exclaimed. 'I have had it up to here with this crap about your dad!'

As soon as he said it, he knew that it was an unforgivable loss of self-control, but suddenly he didn't care. In that moment, he was not Patrick Noonan.

'You bastard,' she said. 'You *bastard*.'

Whitestone regarded her with cold eyes. Then it was as if the demon possessing him was suddenly exorcised, and his shoulders sagged.

'Jesus, babe – I'm so sorry. I didn't mean to say that.'

267

'Get away from me,' she said, brushing away his outstretched hand.

Curiously, as she stood from the table and hurried towards the exit, Martha was almost *relieved* that he had said it.

Chapter Fifty-Six

As far as Jake could see, when he was not hanging around strip clubs or getting drunk in Suki Lo's bar, Tug Viljoen's existence was about as interesting as that of his crocodiles. *Unless, of course, you counted murdering Mombasa gangsters.*

For the last two hours, the South African had been holed up in his rundown caravan, emerging only to berate the two young Africans whitewashing the maintenance sheds at the far side of the compound. Jake, watching from the bough of a mangrove tree overlooking the perimeter of the compound, was in grave danger of seizing up with cramp and plunging thirty feet to the jungle floor. Even the proboscis monkeys in the trees near by had stopped their jabbering and now regarded him with something approaching pity in their mean eyes.

But at least being up here gave him time to think.

And Jouma had given him plenty to think about.

The inspector was sure Viljoen had pulled the trigger on Michael Kili, and that the murder was connected with what had happened up at Dennis Bentley's boatyard the other day.

Jake wasn't so sure. As far as he could gather,

there were any number of people prepared to off the Mombasa gangster, and for just as many reasons. But it was a lead, and he could tell from the haunted look in Jouma's eyes that the little detective needed every friend he could lay his hands on.

'I need you to watch him,' he had said. 'I believe that things will happen today that will precipitate an answer to our conundrum.'

Jake Moore was no stranger to surveillance. Seven years ago, he, Mac Bowden and Tom Kent had spent nearly three months in an attic in Canning Town, watching a flat belonging to an armed robber called Charlie Green. As surveillance went, it had been a textbook job. Green had a big mouth, and right now he was serving twenty years in Belmarsh, along with the rest of what remained of his crew.

But it was now 11 a.m. in a sweltering mangrove jungle, and Jake was no longer as patient as he was when he was a Flying Squad officer. In fact, he was of half a mind to pay Tug a visit and simply *ask* him if he'd shot Kili. At that moment, however, the trees erupted with the piercing alarums of birds, and the monkeys scattered like a gang of teenage vandals routed by a police patrol. Jake flattened himself against the bough as a white Transit van rumbled into view along the dirt track leading from the highway and passed directly underneath him. The van was unmarked and unwashed, and as it swept through the compound gates Viljoen emerged from the caravan and directed it towards a yard behind the storage sheds.

Relieved to have an excuse to get down from his vantage point, Jake shinned down the mangrove trunk and dropped silently on to the soft jungle floor. Staying out of sight in the undergrowth, he followed the line of

270

the perimeter fence round to the rear of the compound. Now between him and the fence was a cleared area that Viljoen obviously used as a junkyard. The dusty ground was littered with twists of rusted metal, plastic containers, stacks of old tyres and, he noted ominously, scattered bones. It provided good cover. Nimbly stepping around the junk, Jake was able to get to within ten feet of the fence and had an unobstructed view of the compound beyond.

The van was parked beside a gibbet on which hung the skinned remains of a crocodile, its marbled flesh rotting sweetly in the heat of the sun. There were two Africans in the cab in T-shirts and ragged jeans, and Jake saw them flinch with revulsion as they jumped down and began stretching their stiff limbs. He also saw that both men had machine guns slung over their shoulders, the familiar crescent-shaped magazine telling him that they were AK-47s, the paramilitary's weapon of choice.

Viljoen approached them, barking sharp instructions in Swahili. The two men scuttled round to the back of the van and unlocked the rear doors. Viljoen looked inside and nodded. The doors were slammed shut as the three men left the yard in the direction of the caravan.

Jake waited until they were out of sight, then crept forward to the fence. It was made from cheap plastic-coated metal that provided no obstacle as he climbed over it into the compound. Keeping as far away as possible from the corpse of the dangling reptile, he went to the rear of the van and opened one of the doors. The interior was dark, empty and smelled of sweat and piss. In the roof was a single air vent and at the far end, stacked against the cab wall, were three plastic buckets.

It was a good job Viljoen's voice could strip paint at ten yards, because if he hadn't heard the croc owner tearing a strip off one of the men with guns Jake would not have known they were returning.

Shit! Realising in an instant that there was no way he could get back to the fence without being seen, and with no other place to hide than under the vehicle's chassis, he leaped up into the van, scrabbling at the lock housing on the inside of the heavy doors in a desperate attempt to close them behind him. As he flattened himself behind the wheel arch bulkhead, he could hear Viljoen shouting orders and the intermittent subservient grunt of the gunmen. Then there were footsteps and Jake froze as a shadow passed in front of the tiny crack of light between the doors. If they were opened now, there was precisely nowhere for him to go. And if, as he suspected, the Africans were twitchy with their guns, then—

But the front doors slammed shut, and he felt the vehicle lurch as the three men climbed into the cab. The only light now came from the vent above his head, a narrow sliver of brightness in what was otherwise pitch dark. The metal panels of the vehicle shuddered as the engine kicked into life, and Jake's brief moment of relief that he had not been caught was now consumed by the realisation that he was locked in.

Chapter Fifty-Seven

Nyami had talked long into the night, reticently at first but then spilling out names and dates with such enthusiasm that Jouma had had to slow him down in case his words were not caught clearly on the tape machine in front of him. When he had finished, it was nearly dawn and four cassette tapes were full. Only then had he slept.

When Jouma roused him upon his return from his meeting with Jake Moore, it was shortly before 10 a.m. Nyami and Jemima listened as Jouma told him what he had arranged, at which point the disgraced sergeant – who had glumly assumed he was going to spend the rest of his life behind bars – burst into tears.

Now it was 11 a.m. and, as he and his wife boarded the rusting hulk of *The Arturet*, knapsack dangling over the shoulder of his cheap jerkin, Nyami's expression still mirrored an ongoing internal conflict between bewilderment, fear and relief. He looked like a small child accompanying his mother on his first day at school.

Jouma watched from the dockside as Aristophenedes, who could not have been more welcoming if his passengers were the king and queen of Greece themselves, greeted his passengers at the top of the gangplank. Nyami glanced back one more time before the Greek skipper's muscular arm clamped around his bony shoulders and led him away out of sight. In two days, he and Jemima would be in Somalia. There – well, there it was entirely up to them whether they thrived or wilted on the vine.

As he turned away and began walking along the quay towards his car, Jouma reflected that at least he had given Nyami a chance. And in many people's eyes that was more than the sergeant deserved for his treachery.

He got into his car and headed for police head-quarters on Mama Ngina Drive, suspecting that this would be the last upbeat moment he would enjoy in a day that promised to be long, fraught and possibly his last on this earth.

Chapter Fifty-Eight

The luminous dial on Jake's watch told him they had been travelling for two hours, the smooth ride indicating that they were most probably headed inland on one of Kenya's few main arterial roads worthy of the name. It would be ironic, he thought bitterly, if they were at this very moment speeding through Mazeras township on the Nairobi highway. Maybe Tug and his goons would stop to let him pick up the secondhand ship-to-shore radio from the address Harry had given him.

The road surface was one blessing, but there was little else to cheer him up. The heat in the metal-lined container in which he sat was proof that the vent in the roof was next to useless and that if he didn't get out soon he would run the risk of suffocation. His clothes were sodden with sweat, the material chafing against his skin as he constantly shifted against the sides of the van in an effort to get comfortable. He didn't want to have to kick open the doors and dive out of a moving vehicle, but pretty soon he would have no choice.

After a while he must have dozed off, because when he snapped awake again the van was slowing to a halt. As the engine rattled and died, Jake hunched down behind the bulkhead again, his body tensed and ready for the moment the doors swung open. Against two guys with AK-47s, the element of surprise was just about all he had – and even then he didn't fancy his chances. He might be able to tackle one, but two would be stretching it, and he doubted Tug was unarmed. He also doubted whether being a casual drinking acquaintance would cut much ice with the psychopathic South African. But instead he heard the cab doors slam and the sound of voices retreating into the distance.

He waited for a few moments, in case Viljoen or one of the gunmen were still in the van. Then, fumbling in the dark, he found the inside bolt handle and fired open the lock. Bright-white light flooded the interior, blinding him, and he tumbled inelegantly out of the back of the van and on to the dirt. He scrambled under the vehicle on his belly, expecting at any second to hear shouts of alarm and the crash of automatic weapons being cocked. But there was nothing, save the tick of the cooling engine and the chafing of cicadas.

The truck was parked outside a remote roadhouse, fifty yards from a two-lane highway that sliced through featureless bush landscape towards a hazy range of hills in the far distance. The building was jarringly sophisticated considering it was the only one for miles around, with a crisply whitewashed adobe façade, a thatched roof and a row of broad picture windows tinted against the glare of the sun. The two Africans were lounging in the shade outside, smoking cigarettes. They appeared to be unarmed. Viljoen, he assumed, was inside. But was he feeding his face or taking a leak? The difference could be crucial.

For now Jake had to take some decisive action.

He knew he was only marginally less vulnerable under the van as he had been in it. He also had no idea where he was. Apart from the roadhouse and the hills in the distance, the only other landmark worthy of note was the highway.

And somehow he needed to get a message to Jouma.

Christ – how had this happened? The plan had been so simple: observe Viljoen, then relay his report to the inspector by phone from Flamingo Creek at the end of the day. It was the kind of job that shouldn't tax a rookie special constable, let alone a former detective sergeant in the Flying Squad. Yet somehow, whether through bravado or sheer pig-headed stupidity, he had ended up taking an unscheduled road trip into the Kenyan wilderness. And what made matters worse, there wasn't a sniff of a contingency plan. As he had sheepishly explained to Jouma, he didn't even have a cell phone.

It was Keystone Cops time all right – except as far as Jake was concerned there was nothing remotely funny about it.

Yet just maybe . . .

Running alongside the road were telegraph poles supporting thick loops of cable. Where the highway met the dirt track leading to the roadhouse, a line of cable branched off to a junction box on the other side of the building. As he eased himself carefully out from under the van, Jake prayed that the box meant what he thought it did.

Keeping low and out of sight of the Africans behind a row of parked cars, he ran to the far end of the roadhouse, then crept along the wall beneath the windows. At the corner he turned and at that moment he could have punched the air as he saw that the box was indeed connected to a glass and metal phone kiosk situated at the rear of the building, beside a flyblown garbage dumpster and a door which presumably led to the kitchens.

He ran to it, then stopped and stared in disbelief: the receiver dangled uselessly on its wire and the phone casing swung open where the machine had been raided for its stock of shillings.

There was only one option open to him now if he wanted to keep tabs on Viljoen, and that was to get back into the van. But as he reached the corner of the building Jake saw to his dismay that the two Africans were already sauntering back across the car park towards the vehicle. He saw one of them stare with a puzzled expression at the open rear doors, then shrug and kick them shut. A few moments later, Viljoen emerged purposefully from the diner, zipping up his flies and tightening his belt, and the three men climbed back into the cab. The engine started up first time and the truck swept back on to the highway and sped away in the direction of the hills.

Jake hurried into the car park. There were three vehicles parked in an erratic line; two of them he immediately dismissed – a flatbed truck containing crates full of chickens and an Austin Allegro with one flat tyre. He ran across to the third, a busted-up Ford with a sign on the roof that said KAGONI SCHOOL OF MOTORING. It was unlocked. Jake slid into the driving seat and in a second had rived the ignition housing free. A moment later the two connector wires crackled and the car coughed into life. But he had only gone a few yards when every light on the dashboard came on and the Ford wheezed to a standstill.

Shit! He grabbed the two connectors and frantically sparked them together, but the engine resolutely refused to bite.

'You are the repairman?'

He looked up to find a tall academic-looking African standing by the car.

'You are the repairman?' the man asked again, poking his head through the open passenger window. 'My name is Johnstone Kagoni of the Kagoni School of Motoring. I called for a repairman four hours ago.'

Ignoring him, Jake got out of the car and ran to the highway. A black SUV was approaching fast, kicking up a huge dust cloud as it headed towards the hills. He flagged it frantically but in a second it was gone. Suddenly bone-weary and defeated, Jake trudged towards the roadhouse. There was no way he was going to catch Viljoen now. He might as well go and spend the last of his money on a couple of ice-cold beers. Some fucking policeman he was. He could almost hear Albie Moore's crowing laughter from the smoke-filled vault of the Low Lights Tavern.

Jake turned and took one last look at Viljoen's van disappearing into the heat haze – and was surprised to see the SUV racing back along the highway towards him. His surprise turned to astonishment when it swept into the dirt car park and he saw Martha Bentley behind the wheel.

Chapter Fifty-Nine

Superintendent Teshete sat in his high-backed leather chair behind his expansive mahogany desk in his office with its view over the Indian Ocean. When Jouma entered the office, he crushed a cigarette into an onyx ashtray on the desk and stood sharply, his knuckles hard against the polished surface of the desk.

'Where the devil have you been, Daniel?' he demanded. 'I have been trying to contact you for almost twenty-four hours. Where is Nyami? Why did you release him? And on whose authority?'

'May I sit down, sir?' Jouma said.

Teshete, knocked off his stride, waved at a chair. Jouma sat and primly crossed his spindly legs. It was barely thirty-six hours since he had last sat in this chair, but it seemed like a lifetime.

'In answer to your first question, sir, the reason you have not been able to contact me is that I have been at a safe house, conducting a long and detailed interview with Sergeant Nyami.'

'A *safe house*?' Teshete spluttered.

Jouma bowed his head sheepishly. 'In truth, the apartment of my sister-in-law.'

'What on earth for?'

'For the simple reason that I felt the location was less hazardous to Nyami's health than the cells here.'

'You are making no sense, Inspector! Where is Nyami now?'

'He is safe, sir. And so is his wife.'

Teshete reached for his cigarettes and lit one with a gold-plated Zippo. 'You had better start explaining yourself, Daniel. You know better than anyone else that Nyami is in big trouble. Failing to carry out his duty. Receiving bribes. These are very serious charges. '

'I am aware of that, sir. His failure to act in Michael Kili's office is a matter of record. And I can confirm that, during the course of the last three years, Nyami received in total two hundred and four-teen US dollars in bribes.'

Teshete flipped his ash nonchalantly. 'How can you be so precise?'

'Because Jacob Omu kept detailed records of every shilling he paid on Michael Kili's behalf to Coast Province CID detectives.'

'I see,' Teshete said coolly. 'And where did you find these detailed records of Omu's?'

'They were in a briefcase which he was intending to smuggle out of the country, along with himself, follow-ing the murder of Michael Kili. An understandable insurance measure when one considers the information they contained. Though unfortunately not enough to prevent Omu from being murdered himself. '

'Omu committed suicide,' said Teshete. 'He hanged himself from his hospital bed.'

'No, sir,' Jouma said. 'He was silenced. Just as Sergeant Nyami would have been silenced had I not removed him from his prison cell.'

'Silenced? By whom?'

'By you, sir.'

281

Teshete's eyes bulged. 'Are you mad, Jouma? Have you lost your mind? Do you know what you are saying?'

'Not you personally, sir. But you gave the order for Omu to be exterminated. You, after all, had the most to lose, being the greatest beneficiary of Kili's bribe money.'

Teshete crushed out his half-smoked cigarette and toyed with the still-burning ember in the ashtray. 'I take it you have Omu's documents.'

'Yes, sir. And taped testimony from Nyami. They, too, are in a safe place.'

'And I take it you have informed Police Criminal Investigation Officer Iraki.'

'No, sir. Not yet. But I have made provision for all the information to be passed to him should anything untoward happen to me while I complete my investigations.'

'It seems you have it all worked out, Daniel.'

Jouma shook his head. 'No, sir. All I have is evidence. Names. Dates. Figures. I will never be able to work out *why*.'

Teshete smiled sadly. 'Always thinking, aren't you? You should have been a philosopher instead of a policeman.' He steepled his fingers. 'So what is it that you want? Money? That can be arranged.'

'No, sir. Money does not interest me.' Jouma chuckled. 'Maybe that is why Kili never bothered to offer me any.'

'Then what, Daniel?'

'What I want is unimportant. What happens next is not up to me, it is up to the people whose names are on Omu's list. Only they can make the choice.'

'You do not leave these ... people much of a choice,' Teshete said, as he stood and walked two paces to the window.

Jouma shrugged. 'I have found that in life, sir, there is *always* a choice.'

282

Chapter Sixty

It was one of Patrick's more gung-ho traits that even in Manhattan he always left the keys to his car in the ignition.

'If it gets stolen then I can get another one with the insurance money,' he explained. 'But it costs two thousand bucks in New York to repair a hotwired ignition.'

Martha had never understood the logic of that – but, as she started up the BMW and sped away from the Tamarind restaurant, she was glad that his old habits had travelled across the Atlantic with him. *Bastard.* He could blame jetlag as much as he wanted, but what he had said to her in the restaurant was unforgivable. Leaving the sonofabitch stranded in Mombasa and facing a monumental taxi fare would give him time to consider the error of his ways.

She dodged through the maelstrom of downtown Mombasa and headed north on the Malindi highway. It took her a while to find the turn-off for Flamingo Creek, and longer to find Jake's boatyard. A feeling of desolation swept over her when she discovered that the workshop was locked up, and that *Yellowfin* wasn't at anchor. For the first time since she arrived in Mombasa, the first time ever maybe, Martha Bentley felt completely alone in the world. Her father was dead; Patrick was as good as dead after what he'd done – and Jake Moore, the only person she could think of to confide in, was nowhere to be found.

Then she'd met one of the locals, who'd said that if Jake wasn't out at sea then he would most likely be at a bar called Suki Lo's, and, yes, he would take her there as long as she promised to buy him a beer and a bourbon chaser.

'Jake? No, Jake no here,' said the woman behind the bar, a hard-faced Oriental with rotten teeth who Martha took to be Suki Lo. 'But if you see him tell him I wan' my fuckin' car back!'

Suki said she thought Jake had gone to Mombasa, but she couldn't be sure. If he had, though, then there had to be a good reason, because Jake hated the city like the plague.

'Does he have a cell phone?' Martha asked.

Suki shook her head.

'I wouldn't worry, darling,' said the local who had brought her to the bar. 'If Jake's driving Suki's old heap, then he's in no danger of going missing.'

'What do you mean?'

''Cos you could see that lime-green piece of Jap shit from the moon,' the local cackled.

'Fuck you, John,' Suki said. She looked at Martha. 'You wan' some noodles, honey?' she asked.

But Martha was already heading for the door.

It took her ten minutes to get back on to the highway. Turning south, she headed for Mombasa for another ten until, with a whoop, she saw what she

284

was looking for: a luminous-green Honda parked on a dirt side road next to a sign which said: WELCOME TO CROC WORLD.

The old lag in the bar was right. Suki Lo's car was unmissable. It had stood out like a beacon as she passed it on her way to Flamingo Creek.

'So you win the Girl Guides' badge for persistence,' Jake said. 'But I still don't understand how the hell you found me.'

'I asked a kid working at the croc park. He was shit scared. Seemed to think I was from Customs or something. He said the Boss Man had headed off in a van with some guys with guns about two hours earlier. I figured you wouldn't have wanted to miss the fun.'

'They could have been heading anywhere.'

'The kid said he overheard them talking about the Tanzanian border. I took a calculated risk and headed the only way I know. Looks like it paid off. So now that I've saved your butt, maybe you can tell me what's going on.'

Jake told her what he knew, which wasn't much. Then he peered through the BMW's tinted windscreen at the featureless countryside that surrounded them on all sides.

'So where are we now?'

'The border's about ten miles from here.'

The van was a mile ahead, its dust cloud shimmering against the concrete road surface. As long as the road remained straight, there was no need to get any closer – and the highway showed no indication of deviating from its path towards the Tanzanian border. It reminded Jake of those interminable Interstates in the American Midwest that you could drive along for a whole day without seeing so much as a kink in the road.

'Can you get a signal on your phone?' he asked.

'Barely.'

'Let me have it.'

Jake rummaged in his pocket for the scrap of paper on which Harry had scribbled the address of the secondhand-radio dealer in Mazeras. It all seemed such a long time ago now. Scrawled on the bottom in his own handwriting was the number of Jouma's cell phone. He dialled it, hoping that the signal would last out – and that Jouma would figure out how to answer the call.

Having left Teshete's office, Jouma knew there was nothing else to do but wait. He had done his duty and events were now out of his hands. He left police headquarters and walked the short distance to Fort Jesus. There he sat on his favourite bench in the compound and stared at his cell phone as if it was some strange alien artifact.

When it rang he nearly jumped out of his skin. *Now which was the button Jake had told him to press?*

'Hello?'

'Congratulations, Inspector,' Jake said. 'And welcome to the telecommunications revolution.'

Five minutes later Jouma was running for his car.

Jake had barely ended the call when the Transit pulled off the highway and on to a track leading to a collection of farm buildings a quarter of a mile from the road. Martha slowed as they passed the junction, then continued for another half-mile before swinging the BMW into the scrub where it was hidden from the road. Together they hurried on foot to where the flat terrain was slightly raised, giving them a clear view of the buildings – although not, frustratingly, what was going on there.

They did not have long to wait until a second vehicle left the farm. It was a large truck with military-issue olive-green paintwork and a canvas rear canopy. It swung on to the highway and headed towards them. As it roared past on its way to the Tanzanian border, Jake saw that the driver was a middle-aged African with a cigarette drooping out of his mouth.

'The delivery boy?' he wondered out loud.

'There goes Viljoen,' Martha said, pointing down to the farm.

The Transit was leaving now. They watched it bumping and skittering on the loose surface of the track. It rejoined the main road and set off in the direction it had come. Jake could see that it was sitting lower on its rear axle; whatever he had come here for, Viljoen had clearly taken delivery of his cargo.

Chapter Sixty-One

After thirty-three years in the police force, Daniel Jouma was not easily shocked, and he most certainly did not believe in witchcraft – but that was before he had stumbled upon what was hidden in Tug Viljoen's caravan. Even now, as he gulped down lungfuls of stale jungle air, his legs still felt like jelly and his guts as if they had been turned upside down.

My God, Jouma thought, *what manner of evil was this?*

Croc World was deserted by the time he'd got there. In the yard, he had found the decomposing carcass of the crocodile hanging by its tail from a gibbet and identified it as the source of the foul odour that seemed to permeate the whole site. From there he had retraced his steps back to Viljoen's caravan, where the stink of unwashed dishes, stale alcohol and overflowing ashtrays was almost as bad to the detective's sensitive nose.

Viljoen was clearly a man who took as much interest in the mechanics of running a business as he did in his own hygiene. As he poked around the caravan's cupboards and cubbyholes, the only paperwork Jouma could find was a grubby ledger with a few columns of scrawled figures, and some loose receipts from goods suppliers in Malindi. There was nothing to explain his connection with Michael Kili. Jouma almost felt himself longing for the efficient book-keeping of Jacob Omu.

Then he found the camera. It was stored in a padded bag and hidden in a recess under the floor. It rested on a slim manila folder that Jouma removed and emptied on to the banquette.

It was then that he saw the photographs.

The first was a close-up of a white face and, although the eyes were wide and the mouth open as if screaming, Jouma recognised it instantly from the mug shots circulating Mama Ngina Drive. Dennis Bentley, the missing boat owner.

In the next picture, Bentley was still the subject, but from further away this time and photographed from above. He appeared to be sitting in a chair, like the one bolted to the back of Jake Moore's boat. There was ocean behind him and – Jouma's eyes narrowed as he peered closer at the picture.

No, Bentley wasn't just sitting in the chair: he was *tied* to it.

Heart pounding now, Jouma skimmed to the next photograph. It was the same scene, but now a second person was present. He was scrawny, wearing shorts and a black baseball cap with some sort of white logo stitched to the front. He was standing beside the chair, smiling up at the camera. Another face he recognised.

Well, well, Jouma thought grimly. George Malewe.

There was a sourness at the back of Jouma's throat as he saw that the pickpocket was holding a short-bladed gutting knife in his hand.

He flipped to the next image.

289

Malewe hunkered down in front of Dennis Bentley with his back to the camera.

Malewe stood to one side now, arms covered in blood, proudly displaying his handiwork to the camera: a vivid pink and red incision across Dennis Bentley's exposed white belly, and a pile of blueish-grey guts lying in a heap on the deck between Bentley's knees.

A close-up of Bentley's upturned face, the sight-less eyes staring into the camera lens.

The photographs slipped from Jouma's fingers then and scattered like playing cards on the floor. He looked down at them with revulsion, and then at his own hands as if expecting to see the skin stained with Dennis Bentley's blood.

He could barely remember stumbling out of the caravan. Now he stood sucking in the air and trying to expunge the images that had burned themselves into his mind.

Get the photographs, Daniel. You have to get the photographs.

Shakily, he returned to Viljoen's lair and scooped up the photographs. Then he hurried back outside.

From the wilderness beyond the gates of Croc World, the shriek of birds suddenly alerted Jouma to the fact that a vehicle was approaching along the jungle road.

Viljoen?

After closing the caravan door, Jouma ran to the tar-paper sheds near by and watched unseen as a fat-tyred Porsche Cayenne swept at high speed through the gates and a tall thin figure leaped down from its elevated driving seat.

Chapter Sixty-Two

An hour after leaving the farmhouse, heading east along the highway, a road sign told them they were forty miles from Mombasa. Jake smiled grimly. If the van was heading for the city, then Jouma would be able to arrange a welcoming committee for it at the other end of the Makupa Causeway. All it would take was a call to the inspector's new phone. But a mile later the van abruptly turned off the main drag and began heading north on a barely paved minor road.

'Where are they going?' Martha asked.

'God knows,' Jake said. 'Some of these roads aren't even on the map.'

They had switched driving duties. Behind the wheel of the BMW, Jake used every last scrap of his police training to keep a discreet distance between the two vehicles, but as the road began to disintegrate and the traffic thinned he was forced to rely on the van's dust cloud to hide them.

Another hour passed. The terrain turned from arid wasteland to verdant coastal plane. Soon the thin blue strip of the ocean could be seen intermittently through the jungle on their right-hand side. The van turned right and joined a track that led towards the sea. At last they had reached the end of the road. Jake decided it was time to abandon the BMW and continue on foot.

Using the spiked crowns of the sisal plants for cover, he and Martha followed the track until it spluttered and died at the entrance to a shallow cove. No more than a hundred yards away now, the van had stopped in the sand. Viljoen and the two Africans had climbed out of the cab.

They were somewhere north of Mombasa, Jake was sure of that. But where? This was wild coastline, unfamiliar to him. But then that was the point. Whatever Viljoen was up to, he didn't want prying eyes watching him.

Half an hour passed. Nothing happened. The Africans smoked, Viljoen paced up and down at the edge of the surf. Then he stopped suddenly, his head cocked to one side.

'You hear that?' Jake whispered.

A boat was approaching from around the headland; Jake couldn't see it yet, but he recognised the engine noise the same way a parent can recognise their child's voice in a crowd.

Yellowfin? But Yellowfin was supposed to be moored at Flamingo Creek!

He watched dumbfounded as the thirty-footer hove into view, its lines so familiar to him that he almost wanted to shout out to it. Up on the flying bridge he saw Sammy, the kid's face rapt with concentration as he brought the boat about. *Easy, son*, Jake felt himself whispering. *Watch out for the shallow draught*. But then it struck him that *Yellowfin* was *his* boat, and if anyone was going to pilot it into hazardous shallows it should be *him*.

292

Sammy was not alone, though. As the boat idled at the mouth of the cove, a figure emerged uncertainly from the cabin and peered across at the welcoming party.

Jesus Christ. It was Harry!

'You know that guy?' Martha said.

'Yeah,' Jake said grimly. 'But he's supposed to be somewhere else right now.'

A motor launch was tied to *Yellowfin*'s stern cleats, but it wasn't the two-man vessel that Jake used. This was a broad-beamed model that could hold ten people comfortably. Having anchored the boat fifty yards offshore, Sammy shinned down to the cockpit and dragged the launch alongside with a boathook. Harry eased himself in and it only took a few seconds before the launch was nudging the sand.

'Harry, my man!' Viljoen exclaimed, striding across the beach to pump the tall Englishman's hand vigorously. 'Perfect timing!'

He turned and snapped instructions to the Africans. After slinging their guns over their shoulders, the two men began unlocking the rear doors of the van.

'What's with the guns?' Jake heard Harry ask.

Viljoen grinned. 'You can't be too careful, Harry. It's bandit country out there, and this is a valuable cargo.'

The doors swung open. From where he was crouched, barely fifty yards away, Jake couldn't see what the cargo was – but Harry could, and a sudden appalled expression appeared on his face.

'What the hell is this, Tug?' Harry said in a strangled voice.

'The cargo,' Viljoen told him matter-of-factly.

'No.' Harry took a step backwards, his hands

293

raised defensively. 'No, this is not what I agreed to. *This is not what you said!*'

He began moving backwards towards the launch.

The smile drained from Viljoen's face. 'Now, now, Harry. Let's not be stupid about this.'

In the next breath he said something in Swahili to the Africans, and Jake's blood turned to ice as the two men levelled their weapons at Harry.

Harry stared wide-eyed at the guns, as if not quite believing that they were pointing at him.

'You told me it was *hash*, Tug. A shipment of *hash*.'

'Yeah, well,' Viljoen said, 'I thought that might appeal to you. You being an aficionado.'

One of the gunmen had come to the rear of the van now, and was shouting harsh commands at whatever – *whoever* – was inside. A moment later, Jake saw a tiny black foot appear, then another, and then he gasped as a figure dropped down on to the sand.

It was an African girl, tiny, young, wearing a simple white cotton dress that was stained with sweat and God only knew what else. As she landed, blinking and whimpering against the harsh light, her thin legs gave way beneath her and she pitched forward pathetically on to her hands and knees.

'My God,' Martha murmured.

But the girl was not alone in the back of the van. She was followed by a second girl, maybe a couple of years older, the swell of budding breasts visible beneath the flimsy material of her cotton shift. Then a third and a fourth climbed unsteadily down from the truck, wobbling uncertainly, their arms covering their eyes from the sunlight. Five, six – none of them more than fifteen years old, Jake guessed, all of them with the same fearful expression etched on their wide-eyed, unblemished faces. He thought about the heat and the darkness in the back of the van and could only imagine the discomfort and the terror that the girls must have endured on the long journey from the Tanzanian border.

But still they kept coming. More and more until Jake counted twenty girls huddled together in a fragile circle, as if proximity to each other could somehow offer them protection from the men on the beach.

'Get back to the car,' Jake told Martha. 'See if you can get a signal on your phone. We need to let Jouma know we're still alive.'

'What are you going to do?'

'I'm going to find out where we are. And where *Yellowfin* is going.'

When she had gone, Jake moved forwards through the sisals.

'What do you think, Harry?' he heard Viljoen crowing. The South African was standing next to the little girls, who recoiled from him as if he was some predatory animal. 'Aren't they beauties? I understand they're known as *bait* by the cognoscenti in Europe.'

'You can't be serious,' Harry said, his voice a hoarse whisper that barely carried on the breeze.

Viljoen shrugged again. 'I'll admit they don't do much for me – I prefer my *manyanga* with a bit more meat on their bones and a lot more experience in the sack. But that's not the point, Harry. The point is, they do something for *somebody*, and that somebody is prepared to pay top dollar for the very best merchandise. They go for a hundred grand a pop in Europe, so I hear. Not that it's any of my concern. My job's just to arrange the transport of the merchandise. I'm small fry, really.'

'You sick bastard. I'm having no part of this.'

Jake winced as Viljoen struck Harry a fierce blow with the back of one bearlike hand. Harry staggered backwards and lost his footing on the sand.

'You're already part of this, Harry. Twenty-five grand, remember?'

As he spoke, Jake knew that Viljoen would not hesitate to order his men to open fire if he felt Harry was standing in his way.

'Get them into the launch, Harry,' Viljoen said.

Jesus, do it Harry! Just do what he says!

'Go fuck yourself, Tug,' Harry said.

For a moment Viljoen said and did nothing. Then from the waistband of his shorts he produced a handgun, a sleek silver Glock that looked ludicrously out of place clutched in his pudgy fist. Without saying a word, he went over to where Harry was propped up on his elbows and fired once.

The young girls screamed and from the trees fringing the cove it seemed like a thousand brightly coloured birds lifted into the air at the same time.

'Next time I won't miss,' Viljoen said to Harry. 'And after I've killed you I'll kill the young *kaffir* on the boat. Except I'll most probably take my time over him. So what's it to be, Harry? What's it to be?'

Hidden down in the undergrowth, Jake Moore watched with cold detachment. His anger and his fear had gone. He was in a different place now. He knew what he had to do.

Chapter Sixty-Three

Were it not for the fact that he had not yet started coughing up blood, Conrad Getty could have sworn that his long-suffering ulcer had finally burst under the strain. It felt like someone had inserted a red-hot poker into his mouth and down into his stomach, taking particular care to singe the delicate tissues of his gullet on the way down.

The glorified cart track he had just driven on hadn't helped either. Even the suspension of his Cayenne had struggled to adjust to the ruts and potholes that littered the mile-long stretch from the main highway through the jungle to Croc World. How the fuck Viljoen had the audacity to call it a road was beyond him. It was no wonder his pox-ridden amusement park never had any visitors.

Not that *that* was a problem any more. Oh no – because Sergeant Viljoen wasn't coming back.

The call had come through to his office at the hotel thirty minutes earlier, the crackles and twangs betraying the poor signal on Viljoen's field radio.

'Viljoen – where the hell are you? Why haven't you called?'

'There's been a change of plan, Captain.'

'*What?*' The walls of the office suddenly closed in on him and for a moment Getty thought he was going to faint.

'Don't worry – I'll make sure the transfer goes down. But then I'm gone.'

'Are you insane?' Getty wailed. 'Whitestone will kill us all if he finds out!'

Harsh laughter buzzed down the line. 'Don't you see, Captain? He's going to kill us anyway. We're alive only as long as we've got his precious cargo. That's why if you've got any sense you'll come with me.'

'But—' Getty began, but at that moment he knew that Viljoen was right. 'Where are you going?'

Viljoen told him his plan. In a twisted way, it made perfect sense. *A good soldier always made sure to have an escape route*, Getty thought.

'Christ almighty, Tug. Why didn't you tell me this before?'

'Because you're weak, Captain. Because Whitestone would have found out. Now I suggest you get moving. It'll take you at least three hours to get to the rendezvous.'

'Right. Right. OK.'

It was then that Viljoen had dropped the bombshell and sent Getty's ulcer into agonising overdrive.

'On your way I need you to stop off at Croc World,' he said. 'Something I need you to do for me.'

As the hotel owner sped away from the Marlin Bay towards the mangrove forests, his eyes fixed on the rear-view mirror in case Whitestone had seen him leave, he cursed Tug Viljoen with every expletive he knew in English and Afrikaans.

What Viljoen wanted was simple enough. But every minute Getty spent in this godforsaken hole was time that could be better spent getting the hell out of Kenya. Sweating profusely now, and with the pain in his stomach reaching epic proportions, he began sloshing petrol from a metal canister against the walls of Viljoen's caravan.

'Destroying evidence, Mr Getty?'

Getty whirled round. Standing behind him was a small African in a suit. He was holding a manila file. There was something about him that was vaguely familiar, but the hotel owner's brain was racing too hard to stop and figure out why.

'Who the hell are you?'

'My name is Daniel Jouma.' He reached into his pocket and flashed his detective badge. 'Mombasa police. We met the other night when I brought Miss Bentley back from Flamingo Creek.'

'Of course.' Getty's voice was cracking now, but still he maintained an insouciant façade, no matter how ludicrous their current situation rendered it. 'How can I help you, Inspector?'

'This file was inside the caravan. Do you know what is in it?'

'I have no idea.'

Jouma tossed the file at Getty's feet. The photographs spilled out and the hotel owner recoiled when he saw them.

'I assume Mr Viljoen took them for insurance purposes,' Jouma said. 'Just in case anybody should suspect him of the murder of Dennis Bentley. Proof that the killer was a Mombasa thief called George Malewe. A neat plan, don't you think? Especially as George would never be found. It must have caused quite some consternation when the storm washed his body up on Bara Hoyo beach.'

Getty had turned white. 'I don't know what you're talking about, Inspector.'

'Don't you? I find that hard to believe.'

'Now you listen to me. Julius Teshete is a personal friend of mine, and I'm sure everything can be rectified satisfactorily once I speak to him.'

'I suspect Superintendent Teshete has more pressing matters to attend to. Now – where is Mr Viljoen?'

Getty clutched his chest. For a moment, Jouma thought the hotel owner was having a heart attack.

'What do you want?' he said presently. 'Money? I can get you money.'

Jouma grimaced. *Always money.* 'For the time being some answers would be sufficient. If you would—'

With a single swift movement, Getty pulled a Zippo lighter from his breast pocket, flicked open the lid to ignite it, and tossed it against the caravan. The petrol exploded with a *whumphh*! And as Jouma shielded his eyes from the scorching blast Getty bolted for the maintenance sheds and the yard beyond. Jouma reached for his shoulder holster and grabbed his .38. Having not used his gun for fifteen years, he'd now had it in his hand twice in two days. This was becoming something of a habit, he concluded as he took off in pursuit.

Chapter Sixty-Four

Jake waited until *Yellowfin* had disappeared around the headland before he made his move. The two African gunmen Viljoen had left with the van didn't see him coming.

The fist-sized rock smashed the first's skull with a noise like an egg landing on a stone floor, and he fell to the ground in an unnatural position, his blood leaching into the sand. The second fumbled amateurishly with the action of his Kalashnikov until Jake drove the butt of the downed man's weapon into his guts.

'Where are we?' Jake demanded.

The second man was backed up against the side of the van with his hands in the air and flecks of spittle in the corners of his mouth.

'Where are we?'

The African gestured frantically at the cab of the van. A roadmap was jammed between the dashboard and the windscreen. Jake grabbed it and held it up to the African's face.

'*Where, dammit?*'

The African extended a quivering finger and pointed to a spot on the map.

Jake nodded. 'Where has the boat gone?'

'Meet the big ship,' the African jabbered, waving at the open sea.

'What is the name of the ship?' Jake demanded.

'*I* don't know, Boss. *I don't know!*' the African screamed as Jake pointed the gun at his head.

'Then from which direction?'

'South. Always from the south. Mombasa.' The African brought his hands together in a pathetic entreaty. 'Please, Boss. Don't kill me.'

'Get up,' Jake snarled at him. 'Now get your pal and get in the back of the van,' he said.

The African scrambled to his feet and manhandled his unconscious partner into the Transit. Jake locked the doors after them. The heat of the day was slowly dissipating now, so conditions for the two Africans would not be as bad as they'd been for the little girls. They had buckets to piss and shit in. And there was an air vent that worked intermittently. The cove was a long way from the road, and it would probably take the ambulance a while to find them after Jake made the call. But they'd live. Which was more than they deserved.

He turned and ran back towards Martha's car.

'Thank God,' she said. 'But you're hurt.'

Jake looked down and saw spatters of blood on his shirt. Blood that wasn't his.

'Have you got mobile reception?' he asked.

She nodded.

'Then ring your boyfriend. It's time to kiss and make up.'

'Patrick? Why?'

'Because we're going to need a boat,' Jake said, his voice cold. 'A fast one.'

Chapter Sixty-Five

Whitestone had been toying with the idea of sparing Getty's life once this latest shipment was complete. After all, with Kanga dead and his supply routes from Tanzania in a consequent state of flux, it didn't do to be making too many unforced personnel changes to what was after all his most productive cell in this neck of the woods.

But that was before that *bitch* had left him stranded in Mombasa. And before he had returned to the hotel in a taxi to discover that Getty had decided to make a run for it. Now the hotel owner was going to die. And so was everyone else involved in the Mombasa cell. Not only that, but their deaths would be long and excruciatingly painful. Of that, Whitestone would make sure.

And, after that, maybe he would turn his attentions to dear Martha.

'Excuse me, Mr Noonan, sir – can I help you?'

Getty's concierge had entered the office. Whitestone peered at the name on his laminated nametag.

'Good afternoon, Loftus. I was just waiting for Mr Getty.'

'Mr Getty has gone out, sir.'

'So it would appear. Do you know where?'

'No, sir. But, if you would care to wait for him in reception, I will most certainly inform him that you wish to see him.'

'Of course.'

But, as he made to leave the office, Whitestone was suddenly gripped by a wave of irrational fury once again. Who the hell were these people to tell him what to do? Didn't they understand who he was? That *he* gave orders, not them?

'Are you all right, sir?'

Just then Whitestone's cell phone rang. He peered at the name in the display and cursed. Now was not the time for tiresome platitudes between two feuding lovers. For a moment his finger hovered over the disconnect button. But then it struck Whitestone that in the last few hours the self-control he prided himself on had been severely eroded. He needed to calm down, to regain his equilibrium. It was time to do what he did best.

'Martha!' Patrick Noonan said. 'Thank God it's you.'

Apart from the flyblown crocodile carcass on its hook, the yard behind the sheds was empty. The billowing black smoke from the blazing caravan gave the place an apocalyptic appearance that was entirely in keeping with the whole hellish surroundings. Getty was nowhere to be seen. At the far end of the yard was a narrow passageway between two of the sheds, the only possible way out without retracing one's steps back towards Viljoen's caravan. Jouma proceeded along the passageway, the gun held close to his chest, his finger resting lightly on the trigger.

'Jesus Christ – *help*!'

The voice came from up ahead. Jouma broke into a run. The passageway ended at the wire perimeter fence, and now the only way forward was to follow a narrow dirt track that ran between the fence and the exterior wall of one of the sheds. This track terminated at a chest-high wooden palisade. Jouma could see marks on the slats where Conrad Getty's feet had scrabbled for purchase as he scaled it. As he peered over the top of the palisade, Jouma could see what a grievous miscalculation this had been.

Beyond the fence, the ground fell away steeply into one of the man-made crocodile lagoons. Getty, who had tumbled down fully fifteen feet from the palisade, now stood up to his knees in brown water, his lightweight suit dripping wet and covered with mud and his carefully arranged coiffure hanging limply from his skull.

'Are you all right, Mr Getty?' Jouma called down.

'Oh, my fucking God!' Getty said.

Off to the right, something sinuous and log-sized slid into the water.

'The place is crawling with crocs!' Getty exclaimed, as three more reptiles moved towards him from a mud bank at the far side of the lagoon.

'Don't move!' Jouma shouted, but it was too late. Getty was already wading through the water towards the nearest bank, his flailing feet kicking up the water around him and ensuring that now every other crocodile in the lagoon was alerted to his presence. Terrified, the hotel owner began clawing his way towards the fence, but the steep mud sides of the lagoon were impossible to cling to and he slipped back into the water.

Jouma turned and ran back towards the yard. The

thought of what he was about to do next turned his stomach, but he knew that unless he acted now his chief witness would not be around long enough to tell him what he needed to know. Holding his breath, he grappled the croc carcass and heaved it off the gibbet. As he did so, a huge cloud of flies lifted furiously from the rancid flesh, blinding him as he threw the stinking length of meat on to the concrete. Fumbling and cursing, Jouma grabbed the rope that was still tied firmly to the reptile's tail and pulled the body with all his might towards the compound, praying at the same time that the rotting flesh would not disintegrate under the pressure.

Getty was backed up against the mud bank at the far side of the lagoon, staring with horror at the slowly approaching crocs. He looked up and saw Jouma.

'For Christ's sake, do something!' he screamed.

Jouma did not have the energy left to waste on a reply. Moving the carcass sixty yards from the yard to the lagoon was like lugging a roll of wet carpet. But finally he managed to manoeuvre it to the chain-link access gate that led from the path to the lagoon. With one final exertion, Jouma dragged the remains of the reptile through the gate and let it roll down the mud bank into the water. The splash, and no doubt the smell, caught the attention of two of the crocs heading for Getty and they turned lazily in the water. To make sure the rest of them got the message, Jouma raised his pistol into the air and fired two shots. Slowly, the remaining crocs began to lose interest in Getty and instead started swimming back towards the other side of the lagoon and the carcass, which was floating belly up on the surface.

It was a matter of seconds before the first of the

306

crocs reached it. Jouma watched with horrified fascination as the creature pounced on the slab of rotting meat, tearing a great chunk of flesh loose with a frenetic shake of its jaws. Then the rest of them were upon it, and the dead croc disappeared beneath a writhing mass of bodies that turned the water around them into a thick red scum as they began to attack each other.

Jouma heard a grunt, and looked across to see that Getty had managed to haul himself up one of the banks and was now teetering gingerly around the perimeter of the security fence in search of a way out.

'Thank you, Inspector,' Getty said through the mesh, reaching out his hand. 'Now if you could perhaps help me to get over this—'

He stopped and stared open-mouthed at the barrel of Jouma's gun.

'I get the impression those crocodiles have not been fed for some time,' Jouma said. 'Once they are finished with the body of their colleague, they will be after more food.'

'For God's sake!' Getty exclaimed, glancing nervously over his shoulder. 'Get me out of here!'

'Are you ready to answer my questions?'

'Yes, yes! Anything!' Getty said.

At that moment, faced with the prospect of death by crocodile or Whitestone, Getty realised the diminutive detective was by far the best option.

Chapter Sixty-Six

After all those hours on the road, and the distance they had covered to get to the Tanzanian border and back, it transpired the transfer had been made just a few miles north of Kilifi. A few miles further to the south was Flamingo Creek.

A cosy get-together of Suki-Lo's regulars right on their own doorstep, Jake thought acidly. They could have had themselves a barbie and a few beers on the beach.

Thirty minutes after leaving the cove, he slewed the BMW to a halt in front of the Marlin Bay Hotel and he and Martha ran through the atrium, past the lizards by the pool and down to the marina. Patrick was waiting for them. As they ran towards him, Martha called out his name and it seemed to draw him out of a dark pit of thought.

'Martha! Jake!' he exclaimed, blinking behind the lenses of his Ray-Bans. 'Are you all right? I—' He saw the AK-47 slung over Jake's shoulder and his eyes widened. 'Whoa!' he said, backing away. 'What's going on, man?'

'Is your boat ready, Patrick?'

'Yeah, but—'

'Then let's go. I'll explain on the way.'

Patrick seemed to freeze for a moment. Then he nodded. 'This way.'

Seventeen thousand dollars, Harry thought miserably. *Seventeen poxy grand.* Back in the day, such an amount would have barely covered his quarterly entertainment and travel expenses.

Now it was going to get him killed.

What the fuck had he done?

He was tied with fishing wire to *Yellowfin*'s fighting chair. The chair was turned so that it was looking back up the boat towards the cabin. The cabin door was closed and secured shut with rope, which was just as well because Harry didn't want to see the African girls stowed in there. The very thought of them made him feel physically sick.

Up on the flying bridge, Tug Viljoen was cracking jokes with Sammy, who was piloting the boat out to sea on a southeasterly heading. The bait boy wasn't laughing. He had seen what had happened and knew that there was nothing to laugh about.

Harry looked down at his swollen wrists and felt his bonds chafing at his exposed sun-reddened skin. He wondered what Jake would think if he knew what he had done. But right now Jake would be on his way back from Mazeras township, sent there on a wild goose chase to an address that did not exist just to keep him out of the way.

'You all right down there, Harry?' Viljoen called down cheerily from the flying bridge.

'Fuck you, Tug.'

'That's the spirit!' Viljoen leaned over the bridge rail. 'You know it's funny, Harry. The line people draw between what is acceptable and what isn't.'

'If this is a lecture, Tug, I'd rather not hear it.'

'You read the papers and you turn on the news and everywhere you look there are innocent kids getting shot to shit, or hacked to pieces, or burned alive, all in the name of democracy or some other greater good. Even in fine upstanding countries like this one.' He gestured down to the locked cabin. 'Take those kids in there. Where they come from, their lives are no better than a dog's. Yet, when you try to take them away from all that, what happens? You're a pervert. A child trafficker. The lowest of the low.'

Harry looked up at the flying deck. Revulsion surged through him. 'Trust me, there's a difference.'

'You agreed to do this,' Viljoen reminded him.

'No. I agreed to smuggle drugs.'

Viljoen snickered. 'Yeah, you did – so don't get all high and mighty.'

'Smoking hash isn't the same as abusing kids.'

'I don't remember you playing the concerned citizen when you heard how much you'd be getting paid.'

'You lied to me, Tug.'

'Ah, that's what dear old Dennis said when it was *his* first time.'

Harry felt like he had been slapped in the face. '*Dennis*? Dennis Bentley?'

'Oh, yeah. Dennis started off with all the same conscientious objector bullshit as you, but he soon changed his tune when the money started rolling in. Trouble with your business, Harry, is that it's just a big black hole that eats up your dollar bills. You don't need me to tell you, as soon as you get it, it's gone. But then Dennis decided that he wanted out. Said he couldn't do it any more. Said he'd rather go bust. Of course, we couldn't let him do that.'

310

'You killed him.'

'It was business, Harry.'

'And Tigi? Was that business as well?'

'The bait boy? Ah, it was a pity about him. I respect loyalty, and that boy sure stood up for his boss. Put up quite a fight. But believe me it was quick. Pop, pop! A couple of taps to the back of the head and over the side. He wouldn't have felt a thing.'

Beside him on the flying bridge, Sammy turned and stared at Viljoen. The South African noticed and struck the boy across the face.

'Keep your eyes front and mind your own business, boy!' Viljoen snapped.

In the fighting chair, it suddenly dawned on Harry that Viljoen had no idea that the boy piloting the boat was Tigi Eruwa's elder brother.

In the low-slung cockpit of the Sonic, Jake told Patrick everything he knew.

'I expect they'll be shipped to Europe,' Jake said evenly. 'Most probably Eastern Europe. Russia. The former Soviet states. The Balkans. Sex trafficking is a thriving business over there.'

Patrick looked shocked. '*Sex?* But you said they were just kids.'

'That's the selling point for the sickos who buy them up. I've heard of kids as young as four years old being bought and sold like cheap meat. They used to say trafficking of women and children into forced prostitution was the third largest source of profits for organised crime after drugs and guns. But that was in my day. Christ only knows what it is now.'

'But why did your partner get involved?' Patrick said.

311

'Because he's a damn fool who couldn't bear to see the business go bust,' Jake sighed. 'And because Viljoen needed a replacement for Dennis Bentley.'

'*Dennis?*' He looked across at Martha, who kept her eyes firmly on the ocean ahead of her.

'Viljoen was offering him twenty-five thousand bucks per trip. Dennis was going bust. The money would have come in real handy.'

'But trafficking *kids*?' Patrick said. 'Jesus.'

'At first Viljoen would have spun him a yarn about a one-off shipment of drugs or guns or something else. I don't believe for one minute Dennis would have done it if he'd known what Viljoen was really trafficking. But, once he was hooked, there was no way they could let him walk away. Now it's Harry's turn.'

'Shit,' Patrick said. 'That's fucking terrible.'

Martha said nothing. A tear materialised from behind her sunglasses and rolled briefly down her cheek before the force of the wind obliterated it.

Patrick blew out his cheeks and whistled loud enough for the sound to carry against the rush of the wind and the hollow boom of the speedboat's hull against the swell.

'So where do you think they're headed?' he said, still eyeing the AK-47 on Jake's lap warily.

'The goon I talked to seemed to think they were meeting up with another vessel. A freighter maybe. He said it was coming from the south. *Yellowfin*'s range is no more than a hundred miles.'

'That's a helluva lot of ocean,' Patrick said.

'Then maybe it's time we used your state-of-the-art tracker system, Patrick.'

Three coastguard helicopters roared low in formation

over Nyali Bridge, then sheared away from each other and out to sea. Standing at the rail at the far end of the bridge, Jouma watched them go with a desperate sense of helplessness. He knew that the choppers could cover vast areas, far more than any boat, and in a fraction of the time; but he also knew from his own phobic aversion that there would always be swathes of ocean still to cover.

He couldn't help thinking that their inadequacy mirrored his own. For no matter how much corruption and stinking evil he uncovered, it seemed there would always be more.

Somewhere out there, beyond the horizon, was a boat. A pinprick of such insignificance it might as well not exist. On it, a psychopathic monster and a cargo of innocent children bound for a life of unspeakable degradation in a land far from their own. And here he stood in useless isolation: a man who had once taken an oath to protect them.

He had done what he could. Conrad Getty was crumpled in the back of Jouma's Panda, his hands cuffed to the hand strap, and if there was any justice the hotel owner would never breathe the air of freedom again. But Jouma knew that there were a hundred, a thousand, just like him over that seemingly endless horizon.

Yes, he had done what he could. It was up to others now. All he could do was wait and pray.

They were maybe ten miles off the coast now, and on another day Jake might have marvelled at how quickly they had covered the distance. But Patrick was right. It *was* a big ocean. And, even if they found *Yellowfin*, he didn't like to think what they might find on board.

313

'There!' Jake shouted. 'That's it!'

A large distinctive silhouette had appeared off the starboard horizon, just as the tracker on the dashboard had predicted. It was a freighter, low in the water, ploughing a northerly course against the current.

'You sure, Jake?' Patrick said, turning the steering wheel so the Sonic was on an intercept course.

Jake slung the AK-47 over his shoulder. 'Is there a ship-to-shore on this boat?'

'There's a radio below in the cabin.'

'Show me.'

Two miles to the north-east, Viljoen had spotted the freighter too. He grinned and barked an order to Sammy. The boy brought the wheel round and *Yellowfin* began to loop back on itself.

The Sonic's cabin was accessed by a fold-down step at the rear of the cockpit. It was basic and functional, consisting of two narrow banquettes either side of a low folding table.

'I don't see your radio, Patrick,' Jake said, stooping low as he entered the shallow space and laid the rifle on one of the banquettes.

'That's because there isn't one, Jake.'

A foot landed squarely between his shoulder blades and Jake sprawled forward into the cabin. His head struck the metal spar of the table and for a moment he saw stars. As his vision cleared, he heard the ominous clatter of the AK-47's breech mechanism and saw Patrick hunched down in the cabin entrance, the automatic weapon in his hands.

'Get up,' he said, in a voice that was no longer Patrick's.

314

'Easier said than done,' Jake said, as the Sonic pitched and swung into the waves.

'You're a seafaring man, Jake. You can do it. But do it slowly. Understand?'

'Whatever you say.'

Maybe he should have been shocked at Patrick's duplicity, even outraged that Martha's jet-setting boyfriend was suddenly pointing a gun at his head.

Instead, it all made perfect sense.

All along Jouma had been talking about pieces of a jigsaw, and slowly they had been coming together to reveal the truth. George Malewe, Dennis Bentley, Michael Kili, Tug Viljoen, the sickening traffic in human cargo. But until now there had been one question – one crucial piece of the jigsaw – that for Jake had remained tantalisingly elusive.

Who was pulling the strings?

That it should be Patrick Noonan – if indeed that was his name – did not surprise him. Why should it? Under the pretence of an international bonds dealer, he had carte blanche to travel anywhere in the world without raising suspicion. And as for Martha? She admitted they hadn't seen each other more than a few nights since they met in New York. Patrick probably had a Martha Bentley in every city he visited. He was the consummate operator, invisibly controlling his empire through a network of cutouts and dupes. And it would have undoubtedly remained that way if it hadn't been for a charred and mangled body washing up on a remote Kenyan beach, and the dogged enquiries of a Mombasa detective. Now the puppeteer had been forced into the open, and Jake knew time was short before he disappeared into the shadows forever.

He grabbed the table with one hand and levered

himself into a kneeling position. Something wet was sliding down the side of his face, and when he touched it his fingers came away covered in blood.

'So how did you get involved in all this, Patrick?'

'Like you said, it's a long story.'

'Does Martha know?'

'Why let reality get in the way of true love? Now get on your feet and move slowly towards me.'

Jake did as he was told until he was stooped at the bottom of the steps leading up to the cockpit. Patrick had edged backwards to the stern of the boat so that his back was resting against the engine bulkheads. The gun remained steady in his hands.

'OK. Up to the front. I'm right behind you.'

In the driver's seat Martha steered the boat oblivious to what was going on behind her. Jake could see they had made considerable ground on the freighter. The Sonic was now near enough to see the name *Medusa, Istanbul* written in five-foot-high letters across the rusted metal plates.

'Sit down next to Martha,' Patrick ordered.

Clinging to the safety rail, Jake carefully picked his way along the cockpit to the passenger seat and collapsed into its yielding white leather. Martha looked at him and her eyes widened as she saw the blood on his forehead.

'Jake, you're—'

'I know,' he said, nodding at Patrick.

'Just concentrate on steering the boat, honey,' Patrick said smoothly. He slid on to the couch seat behind them and jammed the barrel of the AK-47 under Jake's left ear.

Martha stared at him in disbelief. 'Jesus Christ, Patrick!'

316

She looked at Jake, whose expression told her everything.

'Patrick?' Her voice was a confused whimper, blasted by the wind.

'He's part of this whole operation, Martha,' Jake said, his eyes fixed on the looming hulk of the freighter. 'Running it, I'd say. Isn't that so, Patrick?'

'Yeah.' Whitestone emitted a hollow laugh. 'But never delegate, Jake. Here endeth the lesson.'

Martha's hand reached for the throttles and the Sonic abruptly slowed in the water. She turned in her seat and her eyes were burning.

'Tell me what the hell is going on here, Patrick. Right now!'

Keeping the gun pressed to Jake's head, Whitestone's fingers closed around Martha's hand and eased the throttles back up.

'Move it again, baby, and I'll blow his head off,' he said matter-of-factly.

'Do what he says, Martha,' Jake said.

Whitestone nodded. 'That's good. Now just keep heading towards that big ship over there and everything will be just fine. If you do as I say, I'll be out of your hair and you can get on with the rest of your day.'

Jake didn't believe that for a second. He knew that, as soon as they reached the freighter, Patrick would kill them both.

'Is that how it works, Patrick? You pick the clients while animals like Tug Viljoen do all the dirty work?'

'Something like that.'

'Presumably it was your decision to have Dennis killed.'

Whitestone grimaced with feigned affront. 'Oh,

317

that's a low blow, Jake. A really low blow bringing that up with Martha sitting here. For the record, honey, I was pissed that they killed your daddy. From what you say, he was a really nice guy. But that's the way it goes sometimes.'

'And what about me, Patrick?' Martha said, and from somewhere there was steel in her voice. 'What was I? A perk of the job?'

Whitestone shrugged. 'You might not believe this, Martha, but I really had a thing for you. Chico, I never liked too much, I have to admit.'

'You bastard,' Martha hissed.

'Oh, come on, baby. Don't tell me it wasn't fun.'

Jake saw Martha's knuckles whiten on the Sonic's steering wheel. The boat was now close enough to *Medusa* that gesticulating figures could be seen milling against its stern rail.

'Remember Howard Miller, Jake?' Martha said suddenly. 'The insurance guy from Nairobi? You know – the day my daddy let me drive *Martha B* for the first time?'

Jake blinked, then understood. 'Yeah. I remember Howard Miller.'

The instant he finished speaking, Martha slammed the throttles forward as far as they would go. In that same instant the massive Cobra 1100-horsepower engines engaged fully and Jake clung on to the forward safety rail as the boat shot like an arrow straight towards *Medusa*'s hull.

Behind them, Whitestone was caught unawares by the sudden forward movement and he reeled backwards and sideways on the slippery leather couchette. The gun clattered under the front seats and Jake heard cursing as Whitestone scrabbled for purchase.

'*Turn it! Now!*' Jake yelled, and then held on for

dear life as Martha yanked the wheel to the left.

The Sonic slalomed between the two lips of *Medusa*'s wake and then took to the air as it crested the swell left by the huge freighter. Jake whirled in his seat and saw that Patrick was crushed up against the starboard rail. There was a look of impotent rage on his face as he battled the sudden debilitating G-forces.

'Never were a sailor, were you, Patrick?' Jake said, then punched him in the face with all his strength.

The American's head fired backwards and his limbs went slack. Then the Sonic weaved back into the freighter's wake and Whitestone was flung up and over the side like a gutted fish. One hand gripped the rail, and Jake met the American's eyes as the boiling bow wave buffeted him against the side of the boat.

'Turn it again, Martha,' Jake said calmly.

As Martha whipped the boat round, the thin metal rail first buckled then popped from its securing bolts. For a moment Whitestone clung to it as it swung out like one of *Yellowfin*'s outriggers, then the immense vortex generated by the Sonic's propellers dragged him under.

'Jesus, Jake,' Martha said. 'Is he ...?'

'He's gone,' Jake said.

'Looks like we got company, Harry,' Viljoen reported from the flying bridge.

But Harry had already seen the Sonic appear from behind *Medusa*'s superstructure like a tiny exotic bird buzzing around a hippopotamus. Now it was heading towards them, closing the gap rapidly.

Viljoen was chuckling as he climbed unsteadily

319

down the ladder into the cockpit. 'What do you reckon?' he said. 'The cavalry?' He reached to his waistband and produced the Glock. 'That's a pity.'

'Why don't you let the boy go, Tug?' Harry said. 'You said it: it's none of his business.'

'I dunno,' Viljoen said, rubbing his chin theatrically. 'He's a good-looking kid. Strong. Good teeth. Folks'll pay a lot for him, I reckon. And I'm damned if I'm coming out of this little escapade empty-handed. I've got overheads to consider.'

'Please, Tug.'

Viljoen looked at him contemptuously. 'It's the English way, isn't it, Harry? Let the women and children go first. Well, I'll tell you what – let's see just how much your friends think the boy's worth, eh?'

From two hundred yards out, Jake could see that Harry was tied to the fighting chair and that Viljoen had a gun pressed against his head. In that instant he was transported back to an East London post office, and a scared-eyed kid with a handgun and a hostage. But, as Martha brought the Sonic alongside *Yellowfin*'s stern, he saw there was nothing in Tug Viljoen's eyes but cold murderous intent.

'Jake! What a surprise!' the South African called out. 'And the lovely Miss Bentley, I take it.'

'You all right, Harry?'

'Never been better,' Harry said with a weak smile.

Jake saw that his friend's skin was bright red and his lips were cracked. The bastard had clearly kept him out in the chair without water or shade since they had left the mainland. Up on the flying bridge, he saw Sammy peering anxiously out.

'It's over, Tug. Your boss is dead. So why don't you let them go? You don't need them any more.'

320

Viljoen grinned. 'Whitestone's dead? That sure is a weight off my mind, Jake. Trouble is, there's a seaplane waiting for me about eighty clicks north of here at Sabaki river and it sounds like I need some insurance to get there safe and sound.'

'Let Harry and the kids go, Tug. I'll take you to Sabaki.'

'That's very noble of you. But I don't think so. I'd have to have eyes in the back of my head all the way, and I don't fancy that. I'm all for the quiet life, see. No, I'll just take Sammy here. He seems to know one end of the ocean from the other. Oh – and I'll take your boat too, if you don't mind. Can't see too many people catching me, can you?'

As Viljoen talked, Jake could see the snout of the AK-47 peeking from underneath the Sonic's front seats. He knew that the only hope of stopping Viljoen now lay with the automatic weapon. But how to get it?

Viljoen's thumb caressed the safety of the pistol that was still pressed hard against Harry's head.

'Throw the keys across, Jake. Nice and easy.'

Martha tensed, but Jake nodded. Reluctantly, she removed the keys from the ignition and handed them to him. Jake tossed them on to *Yellowfin*'s cockpit.

'That's good,' Viljoen said. He clicked the safety back on the Glock and lifted it from Harry's head. 'I really do appreciate what you've done for me, Jake, and I'm sorry to leave you and Miss Bentley in the lurch – but you'll understand that I've got a pretty good hand here.'

Jake inched his foot slowly towards the AK-47. But, as he did so, the Sonic was hit by a wave and the gun slid agonisingly out of sight. With it, he knew, was their last chance of stopping Viljoen.

'Now I want you and the little lady to move to the stern,' Viljoen ordered. 'Then I want you to jump off and start swimming away from the boat.' He cackled. 'You see, Jake, I'm not the monster you think I am. I only kill people when I have to.'

Jake looked at him with pure hatred. 'If anything happens to the boy, I'll track you down, Viljoen. Wherever you are in the world, I'll hunt you until I find you.'

Viljoen nodded impatiently. 'I'm sure you will, Jake. Now get in the water before I change my mind.' Then, without bothering to look up at the flying bridge, he said, 'Get down here, Sammy, and say your *kwaheris*. We're leaving.'

Something silver glinted in the sunlight and Viljoen stiffened, his eyes wide with surprise. He staggered slightly, then turned to peer quizzically at Sammy, who stood at the rail above him with the harpoon gun in his hands. A taut rubber cable connected the barrel of the gun to a foot-long spear that now neatly bisected the South African's skull an inch below the brim of his cycle cap.

Viljoen's mouth moved silently, then his eyeballs rolled up into his head and he sank to his knees on the deck before pitching forward on to his face.

'*Sammy!*'

Jake's shout snapped the boy out of his stupor.

'He say he kill Tigi, Mr Jake,' Sammy said, looking down at him vacantly. 'He say he killed my little brother.'

322

Day Twelve

Chapter Sixty-Seven

Four miles due east of Flamingo Creek, the land mass of Africa disappears beneath the horizon and you are suddenly alone in an expanse of water that seems to have no end whichever direction you look. It is a good place to have a beer. An even better place to start smoking again.

'How long has it been?' Martha asked.

'Two years, eight months and two days,' Jake said.

'What a waste.'

'What a waste of two years, eight months and two days. Think of all the cigarettes I could have smoked.'

He went into *Yellowfin*'s cabin and raided two Tuskers from the chiller. When he came out again, Martha was sitting in the shade of the cockpit awning staring out to sea as the boat idled in the swell without engines.

'Surveying your new empire?'

She shrugged. 'Just thinking about what changes I'm going to make. Who I'm going to fire.'

'Listen – you're an equal partner of three. Harry and I can still outvote you.'

'Harry's in jail. He doesn't count.'

'Four months is just a rap on the knuckles.'

'He's lucky they didn't throw away the key,' Martha said.

Jake couldn't disagree. When Conrad Getty was looking at life in a high-security prison, Harry had indeed been fortunate that the judge had seen fit to hand him a nominal sentence. It was the first time he had ever heard of well-intentioned stupidity coming into the equation for the defence.

But then maybe Harry was due some luck. Maybe they both were.

'Your business clearly needs someone who knows what the hell they're doing,' Martha had told him. 'Think of me as your silent partner in New York.'

'But your dad—'

'He wouldn't have wanted his insurance money to buy a loft apartment in Manhattan or a condo in Palm Beach.'

'Why don't you stay?' Jake had asked her. 'God knows we could use another skipper.'

'New York's my home now,' Martha said. 'Besides, it's nice to know I can always take the wheel of *Yellowfin* whenever I want.'

So it was that Britannia Fishing Trips Ltd had a new investor. And, when Dennis Bentley's insurance money came through, they might just have enough clout to be able to take on the big boys.

The only person disappointed by developments was Jouma.

'Mombasa police could use a man of your experience, Jake,' the detective had told him. 'Especially now.'

'No thank you, Inspector. My day has been and gone.'

'I understand. But you won't mind if I occasionally call upon you? For advice?'

That had made Jake laugh. 'The man who cracked Mombasa's biggest corruption case wants *my* advice? I'm flattered.'

'*Jake!*'

Martha was shouting at him from the flying bridge.

'What is it?

'We've got a bite.'

Jake looked across at the outriggers and saw that one of the rods was vibrating and twisting in its holder. He went across to the stanchion and with a single movement whipped out the rod and tossed it over the side.

'I've got a confession,' he said. 'I never did learn how to fish.'

Chapter Sixty-Eight

In the basement morgue of Mombasa Hospital, Mr Christie arranged his knives and saws on a silver tray, prodded the cadaver lying on the metal autopsy table and shook his head.

'The thing I don't understand about this whole saga, Jouma, is just who this fellow *was*,' he said.

Jouma shrugged. 'Nobody seems to know. The Federal Bureau of Investigation, the Central Intelligence Agency, Interpol . . .'

'It seems quite incredible in this day and age that someone can exist without existing, if you get my meaning.'

'On the contrary, Mr Christie. I would have thought that it was very easy. After all, you and I only exist because we obey the law and have social security numbers and driving licences and birth certificates and identity cards in our name. This man had dozens of identities.'

Christie selected a scalpel and scored a line down the centre of the cadaver's chest. 'I suppose you're right. Mind you, I don't think I could live on the margins like that. In fact, the state of my memory, I'm pretty sure I'd forget who I was supposed to be.'

The pathologist cracked open the rib cage and

dipped his hand into the cavity. Then he paused and looked across the tiled room at Jouma, who stood in his usual place by the door.

'I take it Conrad Getty is who he claims to be,' he said, a note of consternation in his voice.

Jouma nodded. 'Oh, yes. Of that there is no doubt.'

'Thank goodness for that. That old rogue still owes me money from the last poker night at the yacht club.'

'You may have to wait some time before he pays up. I expect he will be in Rumuturi jail for several years.'

Christie shook his head again. 'Sex trafficking! Who would have thought old Conrad would have been involved in something like that, eh? Viljoen, I can understand. The man was mentally unhinged. But Conrad?'

'Getty was enticed by the prospect of money, but in the end he found he could not escape from its clutches. The same was true of Viljoen, of Dennis Bentley, of Harry Philliskirk. Money was the bait that lured them to their downfall.'

'The root of all evil, eh?'

'More than I ever would have believed.'

Jouma watched as the pathologist removed a shapeless lump of purple flesh from the cadaver's abdomen and dropped it into a set of scales.

'Anyway, what about you, Jouma, old man?' Christie said, and above his mask his eyes twinkled mischievously. 'You certainly stirred up a hornet's nest. Half of bloody Mombasa indicted, and the ones who aren't up for investigation have jumped over the border.'

'I cannot say I am proud,' Jouma said quietly.

'Well, you should be. At this rate you'll be Chief of Police. There's no one else left!'

'As a matter of fact, I was thinking of taking Winifred to Ghana to see her brother.'

'God forbid, Jouma – don't tell me you're treating

329

the poor woman to a *holiday* after all these years?'

'He owns a farmstead near Kumasi. We thought we might stay for a while. Maybe longer.'

Christie straightened. 'Well, I think that's a damn good idea,' he said presently. 'And, although you might not believe this, I shall miss you.'

Then he returned to his work and for a while the only sound was Christie humming as he stitched together the cadaver's chest with thick black twine.

'There we are,' he said. 'All done.'

'Well?'

'The body has been bashed about a bit as you might expect: there are significant internal injuries and as you can see a substantial area of the occipital lobe has been damaged. Propeller damage I should say. Not to mention the standard evidence of prolonged exposure to marine conditions. Where was it picked up, did you say?'

'It was spotted in the water by a Russian freighter.'

The pathologist removed his mask. 'Well, to keep things simple for your paperwork, I'd say the cause of death was drowning. The lungs were flooded with aspirated sea water.'

'Drowning.'

'You sound disappointed, Jouma.'

'When I was a boy, a friend of mine was nearly drowned out at sea. When I asked him what it was like, he said it was like ascending to heaven.'

Christie snapped off his gloves and threw them into a plastic container. 'Well, dead's dead in my book, no matter how it happens. And good riddance to bad rubbish. What name do you want me to put in the report?'

Jouma went across to the table and stared down at the cadaver's scarred and pitted face.

'Identity unknown,' he said.

330